ANNIE HAYNES
THE BUNGALOW MYSTERY

Annie Haynes was born in 1865, the daughter of an ironmonger.

By the first decade of the twentieth century she lived in London and moved in literary and early feminist circles. Her first crime novel, *The Bungalow Mystery*, appeared in 1923, and another nine mysteries were published before her untimely death in 1929.

Who Killed Charmian Karslake? appeared posthumously, and a further partially-finished work, *The Crystal Beads Murder*, was completed with the assistance of an unknown fellow writer, and published in 1930.

Also by Annie Haynes

ANNIE HAYNES

THE BUNGALOW MYSTERY

With an introduction
by Curtis Evans

DEAN STREET PRESS

Published by Dean Street Press 2016

All Rights Reserved

First published in 1923 by The Bodley Head

Cover by DSP

Introduction © Curtis Evans 2016

ISBN 978 1 911095 21 7

www.deanstreetpress.co.uk

TO MY DEAR FRIEND

ADA HEATHER-BIGG

IN LOVING GRATITUDE FOR HER

CONSTANT HELP AND KINDNESS

The Mystery of The Missing Author
Annie Haynes and Her Golden Age Detective Fiction

The psychological enigma of Agatha Christie's notorious 1926 vanishing has continued to intrigue Golden Age mystery fans to the present day. The Queen of Crime's eleven-day disappearing act is nothing, however, compared to the decades-long disappearance, in terms of public awareness, of between-the-wars mystery writer Annie Haynes (1865-1929), author of a series of detective novels published between 1923 and 1930 by Agatha Christie's original English publisher, The Bodley Head. Haynes's books went out of print in the early Thirties, not long after her death in 1929, and her reputation among classic detective fiction readers, high in her lifetime, did not so much decline as dematerialize. When, in 2013, I first wrote a piece about Annie Haynes' work, I knew of only two other living persons besides myself who had read any of her books. Happily, Dean Street Press once again has come to the rescue of classic mystery fans seeking genre gems from the Golden Age, and is republishing all Haynes' mystery novels. Now that her crime fiction is coming back into print, the question naturally arises: Who Was Annie Haynes? Solving the mystery of this forgotten author's lost life has taken leg work by literary sleuths on two continents (my thanks for their assistance to Carl Woodings and Peter Harris).

Until recent research uncovered new information about Annie Haynes, almost nothing about her was publicly known besides the fact of her authorship of twelve mysteries during the Golden Age of detective fiction. Now we know that she led an altogether intriguing life, too soon cut short by disability and death, which took her from the isolation of the rural English Midlands in the nineteenth century to the cultural high life of Edwardian London. Haynes was born in 1865 in the Leicestershire town of Ashby-de-la-Zouch, the first child of ironmonger Edwin Haynes and Jane (Henderson) Haynes, daughter of Montgomery Henderson, longtime superintendent of the gardens at nearby Coleorton Hall, seat of the Beaumont baronets. After her father left his family, young Annie resided with her grandparents at the gardener's cottage at Coleorton Hall, along with her mother and younger brother. Here Annie doubtlessly obtained an acquaintance with the ways of the country gentry that would serve her well in her career as a genre fiction writer.

We currently know nothing else of Annie Haynes' life in Leicestershire, where she still resided (with her mother) in 1901, but by 1908, when Haynes was in her early forties, she was living in London with Ada Heather-Bigg (1855-1944) at the Heather-Bigg family home, located halfway between Paddington Station and Hyde Park at 14 Radnor Place, London. One of three daughters of Henry Heather-Bigg, a noted pioneer in the development of orthopedics and artificial limbs, Ada Heather-Bigg was a prominent Victorian and Edwardian era feminist and social reformer. In the 1911 British census entry for 14 Radnor Place, Heather-Bigg, a "philanthropist and journalist," is listed as the head of the household and Annie Haynes, a "novelist," as a "visitor," but in fact Haynes would remain there with Ada Heather-Bigg until Haynes' death in 1929.

Haynes' relationship with Ada Heather-Bigg introduced the aspiring author to important social sets in England's great metropolis. Though not a novelist herself, Heather-Bigg was an important figure in the city's intellectual milieu, a well-connected feminist activist of great energy and passion who believed strongly in the idea of women attaining economic independence through remunerative employment. With Ada Heather-Bigg behind her, Annie Haynes's writing career had powerful backing indeed. Although in the 1911 census Heather-Bigg listed Haynes' occupation as "novelist," it appears that Haynes did not publish any novels in book form prior to 1923, the year that saw the appearance of *The Bungalow Mystery*, which Haynes dedicated to Heather-Bigg. However, Haynes was a prolific producer of newspaper serial novels during the second decade of the twentieth century, penning such works as *Lady Carew's Secret*, *Footprints of Fate*, *A Pawn of Chance*, *The Manor Tragedy* and many others.

Haynes' twelve Golden Age mystery novels, which appeared in a tremendous burst of creative endeavor between 1923 and 1930, like the author's serial novels retain, in stripped-down form, the emotionally heady air of the nineteenth-century triple-decker sensation novel, with genteel settings, shocking secrets, stormy passions and eternal love all at the fore, yet they also have the fleetness of Jazz Age detective fiction. Both in their social milieu and narrative pace Annie Haynes' detective novels bear considerable resemblance to contemporary works by Agatha Christie; and it is interesting to note in this regard that Annie Haynes and Agatha Christie were the only female mystery writers published by The Bodley Head, one of the more notable English mystery imprints in the early Golden Age. "A very remarkable feature of recent detective fiction," observed the *Illustrated London News* in 1923, "is the skill displayed by women in this branch of story-telling. Isabel Ostrander, Carolyn Wells, Annie Haynes and last, but very far from least, Agatha Christie, are contesting the laurels of Sherlock Holmes' creator with a great spirit, ingenuity and success." Since Ostrander and Wells were American authors, this left Annie Haynes, in the estimation of the *Illustrated London News*, as the main British female competitor to Agatha Christie. (Dorothy L. Sayers, who, like Haynes, published her debut mystery novel in 1923, goes unmentioned.) Similarly, in 1925 *The Sketch* wryly noted that "[t] ired men, trotting home at the end of an imperfect day, have been known to pop into the library and ask for an Annie Haynes. They have not made a mistake in the street number. It is not a cocktail they are asking for..."

Twenties critical opinion adjudged that Annie Haynes' criminous concoctions held appeal not only for puzzle fiends impressed with the "considerable craftsmanship" of their plots (quoting from the *Sunday Times* review of *The Bungalow Mystery*), but also for more general readers attracted to their purely literary qualities. "Not only a crime story of merit, but also a novel which will interest readers to whom mystery for its own sake has little appeal," avowed

The Nation of Haynes' *The Secret of Greylands*, while the *New Statesman* declared of *The Witness on the Roof* that "Miss Haynes has a sense of character; her people are vivid and not the usual puppets of detective fiction." Similarly, the *Bookman* deemed the characters in Haynes' *The Abbey Court Murder* "much truer to life than is the case in many sensational stories" and *The Spectator* concluded of *The Crime at Tattenham Corner*, "Excellent as a detective tale, the book also is a charming novel."

Sadly, Haynes' triumph as a detective novelist proved short lived. Around 1914, about the time of the outbreak of the Great War, Haynes had been stricken with debilitating rheumatoid arthritis that left her in constant pain and hastened her death from heart failure in 1929, when she was only 63. Haynes wrote several of her detective novels on fine days in Kensington Gardens, where she was wheeled from 14 Radnor Place in a bath chair, but in her last years she was able only to travel from her bedroom to her study. All of this was an especially hard blow for a woman who had once been intensely energetic and quite physically active.

In a foreword to *The Crystal Beads Murder*, the second of Haynes' two posthumously published mysteries, Ada Heather-Bigg noted that Haynes' difficult daily physical struggle "was materially lightened by the warmth of friendships" with other authors and by the "sympathetic and friendly relations between her and her publishers." In this latter instance Haynes' experience rather differed from that of her sister Bodleian, Agatha Christie, who left The Bodley Head on account of what she deemed an iniquitous contract that took unjust advantage of a naive young author. Christie moved, along with her landmark detective novel *The Murder of Roger Ackroyd* (1926), to Collins and never looked back, enjoying ever greater success with the passing years.

At the time Christie crossed over to Collins, Annie Haynes had only a few years of life left. After she died at 14 Radnor Place on 30 March 1929, it was reported in the press that "many people well-known in the literary world" attended the author's funeral at St.

Michaels and All Angels Church, Paddington, where her sermon was delivered by the eloquent vicar, Paul Nichols, brother of the writer Beverley Nichols and dedicatee of Haynes' mystery novel *The Master of the Priory*; yet by the time of her companion Ada Heather-Bigg's death in 1944, Haynes and her once highly-praised mysteries were forgotten. (Contrastingly, Ada Heather-Bigg's name survives today in the University College of London's Ada Heather-Bigg Prize in Economics.) Only three of Haynes' novels were ever published in the United States, and she passed away less than a year before the formation of the Detection Club, missing any chance of being invited to join this august body of distinguished British detective novelists. Fortunately, we have today entered, when it comes to classic mystery, a period of rediscovery and revival, giving a reading audience a chance once again, after over eighty years, to savor the detective fiction fare of Annie Haynes. *Bon appétit!*

Curtis Evans

Chapter One

"WHAT a nuisance this confounded play is! What a fool I was to promise to take part in it!" Dr. Roger Lavington flung the paper-covered book in his hand on the ground, and then aimed a kick at it as a further vent to his feelings.

Miss Minnie Chilton—the maiden aunt who had been acting for the past three months as his housekeeper—looked at him in mild surprise.

"Really, Roger—"

"I am sick of the whole thing," the doctor went on, in a much exasperated tone. "Here I come in, wet and tired from a long day's work and, instead of a little peace, I have to learn these wretched lines, and I suppose to-morrow when Zoe arrives there will be nothing but rehearsing. Plague take it all!"

Miss Chilton went on with her knitting.

"I was afraid you would find it a bother, Roger. I told you so when the idea was first mentioned, if you remember?"

This well-meant remark only had the effect of deepening her nephew's irritation. He rose.

"Well, anyhow, I am not going to bother any more about it to-night. There's a new article in the *Lancet* I must look at."

"Roger"—Miss Chilton's subdued, rather plaintive voice stopped him before he reached the door—"I suppose Zoe is sure to be here in time for lunch to-morrow?"

"I suppose so. By rights she ought to have come to-night. One day won't be enough for getting her part up, and so I told her; but one may as well talk to the wind as to Zoe, when she has made up her mind."

He did not wait for any of the further questions which he saw coming, but made his escape with all possible speed and betook himself down the long passage that led to his consulting-room.

Dr. Roger Lavington had only been settled in the village of Sutton Boldon for the past six months, but he was already beginning to doubt whether he had made a wise choice of a locality in which to begin life on his own account, and to think regretfully of the time he had passed in the metropolis, with his uncle, Dr. Lavington, Zoe's father, when he was at the hospital.

The village folk were inclined to look askance at the young doctor, and to regard his new-fangled theories with suspicion; he found it difficult to contend with their ignorance and apathy. Of late a new factor had been added to the situation; an old college friend of his—the Rev. Cyril Thornton—had been presented to a living a few miles away, and had brought his sister to keep house. Somewhat against his will Lavington had found himself drawn into the little circle of gaiety which had been created by the advent of the new clergyman. Thornton was so determined to have him that he told himself it was really less trouble to give way than to refuse; some amateur theatricals in aid of the building fund were the young vicar's latest idea, and he had not rested until he had obtained Roger Lavington's unwilling promise to help.

Only five days before that fixed for the performance, a great misfortune had befallen the little band of performers; the girl who was to take the second lady's part—one on which, in a great measure, the success of the whole thing depended—had fallen suddenly ill, and it was impossible on the spur of the moment to supply her place from the neighbourhood. In her despair Elsie Thornton had appealed to Lavington; she had often heard him speak of his cousin's powers as an actress; she begged him to ask her to come to their assistance now. Lavington had yielded unwillingly, and Zoe had promised to do her best; but she had delayed her arrival until the day of the performance itself, and the rest of the troupe were in despair, fearing that the one complete dress rehearsal—which was all that was possible under the circumstances—would be altogether inadequate to their needs.

Lavington himself was by no means word perfect; but, as he lighted his pipe and turned to his writing-table, he resolved to put the whole matter out of his mind, philosophically concluding that he would manage to get through somehow.

He was deeply immersed in the records of a case which was interesting him considerably, when there was a knock at the door. His strongly marked eyebrows nearly met in a frown as he called out:

"Come in!"

"I shouldn't have ventured to disturb you, sir, only; being as it was marked 'Immediate,' I thought—" the house-parlourmaid remarked apologetically as she handed him a letter on a salver.

"Quite right!" he said, as he took it, his scowl deepening as he saw that the bold black handwriting was that of his cousin Zoe.

"More directions, I suppose," he ejaculated, *sotto voce*, as he tore it open and the servant withdrew. "I really wish Zoe—What the deuce!" He stopped short and stared blankly at the note in his hand. Miss Zoe Lavington's communication was characteristically brief:

"DEAR ROGER,

"I am sorry that I am unable to come to you to-morrow, as I am down with the flu. You will have to get some one else to take the part. I am very much disappointed.

"Your affectionate cousin,

ZOE LAVINGTON"

Lavington gave a long whistle of dismay.

"What on earth is to be done now? They can't get anybody to take the part at a moment's notice, that's certain. The whole thing will have to be put off, and Thornton and his sister will be frantic. Well, I suppose"—hoisting himself out of his comfortable chair with a sigh—"I must go and break it to them."

He went over to the cupboard, and, taking out a box of cigars, filled his case; as he did so he heard footsteps hurrying up the gravel walk leading to the surgery door, and a loud clamouring ring at the bell.

He threw the door open; a woman, hatless, her uncovered grey hair floating wildly about her face, her eyes wild and frightened, almost flung herself upon him.

"You'll come, sir—you must come at once!" she cried, catching desperately at his arm as if afraid he would escape her, her breath breaking forth in long strangulating sobs between her words, as she tried to pour out her story. "It—it is the master—he is dying—dead! Oh, hurry, hurry!"

In an instant Lavington became the brisk business-like doctor.

"What is the matter?"

"I—I don't know!" The woman shuddered, casting furtive, frightened glances into the shadows around. "He was quite well at tea-time. But now he is lying on the floor—and there is blood—"

Her voice died away in a wail of anguish.

"Ah!" The doctor turned quickly to an open drawer and took out lint and bandages, together with a case of instruments and a small portable medicine-case. "Now, my good woman, calm yourself," he said authoritatively. "Where is your master?"

The woman looked at him in astonishment.

"I thought you would know, sir," she said in a more natural tone. "He—he is next door—at The Bungalow."

"The Bungalow." The doctor drew in his lips as, the woman running to keep pace with his long strides, he hurried down the little drive that led to his front gate. That there were curious rumours about the tenant of The Bungalow—a middle-aged artist, apparently possessed of considerable means, who had had the bad taste to refuse absolutely to make any acquaintances—it would have been impossible to live for six months in Sutton Boldon without knowing. The gossips had decided that his disinclination for society argued a disreputable past and, being completely in the dark with regard to his antecedents, had proceeded to invent various discreditable stories which might account for his hermit-like preference for his own society.

Lavington himself had rarely seen his neighbour, an occasional glimpse in the garden having been hitherto his only opportunity, and as he entered the long, low room leading out of the passage he was surprised to see how massive the frame of the man was who was stretched upon the floor, how large and well-formed his limbs.

The doctor's face was grave as he knelt down and made a cursory examination, the woman, meanwhile, standing in the doorway watching him with ashen face and wide-open dilated eyes.

At last he looked up.

"I can do no good here. He must have died instantaneously!"

A sort of quiver passed over the white face of the woman in the doorway.

"I can't think how he came to do it," she said hoarsely. "It wasn't as if he had any trouble. He always said—"

"You are making a mistake, my good woman," the doctor checked her sternly as he rose. "This is no case of suicide. Your master has been murdered!"

"Murdered!" With a cry the woman shrank back and put up her hand to her eyes. "Ah, no, no! He—"

"He has been shot through the brain. And there is no sign of the pistol from which the shot was fired—that alone would be conclusive," said the doctor grimly. "But the position of the wound shows that it could not have been self-inflicted. I should say, probably, robbery was the motive: you can see that his pockets have been rifled."

"What!" The housekeeper started violently. "They were not when I was here. They cannot be!"

"Look for yourself."

The doctor pointed to the prostrate figure. One of the coat-pockets was turned inside out; two or three envelopes and a cigar-case lay on the carpet.

The woman uncovered her face, her eyes looked wild and staring. She glanced fearfully round, at the open door behind her, at the darkness beyond.

"I did not see—I did not know! Who—"

The doctor shrugged his shoulders.

"That we have to find out. The first thing to be done is to let the police know. Is there anyone in the house whom you can send?"

She shook her head.

"I did for him altogether. He was never one to care for many folks about him."

"Then the question resolves itself into this: Will you stay here while I go, or shall I—"

"I—I daren't, sir!" the housekeeper broke in, her agitation becoming almost unbearable. "It is as much as I can do to stay in the house when you are here. I should go mad if I was left alone with him!"

Lavington glanced at her coldly: something in her emotion impressed him unfavourably. For a moment the idea of sending her to his house for help occurred to him, but the thought of the shock to his aunt restrained him.

"Then I will stay here and you must go," he said shortly. "Be as quick as you can, please."

The woman waited for no second bidding; she turned through the door, and Roger heard her running swiftly down the garden path outside.

Left alone, he looked down once more at the dead man. Who was the assassin, he wondered, who had stolen in from the darkness? Was it a thief, tempted by the thought of the gold that he might find? Or was it some one who had been once friend or foe of the dead man? But the blank, silent face before him could not answer his questions; there was nothing more to be done, and he was about to turn to the door when a faint fluttering sigh caught his ear. He paused and looked round. Everything was silent; apparently he and the dead man were the only occupants of the room; but Roger's trained eye caught an almost imperceptible movement of one of the thick window curtains.

He sprang forward and flung the curtain aside. Then he stood as if thunderstruck. Opposite, crouching against the wall, a small packet in her arms, her eyes wide open, dilated apparently in the last extremity of terror, was a young girl, looking almost a child as the lamplight fell on her white face and gleaming, dishevelled hair.

Lavington stared at her in utter amazement.

"What on earth are you doing here?" he questioned at last.

The stiff lips moved, but no words came; the brown eyes gazed back at him with the dazed, uncomprehending stare of a child.

Roger put out his hand and caught her arm.

"Why are you here? What have you done?"

With a hoarse cry the girl wrenched herself free and threw herself on her knees before him.

"Help me! Help me! I must get away. If anyone comes—if anyone knows—I shall die."

Lavington looked down into the anguished, tear-filled eyes, at the trembling lips, hardening his heart by a supreme effort.

"If you haven't done anything wrong there is nothing to be afraid of," he said.

But the great terrified eyes, raised so imploringly, had caught the momentary softening in his, and a gleam of hope crept into them. Slowly, falteringly, the girl raised herself, and faced him, steadying herself by the framework of the French window.

"I—perhaps I have done wrong," she said slowly, her throat twitching convulsively, one slender, ungloved hand still clutching the parcel to her breast, the other clenching and unclenching itself nervously, the delicate almond-shaped nails leaving cruel marks on the rosy palm. "But this will be worse than death. If—if you have a mother—a sister—for their sakes you will let me go!"

Her eyes wandered to the open door; she made a step towards it. Still, Lavington did not move aside, though the stern lines of his mouth had relaxed somewhat. Her appeal had touched a soft place in his heart. He had passionately loved his dead mother; she and the tiny sister who had died just as she had learnt to lisp his name were enshrined in his Holy of holies. What would they bid him do, if the dead could speak, he wondered? Then he recollected how his mother had always been on the side of mercy; his extended hand dropped.

With a sigh of relief the girl slipped by. At the same moment the echo of excited voices reached them from the distance, the sound of heavy measured footfalls. The girl halted and then turned back.

"It is too late! Oh, help me! Hide me! Save me! I am frightened—frightened—for the love of heaven!"

All Lavington's compassion was roused by the very forlornness of her attitude, by her despairing cry. He glanced round. Had he indeed left it too late? Was there no way of saving her even yet—this girl who had cried to him for help?

A sudden thought struck him; he stepped to the French window and opened it softly.

"See," he said, taking something from his pocket, as with a swift grateful glance she slipped through. "The garden will be searched, and all round will be watched; you cannot get away. But if you go across the lawn, step over the low fence and go up to that door next to the window where you will see a bright light, you can let yourself in with this latchkey. Stay quietly in my consulting-room until I come to you, and do not open the door to anyone."

He had no time for more, no means of finding out whether she understood or not. Like a frightened rabbit she scudded across the lawn; and when he turned round, after closing the window, the burly form of the village constable stood in the doorway.

"This 'ere seems a bad job, sir."

"It is indeed." To his intense disgust, as the man's small bright eyes watched him curiously, Lavington felt that his colour was changing. "It is impossible from the nature and the direction of the shot that it could have been self-inflicted," he went on, recovering his matter-of-fact, professional manner with an effort.

"I see, sir." Constable Frost's tone was distinctly non-committal. The constable was on the look out for promotion; it struck him that this case might afford him the opportunity for which he had been longing. He crossed over to Roger, who stood with his back against the thick, dull green curtains. "That window now, sir, I heard you closing it—was it open when you came in?"

"No. I unlatched it for a minute. The room was close."

"Just so, sir." The constable opened it and, stepping outside, listened with his head on one side for a minute. "Seems all quiet here, sir. I have sent over to Harleswood for the inspector, but if in the meantime you will oblige me—" He took out his notebook and set down laboriously Roger's bald account of his summons by the housekeeper, his brief examination of the body and, approximately, the cause of death. Then he looked at the housekeeper.

"And you say you last saw him alive, Mrs. McNaughton?"

"About seven o'clock, it would be," the housekeeper said tremulously. "He had his tea as usual; when I knocked at the door with the tray (he always had afternoon tea), I found him—like this. But I never thought but he had put an end to himself, poor gentleman!"

"Ay, I dessay. But, you see, Dr. Lavington here says that you were wrong. Besides, a dead man can't carry away a pistol. You can't give us any idea who done it, ma'am?"

The woman began to shiver, her eyes looked round the room, anywhere save at that stark, awful figure on the floor.

"I can't tell you anything. I never heard anybody come in." The man stooped and picked up something that lay concealed by the dead man's coat.

"What's this? How did this 'ere come 'ere?"

Roger bent forward and looked curiously at the long dangling object, then a breath of subtle perfume seemed to reach him; with a sudden exclamation he drew back. It was a woman's long suede glove that looked so strangely out of place in the constable's big red hand. As he moved away, some small shining object dropped from it; the constable stooped stiffly to pick it up.

"A ring," he muttered, turning it about in the lamplight. "Diamonds too. This 'ere ought to be a clue, sir."

Roger glanced at it; it looked like some family heirloom, he thought, with its quaint, old-fashioned setting.

"Certainly it ought," he acquiesced.

The amazement grew in Mrs. McNaughton's face, a bewilderment mixed with a kind of curious shrinking horror.

"I can't say—I don't know nothing about it."

Lavington stepped forward.

"Well, if that is all I can tell you, Frost, I will just step indoors. I am afraid my aunt—"

"Begging your pardon, sir, I should be glad if you would stay till the inspector comes. I expect him every minute now."

Lavington felt nettled.

"But my good man—"

"I should be blamed, sir, if I let you go afore he come," the constable went on. "There'll be explanations as'll have to be made. There"—he held up his hand—"I hear wheels. Here he is now, sir."

Chapter Two

LAVINGTON crossed the passage to the consulting-room and opened the door; then he stood still in amazement. His own easy chair was drawn up before the fire, and in it the girl was curled up, fast asleep apparently, one cheek resting on her upturned palm, her golden hair gleaming against the dark cushion. As he watched her, she drew her breath in a little sobbing cry, her delicate features contracted; then suddenly she opened her eyes and stared at him bewilderedly.

"Where am I? Oh!"—her lips trembling, a swift rush of colour flooding even her temples—"now, I—I remember. You sent—you sent me here. You will help me to get away?"

"If I can," said Lavington uncertainly. He came into the room and shut the door. "I could not get away before, until the inspector came; and now they are searching the neighbourhood for a girl, a girl whose glove they have found—a glove with a diamond ring in the finger."

"Ah!" The girl drew a deep breath.

Roger's eyes rested on a tiny crumpled ball of suede that lay on his writing-table, then his glance wandered to the fire-place and he uttered a quick exclamation.

"Why, some one has been burning paper," he said in surprise, as he picked up the largest piece.

With a sharp sound of dismay the girl sprang forward and snatched it out of his hand, not, however before he had had time to read two words in the small neat handwriting. It was the outside of an envelope; part of the address was torn away; only "von Rheinhart" was readable.

"How dare you!" the girl flashed as his fingers relaxed. "You knew that you were not meant to read it."

The very suddenness of the attack momentarily disconcerted Lavington, the softness and the smallness of the hands gripping his, the wrath in the great brown eyes alike took him aback. But, as he saw her tear the offending scrap of paper into the minutest fragments and throw it on the top of the smoking heap in the fire-place, he awoke to the full consciousness of the situation.

"I did not wish to read anything written there," he said gravely. "I had no thought at the moment that it was yours; but I could not help seeing the name 'von Rheinhart' and I know that Maximilian von Rheinhart is lying dead next door and that papers and valuables have been taken from his body."

In spite of her anger, as the last word left his lips, the girl visibly flinched.

"Not valuables—papers. And"—raising her head defiantly—"I took them—stole them, if you will. But he ought to have given them up long ago. He had no right to keep them. Now, they can do no more harm." And with the point of her buckled shoe she pushed the ashes farther down.

Lavington's grey eyes were stern.

"I believe that it is my duty to summon the police at once and to tell them everything."

The girl turned sharply; the anger on her face changed to terror.

"You—you couldn't!" she gasped, catching at her throat with both hands. "Listen—listen! I will tell you—you shall judge. He was a bad man—Maximilian von Rheinhart—a cruel man. There had been a story. Oh, you are a man, you can guess it; it was all over, quite over and done with—but there were letters and he traded on them, he threatened. At last he promised to give them to me, if I came alone, late at night, to-night. I came, and I found—oh, I cannot tell you any more!" shuddering and burying her face in her hands. "It was awful. But I think if I had been your sister, you would have asked another man to be kind to her, you would not—"

"Stop!" Roger held up his hand. "It is for her sake, my child sister's and for my mother's, and because you are a woman, and I have your word for it that you have been sorely tried, that I am going to help you now. But how to do it? That is the question. I don't know—" He paced up and down the small room in perplexity.

The girl watched him with puzzled eyes.

"If you will keep silence just a little while, I will make my way to the nearest station; and then—"

"Nearest station!" Lavington laughed aloud though there was little enough of real mirth in his merriment "Don't you know that every stranger at any of the stations round here will be watched and interrogated? Oh, yes; with the help of the telegraph and telephone, Inspector Stables has done his work well—for miles round the police are searching for the woman who wore the suede glove that lay beside the body of Maximilian von Rheinhart, for the owner of the diamond ring."

The colour slowly faded from the listener's face.

"What am I to do then?" she exclaimed in consternation. "How am I to get away?"

Lavington shook his head.

"At present I can see no way out of it. You are safe here now—but for how long?" shrugging his shoulders hopelessly.

"Do you mean that I cannot get away to-night?" she demanded, her face twitching nervously.

"Certainly not," Lavington confirmed promptly. "It is out of the question."

"But I cannot stay here."

"I am afraid you will have to," gloomily.

The girl stared at him a moment incredulously, then her full underlip began to tremble; to Roger's horror she buried her face in her hands and burst into a perfect passion of tears.

He watched her for a minute or two in a species of helpless fascination, wishing vainly that some form of comfort likely to be efficacious would occur to him; the idea of applying to his aunt for help occurred to him, only to be rejected. Miss Chilton was too old and too frail to be troubled with such problems as this girl's safety involved. The veriest hint of the terrible peril which hung over their guest would be enough to make her absolutely ill, as her nephew well knew. If only his cousin Zoe had been there, he thought vaguely, he would have been able to appeal to her. The recollection of Zoe turned his thoughts to her letter, which still lay on the mantelpiece.

As he looked at it, vaguely wishing he could ask her advice, a sudden idea flashed into his mind. Zoe's place, Zoe's room were waiting for her, his aunt and the servants were expecting her. Suppose, for the nonce, their guest were to become Zoe! The audacity of it almost took his breath away; and yet, the longer he thought of it, the more plainly he saw that it distinctly offered a solution of the difficulty. His eyes turned back to the girl, now sobbing aloud, apparently in the last extremity of despair.

"Can you act?" he asked suddenly.

The very incongruity of the question seemed to rouse the girl. She raised her eyes, tear-filled, her cheeks still wet.

"Act!" she repeated, in bewilderment.

"Yes, act," Lavington returned impatiently. "Because if you could, I think I see a way. I believe we might manage—"

A gleam of hope came into the brown eyes watching him.

"If you would explain, I think perhaps I might."

Lavington caught up his copy of the play.

"Have you ever taken part in any theatricals? Do you think you could help in this?" holding it out.

The girl glanced at it in his hand; a tinge of colour was creeping back to her pale cheeks.

"I think I could. I have always been fond of that sort of thing. But when? I cannot understand."

"To-morrow night," Lavington explained quickly. "My cousin Zoe was expected, but she is down with influenza. Luckily, I have not told anyone that she is prevented; and, if until after to-morrow evening you could take her place, the next day I might go to London with you, and I do not think any suspicion would be roused."

She turned the pages over rapidly.

"I could soon learn the part, but the dress—"

"Oh, that is all waiting for Zoe at Freshfield. You see, the scene is laid in Japan. You are the Japanese maiden who fascinates the hero, while Elsie Thornton personates the English girl who finally wins. But the Thorntons were so much afraid that the get-up wouldn't be correct that they have ordered the Japanese costumes from town. They're all loose, flowing garments, so that it is only a question of height; and I shouldn't think "—eyeing her critically —"that there can be an inch between you and Zoe."

Though the tears were still standing in her eyes, a tiny dimple played for one moment round the girl's mouth.

"That will be all right, then."

"Yes; I think so." Lavington acquiesced. "And now, the sooner we go in to my aunt the better. I will tell her you managed to get away by the last train to-night, instead of the first to-morrow—the one by which she expected you."

"In one moment." She turned to the small mirror over the mantelpiece and, with a few deft touches, restored her hair to order and, after pinning her fur toque securely in its place, pulled a veil over her face.

"Now, tell me what I have to do," she said, turning to Roger with a charming air of dependence.

Lavington briefly put her in possession of the circumstances, and told her all that he thought necessary of Zoe's surroundings. In a very few moments she professed herself ready to accompany him to his aunt.

Miss Chilton was still sitting in the little drawing-room where he had left her, her hands busy with her knitting, her thoughts on household cares intent. Secretly, she was rather inclined to dread the coming of Roger's London-bred cousin, and to feel distinctly glad that the young lady had postponed making her acquaintance to the last possible moment. Her usually tranquil smile was scarcely as placid as usual when Lavington put his head in at the door.

"Who do you think I have brought you, Aunt Minnie?"

Her expression changed to one of real alarm as she said hastily, "Not—not—"

"Zoe!" he finished, with a laugh. "Here she is, to speak for herself. She found she could get away to-night after all."

"And I hope you will not mind?" this new Zoe said, coming swiftly into the room as Roger stood aside. "You must not let me give you any trouble. Really, I was obliged to come."

Miss Chilton took the outstretched hand in hers.

"Do not talk of trouble, my dear," she said with her pretty air of old-fashioned hospitality. "Your coming here is only a pleasure to us, I am sure." Then as if moved by some sudden impulse, she drew the girl down and kissed the fresh, young cheek. "I am sure I shall love to have you, and I hope you will stay a long time with us, if you can put up with my old-fashioned ways."

The brown eyes looked very grateful as the girl returned the kiss heartily.

"You are very kind. I should love to stay with you. But this time, I am afraid—"

"Uncle John is not very well, Aunt Minnie," interposed Roger, coming to the rescue, "and Zoe is his right hand. He could hardly be persuaded to spare her even for the theatricals. Later on, perhaps. But now I am sure that Zoe must be tired and hungry after her journey—perhaps you will just show her to her room, and then we will have dinner."

"Of course, my dear. What was I thinking of?" The old lady rose in a bustle and rolled up her knitting in a ball. "Your room is all ready, my dear, and dinner will be ready in a minute."

There was a grim smile on Roger's face as he closed the door behind them. When his aunt came into the room again she was looking anxious and worried.

"I wish we had known that she was coming tonight; we would have had something nice for dinner. You never told me how pretty she was, Roger."

"Who—Zoe?" The doctor looked puzzled. "I do not think she is. At least"—with a change of front, as he remembered the big, bright eyes, the flushing cheeks of this new Zoe—"I suppose she is. I never thought of it before."

"Really, Roger!" Evidently the old lady was working herself up into quite a state of excitement over her guest. "And her gown—did you notice it?"

"Not particularly," Roger responded, with masculine denseness. "Something dark, wasn't it?"

"Something dark!" Miss Chilton repeated with supreme contempt. "It was dark green of course! But did you notice the cut and the finish and the wonderful embroidery on the vest and cuffs? I could not help saying to her, 'My dear, where did you get that gown?' and she said at once, 'In Vienna.' I thought she was inclined to catch herself up the moment after she had said it, but still—I have heard that Viennese tailors are even more expensive than the Parisian. What do you make of it, Roger? Your Uncle John—"

"Must have more money than sense, by your account of it, I should say," Lavington interpolated brusquely." Don't worry yourself about it, Aunt Minnie. Zoe"—bringing out the name after an imperceptible pause—"has put on her best bib and tucker to dazzle our rustic minds, I expect."

"Oh, well, I don't know," Miss Chilton began, unconvinced. "Oh, there you are, my dear!" with a complete change of tone as the swish of Zoe's silken petticoats, the tap of her high-heeled shoes, were heard.

Looking at her, at the daintily arranged masses of her fair hair, at the exquisite finish of her gown, at the delicate touches of lace falling round her throat and wrists, Lavington found it difficult to believe that this was in reality the wild-eyed, desolate creature who had cried aloud to him for help so short a time before.

But, in the dining-room, he saw that she was making the veriest pretence of eating, and that she was with difficulty preventing herself from starting at every sound. As they were finishing, the front door bell pealed loudly. Roger forced himself to look away from the girl's rapidly changing colour, and to talk with apparent unconcern to his aunt during the pause that followed. At last the house-parlourmaid appeared with a white, scared face.

"Constable Frost would be glad to speak to you a moment, sir. He is waiting in the hall. And, oh, sir, oh, ma'am!"—turning to the astonished Miss Chilton—"they say there has been a murder done next door, and they are out searching for them that has done it! Me and Cook are both frightened out of our wits to stay in the kitchen!"

"What!" Miss Chilton fell back in her chair, white and trembling.

Lavington felt, rather than saw, the change that passed over the face of the girl sitting at his right. He rose.

"You should not alarm Miss Chilton in that way, Mary. Tell Constable Frost I will speak to him in a minute. Aunt Minnie, I did not mean to tell you until the morning of the sad fate that has overtaken our neighbour, Rheinhart. But there is nothing to alarm you."

"He is dead!" Miss Chilton gasped.

Roger nodded.

Through the half-open door Constable Frost's keen little eyes were taking in every detail of the homelike scene—the well-appointed dinner-table, the frail old lady at the top, the pretty pale girl bending over her.

"And—and the murderer is still at large!" Miss Chilton went on, with a little sob. "I am frightened, Roger."

Lavington looked away from the girl who was chafing the old lady's hands.

"I think you are quite safe, Aunt Minnie; I will take care of you. But I must speak to Frost a minute. What is it, constable?"—as he stepped out into the hall—"Any success?"

"We haven't found her so far, sir. The inspector, he seems to think that she must have come through your garden, and he has sent me to tell you he will be compelled to make a search. He thought it well to let you know first in case of alarming the ladies."

Was it his fancy, Roger wondered, or was there a slight indefinable pause before the last word? He glanced up sharply. Constable Frost's face was as imperturbably stolid as ever; his eyes were glancing apologetically at Miss Chilton.

"Certainly. Please tell Inspector Stables to make as complete a search as he likes. Is there anything else I can do for you, constable?"

"No. That is all, thank you, sir," he replied.

Outside, in the hall, the dining-room door closed; Constable Frost became suddenly exceedingly affable with the house-parlourmaid.

"Nice-looking young lady that!" he observed communicatively. "Who might she be, I wonder?"

"She is Miss Lavington, the doctor's cousin. She has come over to take part in the play-acting at Freshfield to-morrow," Mary returned. "Oh, Mr. Frost, I am that upset about this murder, I hardly durst open the door! And as for going to bed, me and Cook mean to sit up all night!"

"That would be a sensible thing to do," remarked the constable satirically. "You can go to bed safe enough, Mary"—with a playful pinch of her arm—"I'll look after you."

Chapter Three

"I AM so sorry, Roger. Zoe says that she will be obliged to go away in the morning. Her father wants her, she tells me. I do think that, coming all this way, Dr. Lavington might have spared her to us a little longer." And gentle Miss Chilton looked quite aggrieved.

"Yes; it is a pity she has to go!" Roger assented absently.

He was standing by the window, his eyes glancing over the garden where Inspector Stables's men had made sad havoc among the daffodils and hyacinths, in the course of their search for the murderer of Maximilian von Rheinhart, the night before.

"Zoe" put her arm caressingly through Miss Chilton's.

"It is awfully kind of you to want to keep me," she said in her pretty, flute-like voice.

"Not at all, my dear," Miss Chilton contradicted plaintively. "Or at least, I am kind to myself. It is often very dull when Roger is away; and you are so good to an old woman. At least, if you cannot stay longer now, you must promise to come again very soon and give us a little more of your society."

There was a momentary pause; then "Zoe" stooped and softly kissed the old lady's withered cheek.

"Thank you very much. I, too, hope we shall meet again before long."

Roger stirred impatiently.

"They are bringing the car round. Come, Zoe. I hope you know your part."

"I am word-perfect," the girl declared, as she followed him out of the room.

Outside in the sunshine, it felt like a typical spring morning. The air was warm and balmy. As Roger helped his companion into the car, his eyes rested for a moment on the low roof of The Bungalow. With a pang of pity he thought of the dead man lying stark beneath.

The drive to Freshfield was not a long one; and it was accomplished for the most part in silence; as Roger drew up before the schoolhouse where the rehearsal as well as the performance was to take place, the vicar came forward and welcomed them.

"Ah, Lavington, this is good of you! And Miss Lavington, I presume," anticipating Roger's hesitating introduction. "Do you know"—as he helped the girl down and led the way across the school-yard— "that all last night my dreams were haunted by the fear that you would fail us at the last moment? It is so good of you to come to our assistance."

The girl smiled a little.

"I was very glad to come, thank you," she replied with more truth than the Rev. Cyril Thornton suspected.

The new vicar of Freshfield was a slight, fair, clerical-looking young man; he was, of course, the centre of an enormous amount of interest among the unmarried ladies, old and young, of his parish; but so far he had shown no inclination to respond to their flattering attentions; to-night, however, he positively ignored them and constituted himself the *preux chevalier* of the new and fascinating cousin of Roger Lavington's.

The new-comer was quite a success at the rehearsal; evidently her promise of being word-perfect was no empty boast, and her knowledge of the lines put to shame many of her fellow-performers who had been rehearsing for weeks. She made an attractive picture, too, in her kimono, her gleaming hair drawn off her face and piled high in the Japanese fashion. More than once Lavington scowled as he saw how the vicar's blue eyes followed her every movement and how his lank, clerical figure was constantly to be seen during the interval in close attendance upon the Japanese tea-girl. At last, feeling distinctly annoyed and out of sorts, Roger made his way across to them, unceremoniously leaving pretty Elsie Thornton in the middle of a speech.

Elsie's eyes grew wistful as she watched him threading his way across the crowded school-room; almost unconsciously she had learnt to think a good deal of her brother's friend; to-day she was learning the state of her own heart, and, at the same time, being shown the utter futility of those shy, sweet hopes that had been springing up of late.

The vicar looked up with a smile as his friend approached.

"Ah, Lavington, I am trying to persuade Miss Lavington to take a different conception of these lines, do you see, when you come on, and she—-"

"I think she does it remarkably well as it is," Roger interrupted brusquely. "Come, Zoe, I am going to take you in to tea."

A sudden flush rose to the girl's cheeks as she heard the masterful tone; for a moment she seemed inclined to hesitate, then she rose obediently.

"Thank you, Mr. Thornton; I will think over the alterations you suggest. Yes, Roger, I shall be glad of a cup of tea."

Lavington started as he heard her use his Christian name as naturally as if they were indeed the cousins they were assuming to be. He glanced down at her flushed, smiling face with a curious tightening feeling at his heart.

"You seem to like Thornton?" He had not in the least intended to say the words; they seemed to come without his own volition.

The girl looked surprised.

"He is very kind," she said simply.

He drew her into an embrasure of the window, in which they were practically alone, as he supplied her with tea.

"I think— Can you manage to be ready to catch the eight o'clock train to-morrow morning? I will drive you over to Overcroft Station."

She stood with downcast eyes, playing with her teaspoon.

"I do not want to bother you, but is it necessary to start quite so early? Miss Chilton is particularly anxious that I should stay until the afternoon and I—"

"I think it is necessary," Roger interrupted gruffly. "I think it is better that you should know; Thornton has just told me that they expect quite a crowd to-night at this play, and he has applied for an extra policeman to keep the door. He has just come and he is Constable Frost of Sutton Boldon."

"Oh!" The girl looked unenlightened.

With a distinct feeling of irritation at her denseness, Roger proceeded:

"He is the first policeman called to The Bungalow last night, and from his presence here, when naturally all the available police are employed in connection with the affair, I cannot help fearing that he may suspect.

"Suspect!" the girl echoed, all her pretty, newborn colour fading from her cheeks. "Do you mean that he has guessed—that he thinks that I—"

"I do not see what else could have brought him here," Roger confessed gloomily. "But I do not think he has anything definite to go upon and by to-morrow—"

"By to-morrow I shall be safe away," the girl said, apparently recovering her spirits with marvellous rapidity as Mr. Thornton, having discovered their hiding-place, suddenly appeared before them.

"We—I think we are going to have a full house to-night, Miss Lavington," he said, beaming upon her benevolently and rubbing his hands together in the approved clerical fashion. "Lady Bunner has promised to bring a big party and I hear that Sir William himself is coming."

"Sir William Bunner!" she repeated, a curious pallor coming over her features. "Do you mean the judge?"

"Yes; he retired from the bench last year," Mr. Thornton replied. "Do you know him, Miss Lavington?" curiously.

"I have heard of him," she replied evasively, as she set her tea-cup down. "Now, Mr. Thornton, if you are ready, I will try if I can go over those lines to your satisfaction."

Roger watched them walk away in gloomy silence; then he made his way to the large school-room which was rapidly filling. Apparently the idea of the theatricals had caught on and the vicar's heart would be rejoiced by the sight of an overflowing audience and the prospect of a goodly sum for his fund.

Lavington did not come on at first; the scene was laid in a Japanese tea-shop, and as the curtain rose he took his stand against the wall in close proximity to the front row. For some time "Zoe" had the stage pretty much to herself, and her graceful acting and clear voice, as well as her beautiful face, evidently found favour with the audience, for her exit provoked a round of cheering.

Under cover of it an old gentleman near Roger leaned forward.

"Who is the young lady? She reminds me strongly of some one; I cannot just remember who."

The young man to whom he spoke consulted his programme.

"Miss Maud Perrin, Sir William, as far as I can make out."

"But Miss Maud Perrin was taken ill after the programmes were printed," a third voice interposed at this juncture. "Mr. Thornton was telling me about it yesterday, and they had to get some one else at the last minute."

"Well, she is very like some one I know," the first speaker reiterated, "though at present I cannot place her. Still, my profession has brought me into contact with a good many people," with a chuckle at his own joke.

Roger shuddered as he realized that this must be the well-known Sir William Bunner, whose severity had earned for him the sobriquet of the "Hanging Judge."

But Mr. Thornton was signalling frantically from the door-way; Lavington became aware that he was due upon the platform very shortly. As he made his way to the door he caught another remark; a girl behind him was leaning forward eagerly:

"Why, father, she is just like Miss—"

Roger did not catch the name; the vicar seized his arm.

"What are you about, Lavington? You will never be ready?"

"Oh, yes, I shall!" Roger returned coolly. "Don't excite yourself, old fellow, everything is going on very well."

"Yes, if you don't spoil it," groaned the vicar. "For goodness' sake, make haste, man."

For most of the audience that night the stage held but one figure; Elsie Thornton, Roger Lavington and the rest of the performers might be all very well, but the whole of the time she was on the stage they were dominated and held by "Zoe's" brilliant, fascinating personality; she allured and she charmed alike by her dainty coquetry, and by her passion as she bade a last farewell to her lover.

Lavington was conscious that he was acting like a stick, but all his thoughts were with his beautiful pseudo-cousin. The presence of Constable Frost at the door had roused the gravest misgivings in his mind, and he could not but fancy that a new source of danger had arisen in Sir William Bunner's half recognition of her—even to himself he would not acknowledge all that he feared this last might imply.

"Zoe" appeared with the rest of the performers before the curtain to bow her thanks to the audience, but Roger fancied that she looked worried and distraite, and somewhat pointedly avoided both himself and Thornton.

He hurried off to the dressing-room to divest himself of his grease paint, resolving to start for Sutton Boldon as soon as "Zoe" was ready. As he was getting into his coat, there was a knock at the door; a boy handed him a note; though he had never seen the handwriting before, a certain knowledge of the writer seemed to come to him as he tore it open and read:

"DEAR ROGER,

"Some friends of mine are here and have offered to give me a lift home, and, as I am anxious to get back to my father, I think it will be best for me to go with them, as it might be inconvenient for you to drive me to the station the first thing in the morning. I am so glad that the theatricals have been such a success. Please remember me to Miss Chilton, and thank her for her kindness to me, and with many thanks to yourself,

> "Believe me,

>> "Your affectionate cousin,

>>> "ZOE."

"P.S.—This will be given you when I am gone."

Roger stared at the words as if thunderstruck, and then read them over again. Was it, could it be possible that "Zoe," as he called her in his thoughts now, had really vanished out of his life for ever with the same dramatic suddenness as she had entered it?

Chapter Four

THE MORNING was crisp and cool and bright; there was a touch of frost in the air; outside in the garden the adventurous little flowers of spring were drooping with wilted heads. A bright fire was burning in the grate; Roger Lavington sat at the end of the table nearest, drinking his coffee and eating his eggs and bacon with a gloomy, abstracted air, his dark, rugged eyebrows drawn together in a frown that betrayed his thoughts to be anything but agreeable.

Opposite, behind the coffee-pot and the steaming silver kettle, Miss Chilton had opened the morning paper and was bending over it, her lace cap quivering with nervousness as she uttered various interested ejaculations:

"Terrible! Terrible! What an accident! Why, Roger—"

Her tone was so excited that her nephew was startled out of his absorption.

"Yes, what is it, Aunt Minnie?"

"Oh, this is dreadful! Wasn't Sir James Courtenay a great friends of yours?"

"Yes: both at Wellington and Magdalen, though I've not seen much of him of late years. But what's wrong with him?"

"Sir James Courtenay, of Oakthorpe Manor, seriously injured. It is feared that amputation of both legs may be necessary. Poor, poor fellow, Roger! Isn't it heart-rending? I think I would really rather be killed outright than mangled in such a fashion. It's that railway accident in the north. You know, it was mentioned in the papers last night."

"But do you mean that Courtenay—" Roger came round and looked over her shoulder.

Miss Chilton pushed the paper towards him.

"You take it; I'm sure that I cannot bear to read about it. Poor young man!"

Lavington caught it from her hand and, standing with his back to the fire, scanned the details, his face very grave as he realized how serious was the injury.

Courtenay and he had been great friends in boyhood and early youth and, though they had seen less of one another of late, the old affection was still strong with Roger. The paths in the life of a struggling doctor and a wealthy baronet must of necessity be far apart, and though Courtenay, after his accession to the baronetcy, which fell to him somewhat unexpectedly, had made many efforts to keep up the old intimacy, the force of circumstances had been too strong for him, and they had drifted away from one another.

Only a few days before, however, Roger had seen the announcement of Sir James Courtenay's forthcoming marriage to the daughter of a well-known political peer; that very day he had been intending to write a letter of congratulation; and now his heart was very heavy for his friend as he realized how suddenly the cup of happiness had been dashed from his lips.

He glanced mechanically down the terribly long list of killed and injured. As he reached the bottom, a short paragraph caught his eye that drove the blood from his cheeks and set his heart beating:

"THE BUNGALOW MURDER.

"It is rumoured that the police are in possession of a definite clue that may lead to the discovery of the assassin of Maximilian von Rheinhart. It will be remembered that at the adjourned inquest a witness testified to having seen a woman go in at the garden gate a short time before the alarm was raised; among the victims of the Northchester disaster is a young woman whose body has not yet been identified, but who is supposed to correspond in every particular with that person who is wanted in connection with The Bungalow murder. It is further stated that the police have found in the pockets certain evidence which places her acquaintance with Rheinhart beyond doubt."

Lavington studied the paragraph until the printed words seemed to dance before his eyes. It was possible, he knew, by driving across country, that the girl whom he still thought of as Zoe might have caught the express which came to such a signal disaster at Northchester.

"It's very sad indeed," Miss Chilton said plaintively, her head shaking with nervous excitement. "Though I never saw him myself, I have heard you speak of him so often that I feel quite upset—I do really! And I know that it must be a shock to you."

Her voice fell on deaf ears; her words could not penetrate the red mist that seemed to enwrap Roger as he pictured the quondam Zoe's gleaming golden hair, all soiled in blood, and the tall, slim form mangled and cut up.

"Roger, don't you think there may be a mistake?" Miss Chilton's voice sounded injured. The poor lady was feeling a bit ill-used; here was an exciting piece of news, and Roger apparently took no interest in it.

But this time her nephew heard.

"No, I should not think there is a mistake," he replied, in an odd, strained tone. "Evidence places her connection with Rheinhart beyond doubt," he repeated to himself.

His lips moved silently as he scanned the lines once more, the paper still open before his face. Was it possible that "Zoe" had been mad enough to keep papers of any kind in her possession?

Then a great pity took possession of him as he recalled the girl's big, terrified eyes, the passion in her voice. Had she been frightened, he wondered, in that awful moment when her soul stood face to face with the Great Beyond? Or had Death come swiftly, suddenly? Had she been one of those who pass through the cold waters all unknowing?

A sick shiver shook Roger from head to foot as he threw the paper on the table and turned to the door.

"Is it one of your long days, Roger, or shall you be in to lunch?" Miss Chilton called out as he was about to close the door. She was bending over the account of the accident again, returning to the harrowing details with renewed zest.

Roger's temper rose.

"I can't tell where I may be."

"But Roger—" The rest of the sentence was lost as her nephew strode down the passage into the surgery, banging the double doors that ensured his absolute seclusion.

He drew his case-book towards him from force of habit, and ran his fingers down the list for the day; but though he was apparently regarding every particular with the deepest attention, in reality he could not have repeated one word from the page before him. He shuddered as he thrust his books aside; and, dropping heavily into the straight-backed chair beside him, sat with his elbows on his knees, his eyes fixed unseeingly straight before him.

At last he rose, and, as if moving without his own volition, opened a drawer, took out a time-table, and turned over its pages rapidly. Yes, there it was—"Sutton Boldon, 10.45; Sheffield, 12.20; Northchester, 1.38." There was ample time for him to get to

Northchester and back, ample time to ascertain who had been killed in the Northchester disaster. A very few minutes for deliberation, and his mind was made up. The fact that his friend, Sir James Courtenay, was among the injured was excuse enough for his action if excuse was needed, and when the 10.45 steamed out of Sutton Boldon Station, Roger Lavington was snugly ensconced in a corner seat of a first-class smoking compartment.

No sooner, however, was he fairly on his way, than, manlike, he began to think he had done wrong in coming, to call himself a fool for his pains. What was it to him what became of the girl? he asked himself savagely. With her departure from Freshfield, the responsibility which had been thrust upon him ceased, the episode was closed.

Opposite him two men were discussing the accident, dwelling on the ghastly details with gusto, it seemed in his irritation. In vain he lighted the meerschaum that had been his unfailing resource since his college days, and tried to detach his thoughts. Scraps of their conversation would reach his ears.

"One poor thing was found with her head jammed back against the woodwork; her neck was broken."

"Was that the woman that they say was wanted for the Bungalow murder?"

"No. She was in the front of the train; this one I'm speaking of was behind. Queer thing that is too. I notice they do not say in the papers what the clue was they have discovered; it might defeat the ends of justice, I suppose. But I see in the late edition that she is quite young, a mere girl. Well, well, I dare say it is best it should end like that. Though, mind you, there was more in that Bungalow murder than meets the eye. I can read between the lines."

The speaker was a short, squat-figured man of middle age, with a white, flat, flabby face bordered by sandy side-whiskers; his expression was one of exasperating complacence. With a muttered exclamation Roger thrust his head out of the window. Withdrawing it presently he became aware that his travelling companions were still engaged in the discussion of the same topic.

"A girl like that does not commit a murder for nothing, I say. Probably Rheinhart thoroughly deserved his fate."

His companions carried on their conversation, casting curious glances at Roger now and then. Roger had an uncomfortable feeling that they thought his manner odd, that they were speculating about him.

They got out hurriedly at Sheffield, and he lost sight of them as he made his way to the Northchester train. It was crowded. Relatives and friends were hurrying down to claim the dead or nurse the injured. Roger had some difficulty in finding a seat. He wondered vaguely whether Courtney's betrothed would be there—whether he would find her by his friend's bedside?

At last Northchester was reached. The station was a big, bustling junction; the actual scene of the accident was some little distance away, but the company had arranged for brakes to be in waiting to convey the friends of the victims as speedily as possible; and Roger, mentioning Courtenay's name and his own profession, found himself treated with every consideration and speedily accorded a seat. It had not been possible to house all the injured at the hotel which was nearest to the railway, but Courtenay and those most seriously injured had been carried there and others more able to bear the journey were taken into the town of Northchester itself.

Roger was shocked to find that the papers had rather under than overestimated his friend's injuries; amputation of both legs had already taken place, and the injury to the spine was at present baffling the doctors.

Near at hand, close to the scene of the accident, there stood a long, low, desolate-looking barn; towards it, across a rough, ploughed field, a constant stream of feet had in the last few hours trodden the path. Roger glanced at it mechanically. A goodly proportion of his fellow-travellers were making their way towards it in groups of twos and threes. Others were coming out. Lavington saw that two of them held handkerchiefs to their eyes. He looked once more at the dark, lonely outbuilding silhouetted against the grey sky, and understood. This then was his goal; this was where he must seek the solution of the doubts that had tormented him for the past few hours.

There was little difficulty in obtaining admission Roger found the mere production of his card sufficient. Three of the dead were yet unidentified, he learned—an elderly man, a middle-aged woman, and a young girl. Seventeen had been killed outright, one had already been removed after the adjourned inquest held that morning, the others lay rigid and silent, on separate trestles, up the centre of the building.

The attendant reverently turned back the cloths from their faces; two of them Roger passed unnoticed, his eyes turned to the third. Here the woman paused.

"You are prepared, I suppose, sir. The poor young thing's head was caught against the woodwork and—"

Roger's eyes were fixed upon the form outlined long and stark beneath the sheet.

"I am a doctor, my good woman," he said impatiently.

"I beg your pardon, sir." The woman drew back the covering. Roger caught the gleam of golden hair upon the pillow, hair that might yesterday have been curled and waved, but that to-day was combed primly back and stiffly coiled. He bent forward.

When he raised his head his face was ghastly white. He turned quickly away; the woman followed him.

"There is the dress she wore, sir. Maybe you might know that— dark-green it is. Poor thing, it will not bear thinking of. They say as she had something to do with the murder of that artist gentleman the other day, but it don't seem to me likely. Why, she was little more than a child, as you may say."

As she spoke, she unlocked a heavy chest and brought out a green cloth coat and skirt. Recognizing the colour, Roger stepped forward, then his expression changed; he bent over the stained, dusty garments more closely.

The woman watched him curiously.

"Can you swear to them, sir?"

Roger waited a minute, then he straightened himself, as if throwing some weight off his shoulders.

"No; I cannot say anything about them."

Outside in the clear, cool air, he lifted his face to the breeze. People were still struggling up to the barn; the undertaker's men, brisk and busy, met him. Half-way across the field he was hailed from behind:

"Eh, Dr. Lavington!"

Roger paused in some surprise; the man who was hurrying towards him, alert, rosy-faced, clean-shaven, was a stranger. He waited.

"I heard that you were in Northchester, that you had been to see Sir James Courtenay, and, as I am anxious to have a little conversation with you, I thought, perhaps, I had better avail myself of this opportunity. But I must introduce myself. I am Detective-Inspector Collins of Scotland Yard."

"Indeed!" Lavington's tone was curt." What can I do for you?"

Inspector Collins joined him on the path.

"I am going your way; if you will excuse me, Dr. Lavington, we can talk as we walk. Perhaps I ought first to have explained that I have been sent here in connection with the Bungalow Murder, and as you were the doctor called in, as well as the first person who saw Maximilian von Rheinhart after he was discovered by the housekeeper, I am naturally anxious to hear what you have to say."

Roger frowned. He pulled his hat low down over his brows, and stuck his hand low down in his trousers pockets.

"I do not know that I have anything to add to the account I gave at the inquest."

Detective-Inspector Collins's sharp little grey eyes glanced obliquely in his direction.

"Quite so! Quite so! I understand," he said in a soothing tone, which somehow aroused an unreasonable amount of resentment within Roger's breast. "But, naturally, I want to hear what you have to say at first hand. You were of the opinion that Rheinhart had been dead some time when you saw him?"

"Some little time; possibly not more than half an hour," Roger assented.

"Just so! Just so!" the detective acquiesced. "Now, this young woman"—he jerked his head back to the barn—"has been identified by a man named Heron as a girl he saw enter the garden gate at The Bungalow half an hour or three-quarters before the murder was committed and you were summoned; he recognized her by her yellow hair, he says; and the description he gave of her dress previously tallies with what she was wearing at the time of the accident. I take it you saw nothing of her there," with another lightning glance.

There was a moment's silence; Roger's thoughts went back to the silent thing lying in that ghastly row with the primly-plaited golden hair; his right hand clenched itself suggestively in his pocket.

"Nothing!" he said in an abrupt, decided tone "She must have made her escape before I came."

Chapter Five

"I AM sick of the whole detestable rubbish! It is worse than useless, I tell you."

James Courtenay was sitting in the wheeled chair, in which he managed to make his halting, painful progression from room to room. Two years had elapsed since that Northchester disaster; but, though the doctors had held out hopes of being able to fix artificial limbs, there were other injuries that complicated matters and so far every attempt had ended in failure, and Courtenay was still absolutely crippled.

"This draught will at least relieve you," Roger Lavington said quietly, as he held out the glass. The past two years had altered him but slightly; there were a few grey hairs mingled with brown near the temples, and an added line or so near the mouth, that was all.

The practice at Sutton Boldon had not turned out a success, and Courtenay, who had heard that Dr. Lavington was selling his practice, wrote to ask him to come to him as resident physician, with a handsome salary.

At first Lavington refused. It seemed to him that it would be giving up his independence. Courtenay, however, persisted; his condition was such as to render the presence of a physician close at hand almost a necessity.

Roger saw that it was no sinecure that was being offered to him, the case was an extremely interesting one from a medical point of view, and the post would afford him besides ample time for carrying on the experiments and the study which he had found impossible at Sutton Boldon.

So, after much deliberation, and due weighing of pros and cons, he had accepted for a time at any rate and though he had only been at Oakthorpe a week, he had found already that his task would be by no means an easy one.

At school and college Courtenay, though easily roused to passion, had been distinguished for his easy-going disposition, and his ready good nature. It would have been too much to expect that, after the terrible injuries he had received in the accident at Northchester, he should remain the same.

But beyond the general captiousness and irritability for which Lavington was prepared, it seemed to him that his friend's whole nature was warped and changed. He had become cynical and hard. In some moods he seemed to positively take a pleasure in making speeches that hurt and stung; and he, who had formerly listened to every tale of sorrow or trouble, and sympathized with the sufferers, often relieving them to an extent which his slender income had then in no way warranted, would now dismiss a tenant who came to him for advice or help, with blunt refusal of either, and in some moods would bring the hot blood to the cheek of the unlucky suppliant with a few contemptuous words.

The only thing which, as far as Roger could see, remained unchanged was the old friendship for himself. Though even with him Courtney would often be unjust and unreasonable, it was not difficult to divine that the old liking was there, that Lavington's presence at the Manor was a real pleasure to him.

To-day the nervous pains in the spine and head were unusually violent. Roger had been employed since early morning in trying to find some means of alleviating them, so far with little success. At last he had determined to administer a sedative. Courtney, however, was not an amenable patient, and it was no easy matter to persuade him to take it.

"The best thing you could do would be to give me something out of that medicine-case of yours that would send me to sleep for ever," he growled, as Roger, glass in hand, stood waiting.

"This will probably make you sleep for a time, and I hope when you wake you will feel much better." Roger set the draught on the table and stooped to readjust the mechanism of the chair.

Courtenay caught up the glass and emptied it.

"I see I shall get no peace until I do," he said recklessly. "And, after all, sleep is the one thing left me. It is something to forget, if only for an hour, the crippled, useless log I have become; to think that I am once more alive! Will you ring for Miller, Lavington? I want to give her some directions about the study."

Roger adjusted the chair to the proper angle, so that his patient could sleep, and touched a handbell.

"Send Mrs. Miller here, please," he said to the man, and then waited till the housekeeper appeared.

He knew that she had been Courtenay's nurse in childhood, and that after the accident she had returned to Oakthorpe and begged to be allowed to assist in the nursing, and that Courtenay had since installed her as housekeeper. Courtenay had hinted, too, at a tragic story in her past. He had spoken of a daughter who had left her home, and whose desertion had well-nigh broken her mother's heart.

So far, however, Lavington had only seen her face by candlelight. As she came into the room now, he was conscious of a certain sense of familiarity. He watched her with some attention. She was dressed in the traditional black silk, her grey hair was rolled back beneath a lace cap, and she wore an elaborate gold brooch and chain. It seemed to Roger, however, that in spite of her stately attire she herself was ill at ease and nervous, that her eyes did not meet his fully.

"Have I ever seen you before?" he asked her suddenly.

She caught her sleeve in something on the table, and stooped to disentangle it.

"I believe you came to spend the holidays with Master James once, when you were both at Wellington, sir. I was with Mrs. Courtenay then."

Roger looked at her again. He had fancied that his recollection of her was more recent; but the memory eluded him. He turned away.

"I suppose that is it, then."

Already Courtenay was nodding in his chair. With a sign to Mrs. Miller to take care that he was not to be disturbed, Lavington left the room.

As he crossed the hall he heard his name. Mrs. Melville, Courtenay's married sister, who was staying at the Manor for the present, was standing at the library door.

"How is he?" she asked anxiously.

Roger went towards her and drew her inside. In their childish days he and pretty Ethel Courtenay had been fast friends.

"The pain will go off now, I trust. He was much easier when I came down."

Great tears were standing in Mrs. Melville's eyes.

"Is it not terrible Roger?" she said piteously. "To think of him as he was and then to see him now."

"He is altered," Roger acquiesced. "But we ought to remember that it must inevitably sour and warp a man's whole nature to be thus suddenly and terribly cut off from all that makes life worth living."

"Yes, of course; I am always reminding myself of that." Mrs. Melville crossed to the window. "I cannot help thinking of poor Daphne Luxmore too," she said, after a pause, during which Lavington had waited in sympathetic silence. "I went to see her yesterday. She looked so thin and worn and haggard and sometimes it seems only the other day that they were both so happy, and we were looking forward to their wedding. You know he will not even see her?"

"Miss Luxmore!" Roger looked surprised "I'd no idea of that. I have not heard her name mentioned since I came here. I knew of the interrupted marriage of course, and I must confess I have sometimes wondered—I have thought that the fact that she had failed him might account for a good deal of his subsequent bitterness."

"She did not fail him." Mrs. Melville slipped on to the broad window-seat and laid her head back against the woodwork. "Daphne Luxmore's love has never wavered. She came to Northchester with her father directly after the accident, and I know how she suffered through those long weary days and nights when we scarcely dared to hope that his life would be given back to us. It was a bitter blow to her when he absolutely refused to see her, and she is still unable to bring herself to believe that his decision is final."

"But do you mean"—Roger's tone was expressive of the utmost astonishment—"that he has not seen Miss Luxmore since the accident?"

"He has not seen her since," Mrs Melville assented. "So far as I know he has not even replied to her letters or sent so much as a message to her since his first refusal to see her."

She stopped and, leaning forward, pressed her head against the glass of the window. Outside, in the garden, the flowers were budding bravely, sweet-smelling narcissus, tall upstanding

Madonna lilies; farther away, across the park, the wild hyacinths shone faintly, a haze of blue amid the trees; the lilacs were peeping forth from their green leaves; over their heads it was possible to catch a glimpse of the tender unfolding pink of the horse-chestnuts. A mist of tears rose to her eyes and blurred the colours.

"It wasn't Daphne's fault, Roger," she went on, with a little catch in her breath. "She has been so noble through it all, I know. She has told me herself that she would have married him in spite of everything; that she would have given up her life in the hope that she might make things less hard for him."

Roger did not speak for a minute or two; his heart was full of trouble for his friend, for the girl whose life's happiness had been thus terribly wrecked. His eyes wandered over the ordered fragrance outside to the broad pasture land beyond. All this was Courtenay's; and yet he lay in his room maimed and useless. The pity of it brought a huskiness to his voice.

"It was very noble of Miss Luxmore. But one can't help seeing that your brother would naturally shrink from letting her sacrifice herself in that fashion."

"That is what I try to believe. But when I see Daphne it is impossible to think he is right. She tells me that every day when she opens her eyes in the morning her first thought is that surely to-day he will write to her, he will send for her; and every day closes in the same dreary disappointment. From her sister, too, I have heard that Daphne still goes every evening to their old trysting-place. She is firmly convinced that some day he will meet her there."

"Poor thing!" Roger said involuntarily. In truth it was a difficult matter to deal with. His better judgment approved his friend's action, and yet it was impossible not to recognize that there were features in the case that made it specially hard.

"Lord Luxmore has seen him several times," Mrs. Melville went on. "And though he, too, was of the opinion that the engagement must be broken off, his pity for Daphne's distress is such that he has done his best to induce James to see her. To no purpose though. I believe James told him that he would rather die than be seen as he is now by her. Lord Luxmore has thought all along, though, that when he is stronger, when the terrible shock to his nervous system has to some extent worn off, he will probably alter his mind with regard to that. What do you think, Roger?" She looked up sharply amid her fast gathering tears.

Roger hesitated. It seemed to him that the time had come when at least some measure of the truth should be spoken.

"I can't help thinking, Ethel, it is best that you should see things as they are, as I feel sure Courtenay has realized. The injuries were so terrible that they could hardly fail to affect the heart; the pain from which he suffers is not altogether neuralgic; there is grave organic mischief."

"You mean that there is danger?" Mrs. Melville stood up. "Tell me all, please, Roger. I am going to lose my brother."

Lavington retained her hand in his.

"It is impossible to say more than that there is serious mischief with the heart; such cases may last for years. They may even, in a measure, recover. But think, Ethel, of the existence to which he is doomed. Would you wish to prolong it, to delay the release for which he is longing?"

Mrs. Melville was struggling with her tears.

"I cannot bear to think of it. We were all so proud of James. He was my mother's favourite child; she was always so interested in his work. If she could have known how it would end! And Daphne"— breaking down utterly—"I was forgetting Daphne. This will break her heart!"

Chapter Six

"I WOULD much rather stay with you, really, James."

Courtenay's face was twisted in a satirical smile.

"I am such an agreeable companion, am I not? Nonsense, Ethel, of course you must go. The rector would never forgive me if I disappointed him. Roger will escort you."

Lavington looked up from his papers.

"Delighted as I should be to be of any service to Ethel, I cannot say that school-treats are much in my line, old fellow."

"Oh, this is the one great function of the year at Oakthorpe, when all classes in the neighbourhood meet for once on an equality," Courtenay observed cynically. "You will have to go, my dear Lavington, or you will be set down as an absolute misanthrope. Here's the programme for you!" He tossed it over lightly.

Roger caught it and glanced over it casually. It did not seem to offer anything very startling in the way of novelty.

"Assembly of the children at the school; march to church; tea at four o'clock, after which the prizes gained for good conduct and punctuality during the year will be distributed by Miss Luxmore." Roger wondered whether Courtenay had observed this last item.

"If I go it will only just be to tea and to see the prizes given; I really couldn't stand the whole afternoon there," Mrs. Melville complained fretfully. "When I come to see you, James, I like to spend as much time as possible with you. I shall grudge every moment at the school-treat."

Courtenay's lips curled a little at the corners.

"You must remember what a satisfaction it is to me to get my good works performed by proxy. And now, since I feel rather inclined for a nap, if you good people would let me be quiet—"

Mrs. Melville rose at once and, after a few words with his patient, Roger followed her. He found her standing in the hall, gazing wistfully at the green freshness of the park beyond. Through the open door they could catch the distant echo of the village band. Evidently the children were already meeting.

"Well, Courtenay seems to have set his mind on our participating in this village festivity, so I suppose we must e'en obey," he said lightly. "What time is it your wish that we should set out?"

"I don't know, I am sure," Mrs. Melville sighed. "I don't feel in tune for any rejoicings. I wish James hadn't taken such an unaccountable fancy. I cannot imagine why he should want us to go.

"It has occurred to me," said Roger hesitatingly, "that perhaps the fact that Miss Luxmore is giving away the prizes may have a little to do with it. He may wish to hear something of her, though he will not admit as much."

"Miss Luxmore giving away the prizes!" Mrs. Melville echoed. "I do not understand— Oh I see what you mean!" breaking off suddenly. "But it is not Daphne who is coming to the rectory—poor girl, she hardly goes anywhere now—it is Elizabeth the younger sister. Surely you have heard of her; she is quite a society beauty. I believe she was considered one of the belles of last season."

"Ah, the beauties of last season are not much in my line," Roger said dryly. He felt somewhat unreasonably disappointed; unconsciously he had woven a halo of romance around Daphne Luxmore; her tragic story, her pathetic devotion to the memory of her lost love, had fired his fancy.

"Daphne was always my favourite of the two naturally," Mrs. Melville went on placidly, "though Elizabeth is a sweet girl; but Daphne has the gentler, more clinging disposition. Elizabeth is all fire and spirit. Still, with all that, there is a great likeness between the sisters. Well, Roger, since we have to go, I suppose it is no use putting off the evil hour. Can you be ready by a quarter to four? That will give us time to get to the Rectory before they begin tea."

"Certainly; I am entirely at your service this afternoon."

"A quarter to four, then." And Mrs. Melville ran upstairs.

True to her word, Mrs. Melville appeared at the right time.

She looked very fresh and dainty in her pretty white cloth gown, with a big black picture hat, and a bunch of malmaisons tucked in her belt. Roger was struck afresh by her likeness to her brother as he remembered him at college; there was the same bright complexion, the same glossy brown hair and square, white teeth. There, however, the resemblance ended. Courtenay had been a tall, broad-shouldered man with a hearty laugh and an infectiously gay manner; his sister was slender and petite, with big, appealing eyes and a plaintively sweet smile.

The clock had already struck four, and the school-treat was in full progress when they arrived upon the scene. The children had been marshalled to either side of the white-covered tables, and willing helpers were hurrying to and fro laden with plates of bread and butter and jugs of tea. Roger was bending over a small boy who appeared to be too much overcome by the surroundings in which he found himself even to eat, when a voice near him struck some half-dormant chord of memory:

"Yes, Jane Mason has done the best this year. Is it not curious how all the Masons in turn have been model scholars?"

He raised himself sharply. Surely, he said to himself, he had made no mistake: it was the voice of the girl who had played the part of the geisha in the Freshfield theatricals, the voice of the girl whom he had found in Rheinhart's room on the night of the Bungalow murder!

He looked round; in the midst of the babble of tongues that surrounded them, it was impossible to be certain from which direction the voice had come. He fancied, however, that the speaker had stood behind him, and depositing his burden of cake with scant ceremony on the table he faced round rapidly. But there was no one in sight who at all answered to his recollection of the girl of whom he still thought as Zoe. There was only one girl, it seemed to him whose hair was at all the right colour, and in her case, instead of being arranged in the artistic tangle that "Zoe" had affected, it was drawn closely together and fastened in a network of plaits at the nape of her neck; and he thought too that the girl herself was taller, stouter than "Zoe."

She was walking away from him. As he stood gazing after her, Miss Marchand touched his arm.

"There is a little girl here who wants a piece of your cake, Dr. Lavington," she said sweetly.

"I beg your pardon," Roger responded vaguely, his eyes still fixed on the golden hair. "I was wondering whether you could tell me the name of that lady in grey over there, the one with the yellow hair. I can't help thinking that I know her."

Miss Marchand did not look pleased as she leaned forward.

"She is talking now to that man in Navy blue with a sailor hat," Roger prompted.

"Oh, you mean Phoebe Gill." Miss Marchand laughed affectedly. "She is our butcher's daughter, Dr. Lavington. I should think it very unlikely that you have met her; only, of course, doctors, like clergymen, have to know every one, don't they?"

Lavington, however, was not looking at her. His eyes had not relaxed their eager gaze.

"A butcher's daughter," he echoed. "No, I do not think—"

"Of course I ought to have said that she has been brought up in an absurd way," Miss Marchand went on eagerly. "My mother always says it has been a mistake. But it appears that Mrs. Gill has a sister who married considerably above her and Phoebe has been invited a great deal to stay with her and naturally has acquired notions which are quite out of place in her position. It is a great pity, but what can one do?" shrugging her shoulders with the air of repudiating all responsibility with regard to Miss Gill's education.

"Of course not," Roger rejoined abstractedly. People moving backward and forwards had come between him and the light hair. With a hurried apology to Miss Marchand, he strode off in the direction Miss Gill had taken. But Fate seemed against him. He had only gone a few yards when the vicar hailed him.

"I was just speaking about you to Lord Luxmore, Dr. Lavington. He wishes me to introduce you to him."

Flattering as was Lord Luxmore's desire, Roger felt at this moment that he would willingly have dispensed with it. It was out of the question, however, to disregard it, and he had to control his impatience as best he could.

Lord Luxmore was a pleasant, kindly-faced man, considerably past middle age. His reputation as a philanthropist, a scholar and a scientist, was worldwide; but as a politician, a character in which of late it had been his ambition to shine, he was scarcely looked upon as a success, even by his own party.

In person he was tall and spare, with bright, eager-looking eyes, a clean-shaven face, save for the scanty mutton-chop whiskers which he had a habit of reflectively drawing through his fingers while he tried to think out some knotty problem.

He buttonholed Roger at once.

"I have been looking forward to meeting you immensely, Dr. Lavington. My attention has been directed to an article of yours in the current number of the *Lancet*, which seems to bear to a certain extent upon my work in the East End. I allude to your remarks upon the frequency of transmission of disease by second-hand clothing. Now do you mean to tell me that—"

Roger saw that, for the present at any rate, it was hopeless to think of escaping and, resigning himself as best he could to the inevitable, listened with admirable patience to Lord Luxmore's theories with regard to certain contagious diseases, and to his schemes for the regeneration of the poor.

Meanwhile, the tea was finished, the children were being got in order by their teachers. Look as he would, Roger could discover no sign of the girl in grey.

Presently Lord Luxmore turned.

"Why, bless me, I don't see Elizabeth! She was to give away the prizes too. Oh, I suppose we must go over there," nodding in the direction of the Rectory.

A table covered with books and prizes stood on the grass; a group of people had gathered round it. Roger distinguished Mrs. Melville's white gown in close proximity to the rector's long black coat. Miss Marchand was talking to a girl in a blue linen frock.

"Well, I suppose we ought to join them," Lord Luxmore said, moving nearer.

But Roger hesitated.

"I think I should prefer to stay in the background; I am quite a stranger here."

Lord Luxmore halted a few steps in advance.

"Well, I don't know but you are right," he remarked genially. "Elizabeth can manage quite well by herself, and old Marchand, though he is a worthy old chap, is a bit of a bore, while his daughter—dare say she is a good sort too, but the fact is"—with a burst of confidence—"I never can stand Constance Marchand myself."

Roger made some inaudible reply; he was leaning forward, his eyes riveted on the girl to whom Miss Marchand was speaking. It seemed to him that there was something strangely familiar about the tall, svelte form, about the very turn of the head and the free, graceful carriage.

Lord Luxmore's flow of conversation fell on deaf ears.

"You must come up to the Hall one of these days, and we will talk over the matter further," he was saying, with the air of bonhomie which made him a favourite with all classes of society. "I spend a good deal of my time down here, as you may have heard. Not that I am particularly fond of the place myself, and the house is little better than a shooting-box, but my daughters prefer it to Luxmore Towers, poor Daphne; I am hoping great things from your residence at Oakthorpe. Dr. Lavington, I am really! I think it is the best thing possible for poor Courtenay."

"You are very kind," Roger said absently. His eyes were still following every movement of the girl who was bending over the books. At last she turned and smiled at the rows of eager little faces upturned to her.

With a stifled exclamation Roger stepped forward. For one moment he fancied that he was back at the theatricals at Freshfield; that he was once more watching the Zoe of a day in her geisha dress. Then the mist before his eyes cleared a little; he saw that the tall girl to whom the rector was now speaking was strangely like and yet unlike that other girl who had been in his thoughts all the afternoon. Her smile, her large brown eyes, her very way of holding herself, all were the same.

But this girl had an air of dignity, a serious purposefulness of manner which were absolutely unlike the varying charm of the girl who had passed as Zoe, and, in place of her golden tresses, a wealth of dusky, nut-brown hair behind the ears and on the nape of the slim, stately neck.

"I think an occasion like this—" Lord Luxmore began presently.

Roger interrupted him with scant ceremony:

"Who is that—the girl standing by Mr. Marchand?"

Lord Luxmore looked slightly surprised as he adjusted his pince-nez.

"That—oh, that is my youngest daughter; she is distributing the prizes to-day. That is my boy next her; he was fifteen yesterday; fine-looking fellow I call him. And yet they tell me he is not strong. I must get you to look at him and see what you think, some day, Dr. Lavington."

Roger murmured something inaudible; he scarcely knew what Lord Luxmore was talking about. With his eyes following every movement of the girl on the grassy platform he was trying to grasp the inconceivable fact that, though her smile, her eyes, her very walk were those of the girl at The Bungalow, she was indeed Elizabeth Luxmore, the daughter of one of the most important men in the country—what had Mrs. Melville called her?—the belle of last season.

His replies grew so wide of the mark at last that Lord Luxmore looked at him in mild astonishment; and Roger himself felt thankful when the children, with their clear, young voices, began one of the glees that had been carefully taught them for the occasion.

When the last prize had been presented Miss Luxmore stepped down and was lost to sight among the children.

Lord Luxmore touched Roger's arm imperatively.

"Come, they will expect me to speak; and I want to show you my boy."

Still moving like a man in a dream, Roger followed him. As they passed through the children, now scampering about in all directions, Roger found himself face to face with the girl in the grey dress with the golden hair that had been his magnet all the afternoon. He turned almost with a shudder from the contemplation of her fair, plump face and complacent blue eyes.

At the same moment Lord Luxmore spoke at his elbow. "Elizabeth, my dear; I want to introduce Dr. Lavington."

Evidently Miss Luxmore was a favourite with the Oakthorpe children. Two or three of them were clinging to her skirts; she held one mite in her arms, its curly head nestled up against her neck. As her father spoke she set it down and responded to Roger's bow with a grave smile.

It was not often that Lavington's self-possession was shaken, but to-day, in face of this girl, with her little dainty air of aloofness, whose eyes, the very counterpart of those others he had seen in The Bungalow, held only cold surprise as they met his, he stood, tongue-tied, embarrassed like the veriest schoolboy.

Miss Luxmore waited a moment, then she said slowly, the same musical inflection in her voice that had rung through the hall at Freshfield:

"What a charming afternoon we have had for our treat, have we not? It is very kind of you to help us, Dr. Lavington. I am sure Mr. Marchand is greatly indebted to you."

It was she, then, whom Roger had heard speak earlier in the afternoon. Was there a spice of raillery in the clear, level tones now, he wondered—a soupçon of mockery in the eyes that were regarding him so steadily?

"I am afraid I cannot claim to have been of assistance," he said slowly at last. "But I have been very much interested—"

"Roger! Roger! I was looking for you" It was Mrs. Melville's voice; she was coming towards them. "I'm going back now if you are ready. Good-bye, Elizabeth, dear," kissing the girl heartily. "It has been quite delightful seeing you, and I should like to stay longer;

but I feel that we ought to go home—that we should not leave James any longer."

Chapter Seven

OAKTHORPE Manor was not a building of great antiquity; there was a tradition that an older mansion had originally stood on the same ground, and that it had been in Elizabethan times the home of the Courtenays.

The old rose-garden was still maintained in all its beauty; but Wilson, the old Scotch gardener, would tell, with a huskiness in his voice, how Sir James had promised to bring Miss Luxmore to see it the very day of the accident, and how the news was brought to Oakthorpe that Sir James would never walk again just at the moment he was expecting them. But, though Courtenay had never visited the rose-garden, the conservatory had remained one of his favourite resorts. He was there to-day, his chair wheeled close up to the fountain in the centre; his shoulders hunched up as he leant a little forward, marking the fresh green of the ferns at the water's edge, watching the goldfish darting to and fro from their leafy shelters.

Farther down, by the door opening on to the grassy terrace, Lavington was sitting smoking. The two men were not talking; Courtenay, who in his youth had been one of the most loquacious of mortals, had developed a curious reserve; he was given to long gloomy fits of silence, and Roger had learned that at such times he was best left alone. To-day, however, Courtenay was the first to speak.

"Have you ever heard that the man who wrote the most exciting stories that have ever been penned was a hopeless invalid, Lavington?"

Roger took out his pipe, and rapped its contents on the ash-tray before he answered.

"I don't quite know that I have, but I should believe it quite possible. Heine was a terrible sufferer, I have heard, and yet it does one good to read his poems."

"When I am lying here, and I realize the hopelessness of everything, or dreaming of anything better in the future, all sorts of queer fancies come crowding into my brain. Sometimes I fancy I shall put them down on paper, and see what the world will think of them. What do you say?"

"Say? Why it's a capital idea," Roger assented heartily, as he rose and strolled over to the fountain.

In truth, it seemed to him that the very suggestion was doing Courtenay good. His eyes looked brighter, his tone was more animated.

"Your travels, too, would give freshness to the setting of your tales," he went on.

"Oh, I don't think I should go in for descriptions of scenery, and that sort of thing," Courtenay said, a satirical smile curving his thin lips. "What I thought of trying was short stories of crime, forgery burglary, murder even, crisp and pithy, putting in the motive in a few words. Some of Maupassant's are examples of what I mean. And I had an old seventeenth-century thing—French too. I think the name was Duvarnois. It professed to be a true and particular account of the Borgia crimes. It was not particularly fine writing, I dare say, but it made you feel Duvarnois ought to be in the library. I wonder whether I could find it?"

He moved his chair forward as he spoke, and Roger followed.

"Now, he ought to be over there on the fifth shelf. I am afraid I must trouble you to reach it down." Roger glanced along the indicated shelf.

Duvarnois was an unpretending little book, wedged in between two bulky volumes of memoirs. He handed it to Courtenay, and then turned back, attracted by the title of a treatise near at hand. He moved a little nearer the light. It was a work, out of print now, that he had seen referred to recently in a medical journal, and had endeavoured to get it in vain. It was curious that he should stumble across it in his friend's library.

A curious stifled sound roused him from his absorption in its pages. He looked up. Something had fallen from the old Duvarnois on to the foot of Courtenay's chair, and he was stooping, trying to reach it.

Roger stepped forward. He was about to speak, but something in his friend's expression restrained him.

Courtenay's thin nervous face was contorted by an ugly sneer.

As Roger hesitated, the lean, yellow hand clutched the white oblong packet and raised it triumphantly. Something fell out. It looked like a curl of yellow hair, Roger thought. Another moment he saw he was right. It was a lock of long, golden hair. It curled round Courtenay's fingers like a living thing. With an oath he stooped forward, his face transformed by rage and aversion, loathing even, and held it up, still coiling and twining itself over his fingers. Then, with a shudder of horror, he hung it from him, right into the heart of the fire.

Roger woke up suddenly to the fact that Courtenay had forgotten that he was in the room, that he believed himself to be alone. He stepped back, and caught his heel on some piece of furniture.

Courtenay started; his face, convulsed as it had been by a very passion of emotion, smoothed itself out in a wonderful fashion.

Roger was resolutely averting his eyes from the fire-place where, to his fancy, the shining curl was winding round the flames as it had twisted round Courtenay's fingers.

There was a faint smell of burnt hair in the air.

"Ah, yes. You are dining at the Rectory to-night, aren't you? I'd forgotten."

Courtenay's voice sounded very tired and far-away now. He leaned his head back against the cushions.

"I should have a nap if I were you, old fellow," Roger said quickly, as he made his way to the door. "Sleep over Duvarnois, and see what you think of him then."

"Well, it sounds absurd. I have been doing nothing but sitting in this chair all day, but I believe I am tired."

"All right, old fellow. I will look you up presently."

Courtenay's air of languor did not deceive Roger for a moment. He knew that as soon as the door closed behind him the head would be raised, all the exhaustion would disappear, and the invalid would give himself up to the contemplation of the memories that had been evoked by the sight of the gleaming golden hair.

Roger could not help speculating as to whom it could have belonged; that some history was attached to it he could not doubt after the scene he had witnessed. For some time now, too, he had seen reason to doubt Courtenay's attachment to Miss Luxmore. It seemed to him that, terrible though his injuries were, they formed no adequate reason for his refusal to even answer his former fiancée's letters. Roger fancied that the yellow curl might explain much, and he felt a throb of pity for the girl who was herself so faithful.

And then a startling thought came to him. Where had he seen such yellow hair before? Ah, he remembered only too well!

Roger Lavington found his thoughts constantly wandering in the direction of Elizabeth Luxmore during the week that elapsed after the school-treat.

Elizabeth Luxmore's great dark eyes haunted him, her extraordinary likeness to the girl who had masqueraded at Freshfield as Zoe seemed so absolutely inexplicable. Sometimes Roger told himself that he must be the victim of some hallucination, that, unconsciously even, his thoughts must have reverted to the Bungalow murder, and that he had exaggerated some chance resemblance. It was impossible that Lord Luxmore's daughter could be related in any way to the trembling, terrified girl he had found at The Bungalow.

Nevertheless, the fact that he was asked to meet Lord Luxmore and his youngest daughter at the Rectory to-night was responsible for his acceptance of the invitation. Much as he disliked the Marchands, they greeted him effusively. There were a retired colonel and his daughter, and a couple of clergymen with their meek, shabby wives. Roger was introduced to each in turn, and gathered that, with the exception of the Luxmores, the party was now complete. They had not long to wait; just as Roger had been informed that to him was allotted the pleasing duty of escorting Miss Marchand to dinner, Lord Luxmore and Miss Luxmore were announced.

It seemed to Roger that the resemblance which had struck him at the school-treat, strong though it undoubtedly was, was less marked to-night than he had fancied it in his recollection. Meeting his glance, Miss Luxmore bowed very slightly; her manner was singularly unlike her father's genial, kindly fashion of greeting him, Roger thought, as he offered his arm to Miss Marchand and followed in the wake of the others to the dining-room.

At the long table he found that he was between Miss Marchand and the colonel's daughter. Elizabeth Luxmore was next her host on the opposite side of the table. Between the ferns in front of him, Roger could catch a glimpse of her dainty, clear-cut profile, of her crown of waving brown hair. She was not talking much. He fancied that she looked weary and distraite; evidently she was not enjoying the good rector's conversation. He was studying her expression, replying absently the while to Miss Marchand's lively sallies, when she glanced across suddenly and their eyes met in the one brief moment before he looked away. He could not help fancying that her glance held a certain veiled hostility, a latent yet perceptible dislike.

All through the rest of the dinner—which was long and pretentious, with weary waits between each course—he found himself puzzling once more over the riddle of Elizabeth Luxmore. What could account for her likeness and yet unlikeness to the girl he had protected at The Bungalow? And what could be the reason for the enmity with which he felt sure he had inspired her? The enigma was still unsolved when the ladies left the table.

Lord Luxmore drew his chair nearer Roger's.

"I am coming to call on you one of these next few days, Dr. Lavington. How is poor Courtenay now?"

"Much about the same, I think," Roger replied, a little surprised at the sudden transition.

Lord Luxmore blew his nose noisily.

"It was a sad thing-a very sad thing! You know, of course, of his engagement to my elder daughter?"

Roger bowed an affirmative.

"Poor girl! It has naturally spoiled her life," Lord Luxmore went on, twirling the stem of his wine-glass in his right hand. "It is a continual grief to her, too, that Courtenay refuses to see her. Of course I can understand his feeling in a measure; the alteration is a terrible one; no doubt he would prefer that she would remember him as he was. But still, when he knows how the poor child troubles about the separation, I think he should put his own sentiment on one side for her sake. I wish you could bring him to see matters in this light, Dr. Lavington."

"I wish I could," Roger acquiesced. "It would be the best thing for Courtenay too. I will do what I can, of course, Lord Luxmore, but at present I am not very sanguine of success. Courtenay is terribly altered."

"Terribly! Terribly!" Lord Luxmore assented, as they rose to join the ladies.

Elizabeth Luxmore was standing by the open window a little in the shadow of the curtain. Lavington's eyes sought her at once. His artistic sense was gratified by the long, straight folds of her white gown, the suppleness of the material showing every line and curve of her slim, rounded figure.

Her father crossed to her at once, Roger following in his wake.

"I have been telling Dr. Lavington that he must come up and see me, Elizabeth."

"We shall be pleased to see Dr. Lavington," Miss Luxmore returned with polite indifference.

Roger and Miss Luxmore were left *tête-à-tête*. Roger hesitated. Now that the opportunity for which he had been longing was his he felt unable to make use of it.

"It is very kind of Lord Luxmore to ask me to the Hall," he said lamely at last.

"Not at all. He will be delighted," Miss Luxmore said, with a small conventional smile.

Roger found himself wondering whether her cold, languid manner was habitual, or whether it was possible that she had taken a personal dislike to himself.

Presently Miss Luxmore looked at him again.

"You are quite a stranger to this neighbourhood are you not, Dr. Lavington?"

"Yes. I have been in practice at Sutton Boldon for some years." Some outside impulse seemed to prompt Lavington. "I wonder whether you have relations near there, Miss Luxmore?"

As if surprised at his tone, Elizabeth raised the big brown eyes that always gave him a sense of familiarity.

"Not relations. Friends, I might say—the Folgates of Norton Priory. At least, the Priory is within motoring distance of Sutton Boldon; we passed through it last week."

Another friend then came to claim her attention, and Roger had no further opportunity of speaking to her.

Chapter Eight

OAKTHORPE Manor was quite one of the show places of the county. Courtenay had been so pestered with requests to be allowed to see the famous gardens that a short time before his accident he had thrown the park and grounds open every Monday, and allowed the public, under the supervision of the gardeners, to wander about at will. Nor had he discontinued the practice since his accident, though every week when Monday came round he was wont to fume and fret, and declare that he would withdraw the permission he called himself a fool for having granted.

To-day, however, was Tuesday. Roger Lavington kicked aside a piece of white paper that lay on the grass, but otherwise there was no sign of the visitors who yesterday had thronged the lawns and shrubberies, admired the choice blooms in the conservatories, and listened to the head gardener's dissertation on the vines in the greenhouses.

Much of the garden and of the park was still unknown ground to Lavington. What with the continual care needed by Courtenay, and his own literary and scientific work, he had but little time to spare. But this evening he had found himself at a standstill, and his thoughts would stray to The Bungalow, to Maximilian von Rheinhart's body as he had seen it stretched on the floor and to the girl whom he had found crouching behind the curtain.

At last, in despair, he had pushed his papers aside and made up his mind to go for a stroll and have a smoke while he thought over his difficulties. It was growing dusk as he passed through the rose-garden that had been planted for Courtenay's bride, and to Roger's mind it all looked deserted, melancholy, as if some shadow of the joy that had so suddenly turned into sorrow, some echo of the interrupted marriage bells darkened it even yet. But here, too, he was pursued by the ever-recurring recollection of that tragedy at Sutton Boldon. He found himself wondering, speculating as to how Rheinhart had met his death—as to what had taken the girl with the soft brown eyes that were the counterpart of Elizabeth Luxmore's, to The Bungalow. In what relation had she stood to Rheinhart— wife, sweetheart, or victim?

He was still pondering over this baffling enigma as he closed the door of the rose-garden and went on into the park where, leaning up against the trunk of a stout old oak, he gave himself up to the luxury of a quiet think and a smoke.

But in vain he tried to control his thoughts, to fix them on the subject-matter of his article. Elizabeth Luxmore's slim figure, her small straight features, would obtrude themselves. He found himself recalling her little disdainful way of raising her dark level brows, the thick coils of brown hair that were twisted high on her gracefully-poised head.

Roger had no idea how long he had been standing wrapped in a brown study; a sense of the nearness of some living creature close at hand roused him, a feeling that he was no longer alone. He waited expectantly. Everything was quiet; there was no sign of any movement near. A silence seemed to have fallen all round. Roger stood still, every faculty suddenly quickened, his eyes, keen, alert, glancing through the tangle of interlacing branches.

Suddenly out of the shadows and the stillness, a low wailing voice sounded near at hand:

"Ah, how long is it to go on? For ever? Shall I ever be forgiven?"

It sounded so close to him, the sweet pathetic voice was so distinct, that Roger started, feeling bewilderedly that help was needed somewhere. Before he had made up his mind from which direction the cry had come, however, a twig cracked behind him, there was an echo of a woman's sob, the soft *frou-frou* of a woman's dress. Roger caught his breath, as, without apparently noticing his presence, a tall, slight figure in a grey gown with something white and coif-like twisted round the head, passed him so short a distance away that by stretching out his arm he might have touched her. For one moment something in the walk reminded him of Elizabeth Luxmore, and his heart stood still; then the tearful voice was raised again:

"Ah, Heaven, my punishment is greater than I can bear!" The white fleecy shawl slipped back, and he caught a momentary glimpse of fair hair twisted high in a golden coronet on the bent head.

With a sense of prying, of eavesdropping, he drew back and waited. He could hear the cracking of the branches as she passed, the rustling of the leaves under her feet, a distant sighing sob—no more.

The twilight was fast merging into darkness when Lavington walked slowly through the rose-garden and sauntered up the terrace to the Manor. As he let himself in by the glass door giving access from the conservatory to the little-used drawing-room he came suddenly face to face with Mrs. Miller, the housekeeper.

She started back with a slight scream, her hand pressed to her heart. Roger glanced at her with some surprise.

"Did you take me for a burglar, Mrs. Miller?" he asked with a smile.

The housekeeper seemed to recover her breath with an effort.

"N—o, sir, I was only startled for a minute, this room being so seldom used except when Mrs. Melville is here, and me not expecting anyone either. I beg your pardon, sir." She was about to turn away.

"Please do not go away; do not let me interrupt you," Roger said pleasantly.

"It—it was only that I wanted to make sure the shutters were bolted, sir," the woman said in the nervous, apologetic manner that contrasted so oddly with the sober richness of her dress, with her assured position at Oakthorpe. "Sir James is particular about that as soon as darkness sets in in these unused rooms, and it's difficult to be certain unless one comes round oneself."

Her hands, long, thin and nervous, were busied feeling for the bolts. Her back was towards Roger.

He watched her, wondering what might be the secret of her extraordinary manner. Though he could not doubt her whole-hearted devotion to Courtenay, he had never been able to bring himself either to trust or to like the housekeeper fully. Her nervous, disjointed manner of speaking, her way of glancing at him in a stealthy, sidelong fashion, all gave him a vague sense of irritation for which he was inclined to chide himself as unreasonable. It seemed now that she was taking an unnecessarily long time over her task.

"Mrs. Miller," he said at last, "I have been for quite a long ramble in the park this evening. That is a pretty little stream on the south side beyond the rose-garden."

"Yes, sir." The thin fingers tugged restlessly at a stiff bolt.

Was she trying to unfasten the window? Roger wondered.

"And the wood on the other side is very pretty," he went on. "There are some grand old oaks."

"So I have heard, sir. It would have been a rare shame to have cut them down as they say the last owner was near doing when he was short of money." The housekeeper was stooping down now.

"The last owner, Sir George Courtenay," Roger repeated in some surprise. I had no idea he had ever been in any sort of difficulty. I was under the impression that he was a very wealthy man."

Mrs. Miller moved to the farther window, bestowing upon Roger as she passed one of the furtive, questioning glances which he had surprised more than once during the last few days when she had been attending to Courtenay under his directions.

"Not Sir George, sir," she said at last. "It—that part never belonged to him. The stream is the boundary of the Courtenay property on that side; the other bank and the wood belong to Lord Luxmore."

"To Lord Luxmore!" Roger drew in his breath. "I had no idea his property was so near. The Hall itself is some distance away, isn't it?"

"It is if you go by the road." Mrs. Miller seemed satisfied with the window fastenings and edged towards the door. "But if you go straight as the crow flies, as they say, it is but a step. A footpath through that wood leads you right up to Luxmore Hall. Some people say that that little bridge you spoke of—it is where Sir James and Miss Luxmore used to meet. And I have heard that it isn't often a night passes but Miss Luxmore goes to the old place still, poor young thing!" She had paused near the door, and with her handkerchief was carefully wiping a speck of dust from the face of a mirror that hung on the wall; her haggard, scared-looking eyes watched the reflection of Lavington's face anxiously.

"Ah," Roger said slowly, an instant certainty as to the identity of the woman he had seen in the woods flashing across him, "a lady was walking down the path between the trees just now; that, then, would be Miss Luxmore?"

"I should say so, sir." There was a curious reserve in the woman's voice. "Poor young lady! It has been a terrible thing for her as well as for Sir James. And they say she frets so at him not letting her see him. Though one can't wonder at that with him—the wreck he is."

"Perhaps not." Roger acquiesced doubtfully. He was recalling the thrill in the passionate, tragic voice, the wail of an anguish that had rung through the tones. "Shall I ever be forgiven? ... Ah, Heaven, my punishment is greater than I can bear!"

What relation could these words have to the life story of Daphne Luxmore as the world knew it?

"Is Miss Luxmore considered like her sister?" he asked at last.

Mrs. Miller bent forward. The speck on the glass was troublesome; it needed much hard rubbing to get it off.

"Folks think so, sir. I can't say that I have noticed it myself. But then I have never seen the young ladies together. Miss Luxmore she used to come up sometimes with his lordship when I first came to the Manor and beg to be allowed to see Sir James. But the doctors would not consent, and in the end she gave up. But she always looked pale and sad, poor Miss Daphne! And Miss Elizabeth is that lively you can't compare them."

Lavington had never seen Elizabeth Luxmore very lively—bright and lively were not exactly the adjectives he would have applied to her stately young beauty. But he stood silent, tongue-tied. A new bewildering idea had suddenly occurred to him.

Mrs. Miller slipped her handkerchief in her pocket and glided through the door; in another moment she would have drawn it to behind her.

"Mrs. Miller!" Roger's voice sounded husky. "Oh, it's nothing," he added with forced carelessness. "I didn't know you were going. I was about to say that Miss Luxmore's hair is not the same colour as her sister's, is it? That must make a considerable difference in their appearance."

Seen by the electric light in the hall, silhouetted against the dark oak wainscoting, Mrs. Miller's face looked ghastly white; her eyes glanced round with a hunted expression; she laid one hand on her heart as if to still its beating. Lavington had not moved out of the drawing-room.

"Yes it does, sir," the housekeeper answered, moistening her dry lips with the tip of her tongue. "Miss Elizabeth is dark, you see, while Miss Luxmore—"

"Yes?" Roger's tone was distinctly interrogative.

"She is fair, sir." Mrs. Miller moved across the hall, catching at a table near the farther end as she passed.

"Ah!" Roger hesitated a moment as if uncertain what to do. Then he turned back into the drawing-room.

Chapter Nine

"VERRALL will have to go. This is the third half-year his rent has not been paid."

A shaft of sunlight fell athwart Courtenay's head. To Roger's fancy there was something cruel in its very clearness. It brought out with pitiless accuracy the yellow, parchment-like hue of the skin, the deep furrows that had been graven by bodily suffering. It showed, too, how the lips that used to lend themselves to facile laughter were now compressed in this straight line.

Opposite, at the writing-table littered with papers, Gorringe, who had been steward at Oakthorpe for more years than he would care to count, watched his employer with puckered brows and anxious, worried-looking eyes. He stirred uneasily as Courtenay spoke.

"Verralls been at the Mill Farm for near a hundred years, Sir James."

Courtenay's laugh was not exactly pleasant to hear.

"All the more reason they should make way for some one else now."

Old Gorringe looked across at Lavington as if imploring his aid.

"These two seasons have been bad ones, Sir James, and the Verralls have had family troubles; the eldest son died, and Mrs.

Verrall has been ill, and they have had big doctor's bills to pay. Things have been hard on the Verralls lately, but they have every hope of making up now, if only they can have time. If you would wait until Christmas, Sir James."

"It was just the same tale a year ago. I yielded to you and waited, and what has come of it? I shall lose double what I should have done if I had followed my own inclination. No! If he does not pay, he must go. That is my last word on the matter!"

His tone had all the accent of finality. Gorringe opened his mouth tentatively as if to offer some remonstrance, but recognizing its utter futility, began to put his papers together in silence.

"Very well, Sir James, I—I will do my best." It was plainly to be seen that only by a great effort was he repressing his natural indignation. As the door closed behind him, Courtenay gave vent to a sardonic chuckle. Meeting Roger's eyes, he stopped suddenly.

"Well, old sobersides, what have you to say?"

Roger looked at him fully.

"I was wondering why your whole nature should be so strangely altered by your accident, Courtenay. Do you remember how harsh old Pounceby used to be to his tenants, and how you used to criticize him and yet even he—"

"Had his good points, I dare say." Courtenay finished the sentence in his own fashion. "It is a very different pair of shoes, let me tell you, when you are a landowner yourself, Roger; you look at things from another point of view altogether. Besides"—his tone hardening—"why should I let Verrall off? He has his health and strength, all the things I covet most—why should he expect to go through the world without trouble any more than the rest of us?"

"The very fact that there is so much trouble in life is the very reason for each one of us doing our best to lessen the sum of human misery, not to add to it, Courtenay."

Roger's tone was significant, but it apparently made small impression. With a grunt Courtenay turned his head away as if tired of the conversation. Roger picked up the *Times* which lay at the foot of the chair, and carried it over to the window. Courtenay was invariably trying in this mood; the only thing to be done was to leave him to himself and trust that reflection might bring him wiser counsels.

Roger's eye wandered idly down the columns; then, in a corner of the paper, his attention was arrested suddenly by a paragraph in small type, headed by the words "The Bungalow Murder" in larger type. Roger's breathing quickened as he read: "It will be within the recollection of our readers that in spite of the police the murderer of Maximilian von Rheinhart at Sutton Boldon two years ago is still at large. It is rumoured that within the last few days the police have discovered a valuable clue, and, though they are naturally reticent about the matter, it is probable that an arrest will be made within the next few days."

Lavington read it over a second time. Its very vagueness rendered it more alarming. Roger repeated the words mechanically, "It is probable that an arrest will be made within the next few days." Whose arrest? His face paled beneath its bronze as he asked himself that question. And what could be the clue the police had discovered after all that time? Roger racked his brains in vain. He had imagined that the Bungalow Murder was long ago relegated to the list of undiscovered, half-forgotten crimes. The last thing he had expected was to see the whole matter was likely to be raked up again.

Once more he recalled the ghastly details of that night two years ago. Once more he heard the gasping breath as he drew back the curtain. The girl with Elizabeth Luxmore's eyes was pleading to him for mercy and help. Then, with a shudder, he thought of the form that had lain last on that row of trestles in the barn, of the golden hair so primly straight and the face that merciful hands had veiled.

How had she come into Maximilian von Rheinhart's room, the girl who had passed as Roger Lavington's cousin for one long day? Had she been tricked, deceived? The man's very brow grew crimson as he pictured what might have been; the love dishonoured; the intolerable insult; the sudden swift revenge.

And now they were to arrest some one for the murder. Who was it? Had he been mistaken, after all, in thinking of the girl he had protected as killed in the railway accident?

An exclamation from Courtenay startled Roger. The old butler had opened the door.

"Lord Luxmore has called, Sir James. He hopes that you will be able to see him for a few minutes this morning."

"I won't," Courtenay returned irritably. "Have I not told you, Jenkins, that I never see anybody? Tell Lord Luxmore that I regret I do not feel equal to seeing visitors to-day—"

"Not now, my dear James, that will not do." Lord Luxmore thrust the man aside and bustled into the room. "Really, you know, we can't let you shut yourself up in this way—we really can't. It's the worst possible thing for you."

"I do not agree with you," Courtenay said grimly, wincing as Lord Luxmore pressed his hand. He had raised himself slightly in his chair, but his gloomy countenance did not relax as he met his visitor's genial smile.

"Oh, come! I don't think you are the best judge of that. You must let your friends decide for you." Evidently Lord Luxmore was not inclined to take umbrage at the coolness of his reception. He turned to Roger. "How do you do, Dr. Lavington? My visit is partly to you to-day. I had intended to call before, but there has been some trouble at the Home Office, and I had to go up to town at the beginning of the week, and only got back last night. Still, I have availed myself of the earliest opportunity," with another infectious laugh. "Now, do you know what I have strict orders to do? Take you two young men back to lunch with me."

Courtenay had resumed his former position now. One hand was pulling his brown moustache, the other drummed restlessly on the arm of his chair.

"I thought you understood I never go out."

Lord Luxmore seated himself crosswise on the nearest chair and regarded him benevolently.

"I know you have had some such notion, James. But I think it is time your friends tried to break you of it. You will have to get over it some time, you know. You can't live all your life shut up here like a hermit."

"Can I not?" Courtenay questioned quietly. "I think you are making a mistake, Lord Luxmore."

Looking at him, Roger could see by the tautness of his muscles, by the knuckles that shone white through the tightened skin, the gigantic effort he was making to retain his self-control.

Lord Luxmore, however, apparently noticed nothing of it. He leaned forward.

"There is some one else you ought to think of, Courtenay. She has forbidden me to mention the subject to you, but when I see the poor child fretting her heart out, how can I obey her? Do you never think of poor Daphne, James?"

Suddenly Courtenay's whole frame seemed to relax; he sat farther back amongst the cushions; his hand lay limp on the silken coverlet that was thrown over the lower part of the chair.

"Often." The word seemed to be wrung from the thin, drawn lips.

Lavington, with the true physician's insight, guessed something of the torture his friend was suffering, and longed to put an end to it; but Lord Luxmore was not to be easily turned from his purpose.

"Oh well, that is something," he said heartily. "It will do her good to hear that, poor child! And if you will not come up to the Hall, you will let her see you here some day, Courtenay?"

"Never!" Courtenay's blue eyes were sombre; his upper lip twitched nervously. "Remembering what has been, could I bear her to see me like this?" With a sudden gesture he threw back the gay quilt; he pulled himself up.

With a visible shudder Lord Luxmore shrank back; he looked from the bottom of the chair, with its significant emptiness, to Courtenay's thin, sunken chest, to his rounded back and worn, lined face; then his expression altered; he drew out a handkerchief and blew his nose.

"Eh, I don't know what to say, my poor fellow! it is terribly sad, and I know what you mean; but bless you, Daphne wouldn't look at it like that. Women are not built in that way—not the best of them, anyhow."

Courtenay made no reply. The muscles near his mouth and nostrils twitched painfully as he looked straight at Lord Luxmore's tell-tale countenance.

Lavington stepped forward and replaced the quilt.

"I think I must forbid any further conversation to-day, Lord Luxmore."

"Quite right, I am sure, quite right!" the gentleman assented in obvious embarrassment. "Perhaps I was wrong, but I didn't realize. However"—recovering himself somewhat—"if it is out of the question that Courtenay should lunch with us, I hope you will not be equally obdurate, Dr. Lavington."

"Another day I shall be delighted," Roger said courteously.

But Courtenay looked up.

"I should prefer you to go with Lord Luxmore to-day, Roger. I have some business that must be finished."

Lavington glanced at him doubtfully. He could perceive no ill-effects, so far, from this recent excitement. Roger felt that it would be the truest kindness to Courtenay to accept the invitation to lunch.

"Oh, well, if you have business, old fellow, I shall be delighted to—"

"You will come then?" finished Lord Luxmore, getting up with alacrity. "That is right. I am most anxious to have your advice. Good-bye, James, my boy! I shall run up and see you again one of these days. Good-bye."

He shook hands with Courtenay and used his handkerchief vigorously as he made his exit. In the hall he turned to Roger.

"Terrible! Terrible! Poor fellow! I hardly knew what to say to him. I dare say you saw that. After all, one can't wonder that he should shrink from seeing anyone, can one really, now?"

Luncheon at Oakthorpe Hall was an informal meal. Lord Luxmore bustled into the dining-room.

"I had no idea we were so late. But now I think of it, I can tell you from my own feelings that it is near lunch-time," with a jolly laugh "Where is Daphne?"

"Daphne has one of her bad headaches this morning," Elizabeth returned, as she took her seat next to Roger at the round table laid for four.

Lord Luxmore took up his knife and fork and laid them down again.

"Now that is most extraordinary. She is almost as bad as Courtenay—never well enough to see anyone. And yet this morning when I went out, she was sitting in the drawing-room reading the *Times*, and looking almost her old self. I shall have to speak to her seriously."

The memory of a certain paragraph in the morning's paper returned to Roger. In vain he told himself that he was a fool, or mad. The question would keep recurring to him: "Had Daphne Luxmore read those few lines, and were they accountable for her headache?"

Lord Luxmore, finding Roger an intelligent listener, was inclined to become enthusiastic about him.

"Of course, I can understand that it is a capital thing for Courtenay to have you here, Dr Lavington, and at present I suppose it suits your purpose, as it gives you time for your studies, but I should advise your going to London as soon as possible. Courtenay tells me you were thinking of it when you came to him. Where had you been living before, may I ask?"

"I had been in practice in the Midlands, at a village called Sutton Boldon," Roger answered, toying with his bread. "But I had given that up before I heard from Courtenay."

"Sutton Boldon! Sutton Boldon!" mused Lord Luxmore. "The name seems familiar, but I cannot place my association with it. How is that, I wonder?"

"It is not very far from Norton Priory," his daughter suggested. "We pass the station as we go up."

Lord Luxmore wrinkled up his brows. His pince-nez fell off and hung unheeded by their cord.

"Perhaps that is it. No! I have it. Wasn't there a murder there a year or two ago? I saw it alluded to in the paper this morning. The Bungalow murder, was it not? The police think they have a clue at last."

"What clue, papa?"

"Oh, my dear child, how should I know?" Lord Luxmore said testily. "That is the last thing the police will tell of course, otherwise the criminal might make his escape. No, they will keep that up their sleeves until they are prepared to pounce down upon the murderer, you may be sure."

Elizabeth said no more. She turned to her young brother.

"Reggie, young Cowan is coming over this afternoon. I have just heard from his mother; he wants you to play in the team he is getting up for the wake week."

Young Luxmore's eyes shone.

"Oh I say, does he really? That is jolly."

"Oh yes, things are coming back to me now," Lord Luxmore went on, leaning back in his chair. "An artist was supposed to have been shot by some girl, wasn't he? It was just about the time of Courtenay's accident, and we were so concerned about Daphne that I did not follow the details. Poor thing! I dare say he had treated her badly; one's sympathies must go out to her, after all this time too."

"To some extent, certainly," Roger looked steadily at Elizabeth. "And I dare say nothing will come of the clue. One sees that sort of vague statement so often in the papers."

Chapter Ten

SUTTON Boldon looked very familiar, Roger Lavington thought, as he emerged from the little station and turned into the main road leading through the village. It was lunch-time; the children were playing about in the yard in front of the school; the geese were waddling across the village green to the pond; in front of the inn a few loiterers were standing about in the sunshine.

Roger paused irresolutely. The host of the Crown was an old patient; he made up his mind to go in and see what they could give him in the way of a repast. His visit to Sutton Boldon was the outcome of a couple of sleepless nights; since he had seen the paragraph in the *Times* with regard to the reported clue to the Bungalow murder, he had been unable to divest himself of the idea that trouble threatened Daphne Luxmore.

Though at times he told himself he must be mad to harbour such a suspicion, even for an instant, though he had no grounds to go upon which would justify him in entertaining it, though the likeness which he saw in Elizabeth Luxmore to the mysterious visitor to The Bungalow might be, nay indeed—as he had tried to persuade himself hitherto—must be purely accidental, the thought that Lord Luxmore's elder daughter, Courtenay's betrothed, was the girl he had found in Rheinhart's room would obtrude itself. The strong resemblance which he had been told existed between the two sisters had first suggested the idea to him; the momentary glimpse he had had of Miss Luxmore in the wood had shown him that her hair was the same colour as that of the girl he had saved. Above all, Courtenay's manner had convinced him that some deep tragedy lay behind—that Courtenay's accident could not be the only cause of separation between the lovers.

After a couple of days spent in restless self-questioning, of nights in which he lay tossing from side, in which pictures of the girl who had acted at Freshfield in the prisoner's dock had alternated in his mind with visions of Elizabeth Luxmore's great brown eyes filled with tears, of the sweet arched lips quivering, he had resolved to come over to Sutton Boldon himself, and ascertain, if possible, how the matter stood, and from what quarter danger was to be apprehended. So he turned into the inn. The landlord came forward to greet him, his rubicund face beaming with smiles.

"Why, Dr. Lavington, sir, this is a treat. We were talking of you the other day, me and Sam Doulton, and Sam Doulton he said he wished you was back. 'Nobody never did my rheumatics the good that Dr. Lavington did,' he said."

Roger shook his hand heartily.

"It is pleasant to have a welcome to the old place, Mr. Rose. And now, can you give me a glass of ale and a slice of bread and cheese or some cold meat?"

The landlord rubbed his hands.

"Eh doctor, I think we can do better for you than that. The missus has got a fine sirloin; we don't hold with cold meat on Mondays, we don't."

"I'm in luck's way then," Roger said genially, as he followed to the little bar-parlour.

While the table was being laid, the landlord stood with his back to the empty fire-place, glad to have a chat with a new-comer.

"You are staying with Sir James Courtenay, aren't you, sir?" he inquired conversationally. "Him as had both his legs took off in that accident at Northchester? I remember hearing about it at the time, and you saying he was a friend of yours. Terrible thing it was too! Ah, that was a time; if you remember, it was just after the murder at the Bungalow! You will have heard, maybe, that they are opening that up again?"

Roger poured out a glass of ale, and motioned the landlord to help himself.

"I think I did see something about it in the paper, but it is rather late to do much now, I should think. What have they found? Do you know?"

"Thank you, sir; your health, sir!" Mr. Rose ducked his head towards Roger as he lifted the glass to his lips. "As to what they have found," he went on as he set it down, "it goes more to show they were wrong in the past than it puts them on the right track now, I'm thinking. You remember it was supposed as the girl that did it was killed at Northchester in that very accident we were speaking of just now?"

"Well?" Roger took out his cigar-case. "Help yourself, Mr. Rose. Yes, I remember. Poor thing, she was a terrible sight!"

"Was she really, sir?" striking a match. "Well, as I was saying, while she was supposed to be killed there, it pretty well put an end to the case. But it turns out now that she had nothing to do having with it."

"Nothing to do with it, you say? How have they made that out?"

"Well, it seems that this girl was some connection of Mr. von Rheinhart's, and that accounts for her having found his card in her pocket, which the police thought so much of at the time. They began to make inquiries, and they have identified the clothes and everything this poor thing was wearing."

"But how do they know that this girl was not Rheinhart's visitor? If she were related to him—"

The landlord scratched his head.

"I can't answer for the rights of it, doctor, but I hear that she was at a farewell party somewhere that night, and that there were lots of folks as could swear she was there all the evening, and naturally couldn't ha' been at The Bungalow shooting Mr. von Rheinhart."

"Naturally she couldn't, if that were so," Roger assented. "But I thought that Heron identified her dress?"

"I understand he said it looked the same. But there—what does Heron know about dress?" the landlord said with a jolly laugh. "He said her hair was the same colour too; but there—there are plenty of yellow-haired lassies about. I have always said, if she made straight off to the woods she would ha' been there before the police began to search. I'm real glad the poor thing got off. From what I can make out, Mr. von Rheinhart was a brute. I'm not one as cares to see a woman hung."

A momentary vision rose before Roger's eyes—a mass of golden hair, the brown eyes, so like Elizabeth Luxmore's.

His stiff lips moved.

"No; I don't believe in it either."

Roger took his place at the table; but though the meal was all that had been promised, he could hardly bring himself to eat.

The police-station at Sutton Boldon was a long, low building; the end nearest the station was set apart for the incarceration of prisoners, and was easily distinguishable by its heavy, iron-studded doors; the other side, that towards the village, was the residence of the inspector. A gay little garden sloped down to the high road; offenders against the law at Sutton Boldon were brought to the place of detention up a pathway bordered by hollyhocks and carnations.

Chief-Inspector Spencer took great pride in his flowers: but to-day, though he was strolling up and down the little grass plot, called by courtesy the lawn, he was not thinking of his beloved blossoms: even his pipe had been suffered to go out as he listened attentively and nodded assent every now and then to the little man who walked by his side, talking and gesticulating vigorously.

"Yes, it has been a case that has puzzled good deal first and last," he said slowly. "And I don't say that we see our way through it yet," blinking his eyes and looking round him thoughtfully.

The other glanced at him.

"You agree with me in the main though, I see."

"I am not altogether sure that I do. Still there would be no harm in looking him up. Why, I declare—Who is that?"

"Hallo, who is this?" repeated Inspector Spencer to Detective Collins, as the doctor's tall figure approached them.

Roger Lavington was swinging down the cobbled walk on the other side of the palings. As the inspector spoke he halted beside the wooden gate.

"Good-morning, inspector. How is the world using you?"

The inspector hurried down the gravel path.

"Pretty middling, thank you, Doctor. I'm glad to see you in Sutton Boldon again, sir!"

Roger struck with his cane at a tall, upstanding dandelion.

"I have just come over for the day to see Dr. Marpont; there are a few things to be settled between us yet. How is Mrs. Spencer?"

"Nicely, sir, thank you. She always says she owes her life to you for pulling her through that pneumonia two years ago. Will you step in and take a glass of her home-brewed, doctor?"

Roger pushed his hat back from his forehead; the invitation might give him the very opportunity he had been hoping for. He had at least an hour at his disposal before Dr. Marpont would be at liberty.

"Thank you very much, inspector. I don't mind if I do. I haven't tasted anything like Mrs. Spencer's home-brewed since I left Sutton Boldon."

The inspector held the gate open. His companion came towards them, touching his hat.

"Good morning, doctor!"

Lavington looked at him in surprise, then a gleam of unwelcome surprise flashed in his eyes.

"Why, surely, it is Detective-Inspector Collins?"

The little man's rosy, good-humoured face lighted up with a smile.

"Detective-Inspector no longer. I have retired from the force."

Roger was conscious of a throb of relief.

"Retired, have you? Surely, you are young to give up work?"

Collins caressed his round, clean-shaven chin.

"Maybe I am older than you think, doctor. My looks have always favoured me. I haven't given up work altogether either. I do a little on my own now. It pays me better too. You may have heard of Collins and Mason's Private Detective Agency perhaps? I am the original founder."

"Oh, I see!"

Roger looked at the carnations tied carefully to their stakes; he was not to have it all his own way, then. Collins would have his own axe to grind; the chat over the inspector's home-brewed would resolve itself more or less into a duel.

The inspector was still holding the gate open hospitably.

"The missus will never forgive me if I let you go without speaking to her, doctor."

Telling himself that it could make no possible difference, and that in the remote case of there being danger it would be better that he should know it, Lavington turned in.

"You know your way here, doctor," the inspector cried genially, as he held the door open. "Molly"—as a child in a white pinafore appeared at the end of the passage-"go and tell your mother that Dr. Lavington has come to pay us a visit. Say she is to bring jug of home-brewed for him to taste. Step in, doctor."

The inspector drew forward one of the shiny horse-hair covered chairs.

"Sit down, doctor. The missus will be here directly. Where's your mother, child?" as the little maiden returned stumbling under the burden of the great jug she carried.

"Mother has gone over to Hemington this morning," she announced importantly as she set her tray on the red tablecloth, "and I am keeping house. Did you forget, dad?"

For one brief second the inspector looked rather foolish. He gave an embarrassed laugh.

"It had slipped my memory, Molly. That is a fact. She will be disappointed when she hears she has missed you, doctor."

"I am very sorry too," said Roger politely.

The inspector poured out the ale, frothing up the glass carefully.

Detective Collins seated himself gingerly on the extreme edge of one of the uncomfortable-looking chairs; as he glanced about the room in apparent admiration, one hand planted firmly on each knee, he might have been taken for a prosperous farmer, a well-to-do mechanic—anything rather than a well-known detective.

"Ay, doctor," he said, as Roger took a draught from his foaming glass, "the last time we met was at Northchester. You had been to see the poor thing who was supposed to have shot Rheinhart. You'll have heard perhaps that was all a mistake?"

"Mr. Rose at the Crown was talking about it just now. But one hears so many tales. You don't mean that—"

"She had nothing to do with the affair," the detective said, jerking his head in the direction of The Bungalow. "That is clear enough. She was at a party in Cirencester on April 14th, the night Rheinhart was murdered. At least ten independent witnesses are ready to swear that. So it settles the matter as far as she is concerned, and we shall have to look elsewhere for the lady who dropped her glove."

A cold shiver ran down Roger's spine as he tried to think.

"I have always heard that an alibi is the most unsatisfactory and delusive of defences," he said at last, hating himself the while for the slur he was casting on the dead girl's memory. Where had he heard that the vilest slander of all was to defame the helpless dead?

"I don't say but what I am inclined to agree with it in nine cases out of ten, but this affair of the Bungalow is the tenth. I have sifted it through and through, and nothing is absolutely clearer than that the woman who died at Northchester had no hand in Rheinhart's death. You said at the inquest that he had been dead from a quarter of an hour to twenty minutes when you first saw him."

"About that, I should say," Roger assented. "Certainly not more than half an hour."

Collins took a long draught of beer and wiped his lips meditatively.

"It's a queer thing how she got so completely away. You saw nothing of her as you went into the house, doctor?"

Not a muscle of Lavington's face altered.

"Absolutely nothing. There was no one so far as I could see in the neighbourhood."

"And in the house, in the room itself?" The question had all the sharpness of a sword thrust. Collins was not admiring the colour of the ale now; his eyes were fixed gimlet-wise on the other's face.

Despite his self-control, Lavington's eyelids flickered.

"I did not search when I entered," he said, speaking as naturally as he could. "But I saw nothing to lead me to suppose that the assassin was concealed in the house."

Detective Collins nodded his head as if satisfied.

"Just so! just so! That is what I understood at the time. You may have heard that Rheinhart was shot with his own pistol?"

"No. I had not," Roger said, in genuine surprise. "Have you found it?"

"No. That is what we should particularly like to do," the detective remarked grimly. "Apparently the murderer carried that little piece of evidence away."

Roger finished his beer at a draught.

Altogether it seems as if you were in the right way to discover the criminal at last, inspector."

"Oh, I could not say that, doctor! The time that has elapsed is all against us. Still, it does not do to give up hope."

"Decidedly not!" Roger stood up. "Well, I expect Dr. Marpont will be ready for me now. Thanks for your hospitality, inspector. I am sorry not to have seen Mrs. Spencer. I dare say I shall be over this way again before long."

"I hope so, I am sure, sir." Despite Roger's remonstrances both men insisted on accompanying him to the garden gate, pointing out various choice blossoms on the way, and finally taking leave of him effusively.

"What do you make of him?"

Collins pursed up his lips.

"Pretty much what I made of him at the time," he said enigmatically.

The inspector made no rejoinder until they had turned into his room at the official end of the station, then he nodded his head at the bureau which stood in a recess near the door.

"You did not tell him of that?"

Collins looked at him.

"What do you take me for, Joe Spencer—a green-horn? Let alone that, at present, there is not much to tell anyone."

"Well, I don't know." The inspector unlocked the drawer and took out a wooden box.

Collins opened the lid and lifted some oblong, gleaming object tentatively in his fingers.

"It seems to me," the inspector said slowly, "that with that and Matthew Wilson's evidence we ought to do something."

Chapter Eleven

IT WAS growing dark when Roger stepped from the train at Oakthorpe. Coming out of the station there appeared to be nobody to meet him, and a cab was an unheard-of luxury at Oakthorpe. With a feeling of irritation he realized that there was nothing for it but to make his way to the Manor on foot.

It was quite half a mile to the village. Half-way down the rustic street there was a bypath leading to the Manor; Roger thought with a feeling of pleasure of its green freshness. A child came out of one of the cottages near; its mother stood at the open door.

"Now, you'll tell her I will let her have it first thing in the morning, Mary Ann. Say I am very sorry I could not oblige her to-night. And mind you make haste."

"Yes, yes. I will be quick."

The girl's head was turned behind her as she ran across the road. At the same moment there was the hoot of a motor coming round the corner just beyond; puzzled, frightened, not realizing from whence the sound came, the child hesitated, turned back, then started again.

But her indecision was fatal. It was evident that the car was driven by an inexperienced chauffeur. There was an ineffectual attempt to stop, too late; and Roger, springing forward, managed to catch the child in time to save her from the worst of the collision, but not soon enough to avoid an ugly blow from the rear guard. The force of the impact threw him face downwards on the ground. As he raised himself he saw that the car stood farther down the road and the occupants were hastening towards him. Little Mary Ann's mother was already bending over her; Roger took the child from her and felt her all over carefully.

"Oh, Dr. Lavington, have we killed her?" Roger recognized Elizabeth Luxmore's voice.

He turned and stared at her stupidly, dazed by his fall.

"You here!"

"Yes, yes." The girl took hold of his arm. "Don't you understand we—Reggie and I—were in the car? I was driving. I made the chauffeur sit behind. I thought I could drive well enough to do it alone now, and it was such fun. Now it has ended like this." She finished with a dry sob.

Roger pulled himself together; he took her trembling hands in his.

"It is not so bad as you fear, Miss Luxmore. The left arm is broken, the child is stunned by the shock and the fall, but I do not think we need fear any more serious results."

"That is bad enough," the girl said, her breath catching in her throat. "And it is dear little Mary Ann Sturt—whatever you say to me, Mrs. Sturt, it will be no worse than I am saying to myself."

Lavington had the child in his arms now. He was carrying her across to the cottage. The mother turned to Miss Luxmore. Her face was white and her eyes full of tears, but her voice was steady. She laid her hand on the girl's.

"Eh, Miss Elizabeth, I'm not going to blame you. I know it was naught but an accident, and I'm saying to myself that I should have had more sense than to send the child out alone at this time of night."

"You are very good to me," Elizabeth said wistfully, "but I can never forgive myself—" She broke off as they entered the cottage. Little Mary Ann's eyes were open now; she tried to smile at her mother.

Lavington laid her down.

"Now we must try to make this poor arm well. I shall want some long strips of lint or linen, Mrs. Sturt—those long, thin sticks over there will make capital splints. You must be very brave for a few minutes, little girl!"

Mary Ann made a good patient; more than once Roger said an approving word. Elizabeth Luxmore proved very efficient as a helper; she seemed to know by instinct when anything was wanted and exactly how Lavington's instructions should be carried out.

When all was finished, and Mary Ann lay back on her pillow, pale but smiling, Roger turned.

"There, that is all that can be done for the present, I fancy. Now, Miss Luxmore, how are you going to get home? This has been too much for you, I am afraid," looking compassionately at the girl's quivering lips.

"Oh, what does it matter about me?" she cried passionately. "I am all right, and I dare say Reggie is about somewhere," vaguely. "Mrs. Sturt, please get anything—anything that Mary Ann would like; and mind you keep your own strength up! Put your washing aside and give yourself up altogether to nursing. That will be my affair entirely."

"You are very good, Miss Elizabeth; and don't you worry. It must have been sent for our good or else it would not have happened."

Mrs. Sturt accompanied them to the door, with an incoherent torrent of thanks and explanations. Outside, the dusk had merged into darkness. Lavington looked round.

"I don't see your car, Miss Luxmore."

At the same moment Reggie Luxmore spoke close at hand.

"How is the kid now? I shall take jolly I never let you drive again, Elizabeth!"

"Hush!" Roger interrupted peremptorily. "Don't you see that your sister had gone through enough. Where is the car?"

"Down the road. I told Peters to wait at the end of the street."

"I shall walk," Elizabeth said determinedly. "Nothing shall induce me to get in the motor. I feel"—with a shiver—"as if I never wanted to see a motor again!"

"Absurd!" young Luxmore said impatiently. "From what I hear there is no harm done, and if we wait to walk up you know how nervous Daphne is. Probably she is worrying herself into a fever about us already, and if she sets the pater off—"

Roger put one hand on the boy's shoulder.

"Don't you see that your sister's nerves are over-strained? She is quite right; it will be better for her to walk up. I should suggest that you go on first, and tell Lord Luxmore how it is. If Miss Luxmore will allow me, I will come on with her more slowly."

Reggie hardly waited for his sister's assent.

"That is a capital idea," he said heartily. "If you are sure you do not mind, Dr. Lavington."

They did not talk much; the little they said had reference to the Sturts. Elizabeth was eager to know all that would be required at the cottage; though scrupulous and neat in their dress, and in their meagre furniture, it was evident that the widow and her daughter were very poor. Elizabeth's penitence for having been the cause of this fresh trouble was very great indeed.

Lavington glanced at Elizabeth. There was a tired droop about her slim young figure; the folds of her long motor-coat clung about her knees and impeded her walking. She had thrown off her veil, and carried it over her arm; its long ends stirred faintly in the breeze.

As she walked beside him, Roger could see the outline of her small head set flower-wise on the long throat; the air caught the soft curls near her temples, and beat them back against her cheek. Her very nearness thrilled him with an exquisite sense of intimacy.

The hall door stood wide open; inside there was a cheerful glow of light and warmth; as they drew near Roger caught the echo of Lord Luxmore's voice.

He paused. The influence of this one perfect moment was upon him. He would willingly keep the memory unspoilt.

Elizabeth Luxmore looked at him.

"My father will wish to thank you. You must come in, Dr. Lavington!"

"Not to-night," Roger said abruptly. "I—Courtenay will be expecting me."

Elizabeth hesitated; she put out her hand. By the light thrown out from the hall, Roger could see that her brown eyes were filled with tears.

"I want to thank you," she said, beneath her breath. "You have saved me from—But for you, what should I be feeling now? Thank you for all." The slender gloved fingers clung to his for a moment; the next she had turned, and hurried up the steps to the house.

Roger stood still and watched, his heart beating high as he recalled her words and glance, the barriers of caste obliterated. Mad, foolish as he knew himself to be, in that moment of self-oblivion, of exaltation, he realized only that she was the woman he loved, that he had been fortunate enough to serve her and that she had thanked him.

As he waited a tall, white-clad figure came swiftly across the hall.

"Elizabeth—oh, Elizabeth! Thank Heaven! Reggie told us—"

Lavington was not near enough to distinguish the features, but the voice, the walk, the shining golden hair were those of the girl who had taken Zoe's place at Freshfield.

He groaned as he drew back. In his absorption in Elizabeth he had momentarily forgotten the dark cloud that hung over her elder sister—a cloud which something seemed to tell him might at any moment burst, and overwhelm her with ruin and disaster.

A letter was waiting for him as he reached the Manor. It was from Zoe. Her marriage to an officer had taken place about three months later than the theatricals at Freshfield, and very shortly afterwards the young couple had sailed for India. But this letter bore the London postmark. Zoe must have returned unexpectedly, for Roger knew that there had been no idea of her home-coming for years, when he saw his uncle some few weeks back.

With a prevision of coming calamity for which he could not account he tore open the envelope, and read:

"DEAR ROGER,

"You will be surprised to hear that I am back again, I know. I landed a fortnight ago and have been meaning to write to you ever since. Father and I both hope you will manage to pay us a visit soon. I expect you have more leisure now that you have left Sutton Boldon. Speaking of Sutton Boldon reminds me that a man called here the other day to see Father on business, and asked him such curious questions about those theatricals.

"You remember I was prevented from coming to them at the last minute by influenza. Now, mind you come up soon. I want you to see baby.

"Your affectionate cousin,

"ZOE LANCASTER"

Asking questions about the theatricals at Freshfield! Roger's face was expressive of the utmost consternation as he repeated the words aloud and then glanced at the letter again. What could it mean?

It seemed to Roger as he stood there with the letter in his hand that Fate had been too strong for him, that slowly but with deadly certainty the web of circumstance was being drawn around the unsuspecting victim.

Chapter Twelve

"Is MY uncle, Dr. Lavington, at home?"

"No, sir. He has been called out unexpectedly."

The house was exactly that of the ordinary London doctor—the tessellated pavement of the hall, the massive umbrella-stand, the impassive-looking manservant. It was all very familiar to Roger Lavington; he knew precisely how the heavy oak furniture was placed in the dining-room where the doctor's patients awaited him; the very words in which his uncle would greet them in the consulting-room to which they would be ushered. Upstairs in the drawing-room Zoe was bending over some flowers, evidently intending to arrange them in the glasses which stood on the table close at hand.

She looked up with a little joyful sound when Roger was announced, and came to meet him with outstretched hands.

"Why, this is good—this is better even than I dared to hope for! You must have come off directly you got my letter. Good boy!"

"Didn't you expect me to take the earliest possible opportunity of seeing you?" Roger felt a hypocrite as he warmly clasped her hands.

The real Zoe bore no faintest resemblance to the girl who had stolen her name for two days; her colouring was fair certainly, but so pale as to be indefinite; her eyes were good, a clear translucent grey, but her great charm lay in her expression, which seemed to vary with every change of mood, and lighted up her small, piquant features with gaiety, or as she listened to some sad story, would make her eyes intensely sorrowful, the tears quiver in her voice.

Roger had always been fond of his pretty cousin, who was some years his junior; he had seen a good deal of her while he was at her father's, and he was genuinely pleased to meet her again. Nevertheless, as she made inquiries about his journey, and asked if he would have some refreshment before luncheon, he realized how entirely his pleasure in the reunion was subordinate to his interest in the Luxmores.

Zoe, however, was placidly unconscious of any other reason for his coming than a cousinly desire for her welfare. She assumed that his interest in her affairs was only second to her own, and having assured herself that there was nothing needed, settled down to a long and detailed account of the reasons that had rendered her home-coming imperative. It was evident that India suited neither her nor the child, she informed him, and her husband was hoping shortly to arrange an exchange.

At last Roger's moment arrived. His cousin made some allusion to her letter; he broke in upon her chatter ruthlessly.

"You said some man had been inquiring about the Freshfield theatricals?"

Zoe brushed out the folds of her dress.

"Oh, yes. Wasn't it funny? He quite thought that I had taken part in them."

"Uncle John—you said he saw the man—would know you had not?"

"No. He didn't remember anything about it. But the man called again yesterday; says he is a surveyor for the County Council."

"Did he say anything more about the Freshfield theatricals?"

"Oh, yes. Quite a lot. He quite thought I had acted in those theatricals, Roger. It was really difficult to convince him that I was down with the 'flu at the time, and had to give it all up at the last minute."

Roger drew in his breath sharply.

"You told him that?"

Zoe glanced at him.

"Why, naturally I did. You do not mean"—her face changing—"that there was any reason I should not?"

Roger hesitated. It was difficult to know what to answer, or how far it was wise to trust Zoe, who had always been an incorrigible chatterbox. There was the question, too, of whether it was fair to involve her, all unknowing, in the tangle in which he himself was enmeshed? But the peril in which he believed Daphne Luxmore stood was his foremost thought now.

"He—I can't explain, Zoe, but for my sake, if you are questioned again, say that you didn't know what he was referring to; temporize, do anything rather than let him know that you were not at Freshfield."

His anxiety, the fear underlying his words, were infectious; Zoe's face paled, her eyes met his questioningly.

"What is it, Roger? I don't understand. What does it matter to anyone whether I played at Freshfield or not? This surveyor—Mr. Gregg, his name was—remembered my name, and said he had admired my acting. I told him it was a mistake, that I had been prevented from going, that was all."

He rose and walked to the window.

"All!" Roger groaned. His eyes saw nothing of the life of the street outside; instead, they were picturing the cool shade of the beech-wood, the shadowed sweetness of Elizabeth Luxmore's smile. Had the blow he had been fearing fallen? Was Detective Collins on the track at last?

Zoe watched him with troubled eyes: she could not help seeing that the question which had seemed so unimportant to her was of terrible significance to him. At last she touched him timidly.

"Can't you tell me what it is, Roger? I am so sorry!"

Lavington did not answer for a moment. He caught Zoe's soft hand and crushed it.

"It was not your fault, Zoe," he said unsteadily. "I ought to have thought—I ought to have warned you! Good heavens, how could I have left one loophole unguarded?"

Zoe's face paled; she was puzzled, frightened; across the trivialities that made up her existence, the sight of her cousin's emotion, though she had no knowledge of its cause, came as an awakening, a thunderclap. All her pretty frivolities fell away from her.

"I didn't know, Roger, indeed. But if I told Mr. Gregg that it was a mistake—that I was thinking of some other time—"

"Gregg! Gregg!" Roger repeated bitterly. His clasp of her hands tightened. "There is no Gregg, Zoe. What do you take that man for?"

Zoe winced. The pain in her hands was becoming intolerable. Lavington had long since lost all sense of what he was gripping.

"He was a surveyor for the London County Council, I told you."

Lavington laughed—a short, hard laugh that was not pleasant to hear. He threw her hands from him; one soft palm hit the corner of the china cabinet, raising a red lump.

"He was a detective! You will hear no more of your new schemes of drainage, Zoe. I think he got all he wanted."

Tears rose in Zoe's eyes.

"How was I to know, Roger?" she faltered. "If I have hurt you, how can I make amends? What can I do?"

At the sight of her emotion, Lavington's better nature reasserted itself.

"You were not to blame. It was I who ought to have known. But now, I wonder, what is the best thing to do? I must think." He turned to the door.

"Where are you going, Roger? Father will be home directly; we will ask him. He will know what is best to be done."

He caught her arm.

"Don't you understand, Zoe? You mustn't say one word of this to any living soul—neither to your father nor anyone else!"

There were great, blue finger-marks on Zoe's rounded when she undressed that night, but she felt no pain now.

"I will not tell anyone unless you wish me, Roger, I promise you that," she said simply. "But you must wait to see Father. Think how hurt he would be to know he had missed you."

Roger laughed recklessly.

"Tell him I was telegraphed for—that I came up to a consultation, and hadn't a minute to spare," he suggested. "No, it is no use, Zoe. I must get back; I must make up my mind what is best to be done now."

Zoe found that further remonstrance was useless, his resolution was taken; and, sorely puzzled and frightened, she had to let him go.

To Lavington himself, the couple of hours that must elapse before he could get back to Oakthorpe seemed an endless time to look forward to. What might not be happening to them.

He thought of Detective Collins's smug face as he had seen him at Sutton Boldon. So he had known then—he had been deliberately laying a trap. Had he walked into it? There had been no allusion in the morning's paper to the Bungalow murder, but Lavington knew enough of police methods to feel sure that the matter would not rest there.

Whatever might have been the supposed clue—the identification of the victim of the Northchester disaster, or some thing, as he was now inclined to think, entirely different—there could be small doubt that Collins was on the right track at last. And suave and pleasant-mannered as the little man might be, Roger guessed that his prey would not easily escape him, that he would work until every little piece of evidence was complete, until not one link in the chain of circumstances was wanting, and then he would pounce upon his unsuspecting prey.

If only Daphne Luxmore would go away out of his reach, if she would hide her identity under another name in a foreign land, it might still be possible for her to escape, he thought. But if she waited, not knowing, it might be that she would not awake to her danger until it was too late. He turned the matter over in his mind. Clearly she must be warned—but how?

A letter was not safe. No. The warning must be given by word of mouth. Then a third course suggested itself. He had been told that Daphne went every evening to the old trysting-place by the bridge; he had seen her there himself. Would it not be wiser to speak to her, to tell her of her danger, there.

Roger had not long to wait. As he came in sight of the bridge a tall, veiled figure emerged from the wood on the Luxmore side. Lavington recognized the graceful gait, the luxuriant golden air that not even the thick motor-veil could entirely hide.

He stepped forward to meet her, raising his hat.

"Miss Luxmore, I have ventured to come, hoping to see you—

At the first sound of his voice the girl halted; as he crossed the bridge she turned and retraced her steps.

Roger hastened after her.

"Indeed, it is not idle curiosity; if you remember Freshfield you—"

In his eagerness to overtake her, he did not notice a gnarled, projecting tree-root. He caught his right foot in it, and came heavily to the ground. He got up with an exclamation of annoyance at his awkwardness, and then looked round in amazement. Of the tall, grey-clad figure of which he had been in pursuit there was not a sign to be seen.

At last, baffled and humiliated, he had to confess that she had eluded him, that he had lost his opportunity. He turned back disconsolately. There, on the ground before him, as he neared the place where he had fallen, lay a book face downwards, evidently dropped. He picked it up. As he expected, Daphne Luxmore was the name on the title-page. Beneath it, in the same half-foreign handwriting, there was a verse of "The Revolt of Islam."

"Then black despair,
The shadow of a starless night, was thrown
Over the world in which I moved alone."

With a feeling as though he had been prying into something not intended for his eyes, Roger shut the book and put it in his pocket; it would, at least, give him an opportunity of asking to see Miss Luxmore, to restore her lost property. But the words haunted him as he turned across the park.

"A world in which I moved alone," he repeated to himself. "Poor girl—poor Daphne Luxmore!" If things were as he feared, of her these words might be well said. Alone she must ever be with the shadow of a terrible dread, black despair separating her from her fellows!

Chapter Thirteen

"Is Miss Luxmore at home?"

"No, sir."

Roger hesitated; the footman, blandly irresponsive, waited with the door in his hand.

"I have found something which I think must belong to Miss Luxmore. Will you be good enough to give it to her as soon as possible?"

"Certainly, sir."

The footman glanced somewhat superciliously at the red seals with which the brown outer covering of the parcel was adorned, and Roger turned away.

This plan, which he had evolved as the result of much agitation, did not strike him as particularly brilliant, but, for want of a better, he had been forced to adopt it. He had written a note telling Daphne that if, as he felt certain, he had met her at Freshfield, circumstances had arisen which made it necessary that he should see her. He begged her to give him an interview, and said that, unless he heard from her to the contrary, he would be this evening where he had seen her yesterday.

As he was going down the drive there was a quick, springy step on the turf; a hand was thrust through his arm.

"I say, Dr. Lavington!" It was Reggie Luxmore's pleasant boyish voice. "The dad is out," he went on familiarly. "Gone up to town for the day. Did you want to see him?"

"Not to-day. As a matter of fact, my business was with your elder sister."

"With Daphne?" Young Luxmore opened his eyes. "Oh, I say, you know. Daphne never sees anyone! If it had been Elizabeth now—"

"I believe I found a book of hers the other day," Roger went on, "and I hoped she might have allowed me to return it personally."

"Bless you, she wouldn't!" Reggie returned easily. "Very queer, Daphne is. Soon be as bad as Courtenay himself I say. But it is no use talking to her. But I was hoping to see you soon, for, you know,

Elizabeth and I are no end grateful to you for saving that kid the other day. It was touch and go too."

"You make too much of it," Roger disclaimed. "I had no time to think; it was all over in a moment—"

Suddenly Reggie broke in, to say:

"I wonder who those fellows are? They have been stopping at the Corbetts' farm for a fortnight or more—at least, the eldest one has. I have only seen the other this last day or two. Cadging sort of fellow the tall one is; he tacked himself on to me the other day, and asked me all sorts of questions; but I soon sent him about his business."

Lavington glanced carelessly in the direction he indicated. Two men were leaning over the palings of the local cricket-field apparently interested in the game that was in progress; one was short and stout, with a bushy black beard; the other tall and thin, with a ragged-looking, ginger-coloured moustache.

Roger did not recognize the faces as belonging to any of the loiterers on the village green with whom he occasionally exchanged a word as he passed. As he turned his head away, however, something familiar about the shoulders, about the whole pose of the figure of the shorter one, caught his eye. Of whom did it remind him, he wondered. Then, suddenly, he remembered. The bushy beard, the rather long black hair were wholly unlike; but the attitude, his gesture, as he turned to speak to his companion, were those of Detective Collins. Just so had he looked when he was admiring Inspector Spencer's carnations in the garden at Sutton Boldon. Lavington glanced at the broad back again. Was it merely a chance resemblance, or was it Detective Collins in disguise come to spy out the land?

Reggie Luxmore was inclined to resent his silence and his preoccupation. He gave his arm an impatient twitch.

"What is it? You have not seen the fellows before, have you?"

"I don't know," Lavington answered dreamily. He was mistaken, he told himself; of course he was mistaken and yet—"I fancy I may have met one of them," he said as carelessly as he could. "Shall we walk round that way, and I shall be able to see whether it is the man I know?"

Reggie acquiesced somewhat sulkily. Lavington's interest in his stories had waned unaccountably.

"You said you had spoken to him?"

"Him? Who?" Reggie inquired ungrammatically; his attention had wandered to the play. "Oh, of course, those chaps! The ginger-coloured one is always trying to make up to me. Doesn't seem to care about it to-day though."

Roger glanced back. The two men had mounted bicycles that had been leaning against the palings beside them, and were now speeding down the road at a pace which rendered any idea of overtaking them out of the question.

Roger was left a prey to torturing doubt. Had he been mistaken by a fancied resemblance—or was Detective Collins like a sleuth-hound already on the trail? Was the secret that Roger would have given his life to guard already known? Was it possible that any minute might bring irremediable disgrace and ruin upon Daphne Luxmore—upon Elizabeth? He dared not think further. Only one point was clear—important as he had deemed it hitherto that Daphne should be warned of her danger, it had become doubly imperative now.

He parted from Reggie, who rushed off to speak to some new acquaintance, and walked back to the Manor, still puzzling over this new problem. It seemed to him that the afternoon was interminable, the hours that must elapse before he could hope to see Daphne were endless.

As soon as the high clock over the stables had chimed six, he started. Would Daphne come? he wondered. Would she suspect his *bona fides*, or would she suspect a trap, and refuse to meet him?

He had not arrived at any satisfactory solution when he came in sight of the stream. His heart beat faster as he saw a tall, slight figure, in white gown, leaning against the bridge.

He quickened his steps. The girl's back was towards him; beneath the white transparent motor-veil he could catch a glimpse of the golden hair.

"Miss Luxmore," he said slowly, as he laid his hand on the railing. She turned her head slowly. The motor-veil was twisted round her hat, and tied in a coquettish bow beneath her chin; the golden hair curling round the temples, the great brown eyes, the haunting, elusive smile were those of the girl he had found in The Bungalow.

"You wanted to see me?"

"Yes." Roger looked round and hesitated. Until this moment he had hardly known that a faint hope still lingered in his heart that, in spite of the likeness undoubtedly borne to her by Elizabeth he might yet be proved to have made a mistake. Now however, when all doubt in his mind was at an end, he was for a time taken aback, tongue-tied.

The girl waited, her brown eyes fixed upon his face, her lips parted. Far away above them, the clear, sweet notes of a lark floated to their ears, the trickling of the brook made murmuring music at their feet. Roger's eyes wandered idly to the tall, upstanding meadowsweet by the water's edge, noted the gay fringe of ragged robins, the faint sweet-scented clover.

"Yes," he assented. "I wanted to tell you—to warn you—"

"Warn! Ah!" The shadow of a terrible fear flashed in the girl's eyes.

Roger averted his gaze.

"The—the girl who left her glove in The Bungalow was supposed to have perished in the Northchester disaster. But lately, within the last few days, the one at Northchester has been identified; it has been proved beyond all doubt that she could not have been at Sutton Boldon that night."

"Ah!" The girl drew a long breath. "Then, I think I understand— you mean that now they will search—"

"For the one who was," Roger finished. "Already they have questioned—they have found out that my cousin Zoe did not take part in the theatricals at Freshfield. To-day, in the village, I saw a man whom I fear—I cannot help fearing—was the detective who was employed in the case at the time."

Even the motor-veil could not hide the pallor of the cheeks beneath now; the little gloved hands clutched convulsively at the lace round the throat.

"He has come here—for what?"

"Who can tell?" Roger's eyes were very pitiful.

Always he had sympathized with the girl he had found in Maximilian von Rheinhart's studio; now that he knew her to be the sister of the girl he loved, his compassion, his desire to help her, were increased a hundredfold. He hesitated, then went on more slowly:

"It has occurred to me that it might be wiser—that it would be safer—to leave Oakthorpe for a while at any rate. If you went abroad—"

"We could be traced at once." The hands were clasping one another tightly now; a button burst off one glove. Roger's eyes fixed themselves upon it absently as it gleamed against the dusty plank.

"If you went away quietly, if you left no address, I think it could be managed," he hazarded.

"Ah! No, no! My father, Reggie, my sister—it would kill them. Indeed—indeed, I couldn't."

Roger did not speak. In truth the position was beset with difficulty; escape was not easy. If the detective's suspicions were aroused with regard to Daphne Luxmore, it might be impossible. The very attempt might not improbably bring about the catastrophe they were trying to avoid.

Miss Luxmore bent forward; she laid one hand on his arm.

"Don't you see that it would kill my father if I went away without letting him know where I was. And, if he knew, it would be impossible to keep it a secret."

With his knowledge of Lord Luxmore, Roger was inclined to agree.

"But if the detective should see him, should tell him, even if the worst should happen?"

She gave a shuddering cry.

"Ah, then—then"—recovering her self-control with a supreme effort—"I can but tell them the truth—how it happened!"

"Yes," Roger said thickly. Mentally he pictured the scene: the crowded court, the row of jurors, the scarlet-robed judge, the girl in the witness-box, telling them "how it happened." The pity of it. The shame of it, that must fall on other heads as well as hers.

A little colour was stealing back to the girl's face. Never had the resemblance between the two sisters been stronger, Lavington thought.

"How did you know—how did you guess that I was—" Her lips faltered over the last words of the question.

Roger did not answer for a moment. Sometimes it seemed to him that his certainty that Daphne Luxmore and the girl of The Bungalow were one and the same was more a matter of intuition than of evidence.

"I could not help seeing the likeness to you in your sister," he said at last. "It seemed to me that it was far too striking to be accidental. Then I saw you meet her in the hall the other day. But before then I had heard, I had put things together, and I guessed—"

She had turned a little from him now; as she spoke she absently picked little splinters of wood from a broken piece of the railing and, dropping them into the water, watched them floating down the stream.

"That was it, was it? Well, Dr. Lavington, and what are you going to do now?" turning with disconcerting suddenness. "Are you going to keep my secret?"

Roger started at her.

"To keep your secret?" he echoed. "Why, surely you know that I would guard it above all things— even at the cost of life itself!" in a lower tone.

The unexpected vehemence of his reply apparently astonished Miss Luxmore; she did not speak for a moment; her great brown eyes gazed searchingly into his face; then, as he met her scrutiny unmoved, her whole face quivered, she drew a little away.

"But why should you do this for me—why should you help me? I have no claim upon you—I do not understand—"

"Do you not?" Roger questioned hoarsely. The muscles of his face twitched; he went on recklessly. "No, you do not know—how should you? that I would lay down my life itself to prevent this thing becoming known; because I have dared to love your sister, that for her sweet sake I would count my life as nothing— nothing, if by any means I might keep shame and disgrace from falling upon her name."

The girl started back.

"What—my sister! You cannot—it is impossible!"

"Would it be possible to see her—Elizabeth—without loving her?" Roger questioned, the passion in his voice deepening and strengthening. "You may think me presumptuous, mad, what you will! She will never know it. And you—you will now be sure that your cause is safe with me, that I would die rather than betray you!"

"You love Elizabeth?" she said unsteadily.

Roger bared his head in reverence; the light of a great love, a great renunciation, burned in his grey eyes.

"I love Elizabeth!" he repeated simply.

Chapter Fourteen

SUMMER though it was, a bright fire was burning in the grate in Inspector Spencer's best parlour; through the open window the scent of clove-pinks, the strong, damp smell of newly-turned earth was wafted into the room. A great bowl of freshly-gathered roses— the old-fashioned cottage great golden Gloire de Dijon, pink La France, and Baroness Rothschild—stood in the centre of the table.

Detective Collins lit a cigarette as he leaned back in his chair, and wiped his forehead with a red bandanna.

"What time did you say Matthew Wilson's train was due, Spencer?"

"At 3.30." The other man looked at his watch. "He ought to be here any minute now."

Detective Collins drew his chair up to the table, and, producing a stiff roll of paper, spread it out before him.

"Yes. This plan of yours will come in useful, Spencer. Let me just understand the position of affairs. C is the room in which Rheinhart was shot, door at the left leading into the garden. H'm! h'm! Window securely fastened from inside; front door left open by the housekeeper when she called doctor. Exactly. Then this spot marked D is where the woman was met by Henson, the woman with golden hair, who asked the way to The Bungalow. Just so!"

He studied the plan in silence, frowning and biting his nails as he made various notes on the margin.

The inspector went over to the window.

"Our man is coming now, if I am not mistaken. Ah, I thought so!" as there was a loud knock at the door.

He opened the door; a bronzed man, in a sailor's dress, stood outside.

"Come in, Wilson, come in; Detective Collins is here; he is anxious to hear your story."

Wilson stepped in and touched his cap to the detective, who nodded curtly.

"Now, my man, let us hear what you have to say. Sit down," pushing a chair towards him.

Detective Collins drew out his notebook and pulled his chair round so that he got a good view of Wilson's face, with the light falling full on it.

"What I want to hear, first of all, my good man," he said in his briskest, most matter-of-fact tones, "is why was this story of yours not brought to the notice of the police sooner?"

Wilson stirred his feet uneasily.

"I told the inspector, sir."

"Never mind that; I want you to tell me."

Detective Collins waited, notebook and pencil in hand.

Wilson cleared his throat, and gazed into the corner of his hat as if for inspiration.

"It was in this way, sir; I had signed on as A.B. on the *Thistledown*, for a year's cruise in the South Sea Islands. I was due to join on the 15th, and my sweetheart being in service as housemaid at Dr. Lavington's, I went down unexpected-like on the 14th just to say good-bye to her."

"You put it off pretty late?" The detective was scribbling away in his notebook.

Mr. Wilson looked rather foolish.

"Well, she wasn't expecting me, for we had said good-bye on the Saturday, so to speak; but I thought I would run down just for a last word. Many a man is a bit of a fool when he is in love, you know, sir," apologetically.

The detective nodded.

"We will take all that for granted, my man. Go on!"

"Well, it was dark when I got there of course." Wilson stopped and considered for a moment. "I had sent a bit of a note to Mary, telling her I should be on the other side of the wall at the bottom of the garden, and I was waiting for her there when somebody come across the field on the footpath, same as I had done myself a minute or two before. It being dark, and me leaning against the wall, he didn't seem to see me, but began feeling about the wall as if he was looking for a gate. There wasn't one, of course; so, though he lighted several matches, presently he gave it up, and hoisted himself over the wall. As he did so I heard something drop on my side. I felt curious. Having nothing to do, as you may say, till Mary came, I looked about, and presently I found that silver cigarette-case—that one I give the inspector the week before last, sir. I climbed up and looked over the wall, meaning to give it back, when I see I was too late; he had gone right across the lawn to the house and walked in at the window, just as if the place belonged to him."

"Perhaps it did," the Inspector interposed. "It sounds to me as if it might be Rheinhart himself."

Wilson scratched his chin.

"No, sir; it wasn't. I see his face when he struck the matches—quite plain-like. He was a good deal taller than the other too; I had seen Mr. von Rheinhart two or three times when I had been walking in the fields at the back with Mary."

"Well, go on!"

Mr. Collins was waiting, pen in hand.

The sailor coughed.

"I heard voices, sir, raised like; once the thought came to me that perhaps they were quarrelling. Then, as I stopped there, I heard a little creeping sound to one side of me; the moon shone out brightly, and I saw as there was some one else watching too. It was a woman—young, I judged her to be, with lightish hair; she was standing looking at the house as if she was frightened to go any further.

"The next minute I heard Mary running down Dr. Lavington's garden, and I didn't wait to hear no more of what went on at The Bungalow. When I saw the woman I felt ashamed-like to be prying on her, and I thought I would give the case to Mary to send into The Bungalow next morning."

"And this is all you saw?"

Wilson scratched his head.

"Pretty nearly, sir. Me and Mary walked up and down the field at the back for a while, and just as I was saying it was time I was off, if I was to catch the train, there was a crack behind us. It wasn't very loud, but I thought it sounded like a pistol, and said so. Mary said: 'Oh, it is Mr. von Rheinhart; he has been shooting lately'; and I took no more notice of it, my thoughts being otherwise occupied with Mary, as you might say."

"Didn't it strike you that, as you had seen a strange man enter in that secretive way, to say nothing of the woman who was watching the garden, it was your duty to go back and see whether there was anything wrong at The Bungalow?"

All Detective Collins's suavity had vanished; instead of his usual blank smile, his lips were drawn in and firmly compressed. His eyes were fixed searchingly upon the sailor's face as he waited for his answer, his fingers beating an irritating tattoo on his note-book.

"I can't say as I did, sir." Evidently this cross-examination was not at all to the sailor's liking; his open mahogany-coloured countenance was several shades deeper in hue than when he arrived. "I didn't think the gentleman I saw was likely to be doing any harm. As for the woman—well, her being there only served to put me further off the scent. Besides, my mind was so took up with Mary that I did not give them more than a passing thought anyway."

"I see." The detective spread out his plan once more. "Now, will you show me just where you were standing?"

Wilson bent over the table, his heavy breathing growing harder.

"Just hereabouts, it would be, sir, where the two gardens join. Them'll be the fields at the back," passing a horny finger down one of the lines. "This first, that would be where Mary and me was walking."

"I see. Now point out to me as near as you can where you saw the woman when you looked over the wall."

Wilson stared at the lines and figures, bewildered.

"I couldn't rightly do that, sir. It was afore you got up to the window the man let himself in by; nearer the corner of the house and the front drive, I mean. I should say she was standing on the grass, near some tall bush or shrubs or something of that. I couldn't go further."

Mr. Collins mused a moment.

"Well, after that, what happened? After you had heard the shot, I mean?"

"Well, we got right up to the other end of the field and was leaning over the stile, pretty close together, as you may guess, gentlemen"—looking round with a propitiatory smile—"when, all of a sudden, out of the darkness—for the moon had gone in by then and it was beginning to spit of rain—a man come right upon us in a tremendous hurry; he was walking as if for a wager. Well, we both made way for him, and he threw himself over the stile and went off. As I stepped aside, however, it was borne in upon me as it was the man I had seen getting over The Bungalow wall."

"What made you think that?"

The sailor passed his handkerchief over his forehead and shifted uneasily in his seat.

"I couldn't rightly say, sir; only as I thought he was about the same build, and the way he throwed himself over the stile; to the best of my belief it was the same man, but I'm not prepared to swear it."

"Umph!" Detective Collins was making another lengthy note. The inspector went over and stood near him. Presently Collins looked up.

"Now, my man, you have not told me how it was that all this was not brought to the notice of the police at the time."

Wilson's face brightened up; he was sure of his ground here.

"As I said, sir, I was due to join the *Thistledown* at Southampton on the morning of the 15th. I only had time to catch the mail south, and at the port it was all bustle and confusion, and I never so much as saw an English paper for the next six months. We was to have called for mails at Sydney, but Sir John changed his mind, and they was sent after us later on. It seems as I missed two or three of my letters, and among them one from Mary, telling me of this here murder. Then, when we was thinking of coming home—past a year it was then, for Sir John he had been took with a fancy for exploring like, and couldn't be got away—I got a touch of their nasty yellow fever; they put in at Yokohama, and I was left at the mission-station. That is how it is I didn't get home till a month or so ago, and never heard a word of the Bungalow murder till Mary told me. You might ha' knocked me down with a feather when I understood what had happened. 'Mary, my girl,' I says, 'the best thing I can do is to go straight to the police.' So here I am, sir, and I am sorry I was not here sooner."

Detective Collins did not speak for a minute or two; his brows were drawn together as he gazed, first at the plan and then at his notebook.

"Yes; if we had known this at the time we might soon have brought the affair to a satisfactory conclusion," he said at last. "After two years, it is a very different matter. Still, we must do the best we can. Do you know at all in which direction the man went after he passed you?"

Mr. Matthew Wilson's face was illumined by a sudden smile.

"Why, I declare I was forgetting! He went on across the next field as far as we could see, and then in a minute or two we heard a motor start in the lane as you come out on the opposite side. I have always thought that it had been waiting for him there, and he went off in it; but of course I can't say."

The detective pricked up his ears.

"Which way did it go?"

Wilson hesitated.

"I should say away from the village, on the main road towards Birmingham, by the sound, sir; but I couldn't be sure."

"Probably came the same way too," Inspector Spencer interpolated. "That would account for nothing being seen of it in the village that night."

"I forgot to say that the cigarette-case slipped my memory," Wilson went on. "I put it in my pocket, meaning to give it to Mary, as I said , but there, my mind was full of other things; I never give it a thought again, till I found it in my pocket one day when we was well out to sea. I always took care of it, though, meaning to send it to The Bungalow when I got the chance. But when I saw Mary and heard what had been going on, I thought the best thing I could do was to bring that, too, to the police.

The detective nodded.

"That is all right, then. I don't think we can go any further to-day, inspector, except that I must ask you, Wilson, how long a time elapsed between your hearing the shot and the man overtaking you in the field. Was there time, in your judgment, for the man to have reached you if he left The Bungalow after the shot was fired?"

Wilson looked doubtful.

"I couldn't rightly say, sir, not having taken any particular notice. It seemed to me a tidy time before he come; but, then, he might have climbed the wall or come out at the front door and round by the gate. I couldn't tell; I didn't give much heed to it." He stood up. "Is that all, sir?"

"For the present, yes. You must have a glass of beer and a mouthful of bread and cheese, my man." The detective looked at Inspector Spencer.

But Matthew Wilson shook his head.

"No, sir, thank you kindly, but young Ned will be waiting for me; he has never been the same since he was at Dr. Lavington's; them nasty fits are always coming on him, and he's frightened like of most folks; but he has took a bit of a fancy to me, so, as me and Mary are spending the day over at Coton, at her mother's, I promised I would make haste to get back." Touching his hair once more to the detective, he went to the door.

Inspector Spencer opened it and watched him walking down the path.

"I shouldn't wonder if we are in for a thunderstorm later," he remarked, gazing at the dark clouds on the horizon, and drawing a deep breath of the cooler air outside before he turned back to the parlour. "Well, Mr. Collins, what do you make of it?"

"Darned if I know what to make of it!" The detective was frowning at his plan as if to vent his irritation on that. "Did she get in and shoot him directly the man had gone, or did he shoot him and then clear off?"

"Or did the two of them do it together? I mean, were they both in it?" Inspector Spencer questioned. Mr. Collins moved his hand impatiently.

"No, no; that is out of the question. Matthew Wilson's evidence all goes to prove that they had no connection; they came independently and left separately. What we have to ask ourselves in the first place is, which of them shot Rheinhart? And I'm blessed if I can answer it anyway. In the second, who are they? And why did your precious doctor mix himself up in the affair?"

The inspector pinched his chin thoughtfully.

"Ah, that is a mystery, that is!" he acknowledged. "I didn't care for his manner from the first; but still, I wasn't prepared—"

He stopped; there was a knock at the door; his wife put her head in. "Here's a telegram for you, Sam; the boy's waiting to see if there is an answer."

Inspector Spencer tore the brown envelope open and read the contents over once—twice.

"There is no answer, Mary; tell him." Then he held out the sheet of flimsy paper to the detective. "This ought to help us, sir: 'Identified. Leaving for Sutton Boldon to-night—Carton.'"

Mr. Collins permitted himself a low whistle.

"It should be plain sailing now. If the owner of the diamond ring is found, why, we shall soon know the answer to my second question, inspector."

Chapter Fifteen

"I WONDER whether it occurs to you, Roger, that a dose of strychnine would be the truest kindness?" Courtenay was making his slow progression in his wheeled chair backwards and forwards on the terrace. The moving of this chair himself by using the propeller was the only means of exercise possible to him. Knowing its value, Lavington encouraged it as much as possible. He made no reply to Courtenay's speech, beyond slightly raising his eyebrows, as he read his paper.

Courtenay paused beside his chair.

"Any news, old fellow? I'm sick of these wretched elections. Any probability of the long-prophesied war coming off?"

"I don't think so; not immediately at any rate." Courtenay's mouth twisted sardonically.

"When it does, a few more men will know what mutilation is like. Oh, Lavington, what would I give for just one day of the old life! To move as I wished, to feel the grass under my feet, if only for an hour!" He wheeled himself off as he spoke. Roger looked after him with a very real pity and understanding. In truth, it was a terrible life; it was small wonder that he rebelled.

Presently he came back again.

"I saw something about the Bungalow murder the other day—that it was likely to be raked up again; but it seems to have ended in smoke. I suppose you would hear that talked about when you were at Sutton Boldon?"

Roger was filling his pipe. This sudden mention of the subject that was uppermost in his mind rather took him aback.

"More than I wanted," he answered slowly. "I was the doctor called in; and the whole thing took up considerably more of my time than I could afford to spare."

Courtenay stared at him apparently in bewilderment.

"You were the doctor called in! I was under the impression that you had only been there a short time."

Roger shrugged his shoulders.

"Two years is not a very long time, is it?"

"N–o." Courtenay pondered matters a minute or two. "Still, I do not know how I came to make such a mistake. You were called in you say? What opinion did you form?"

"What opinion could I form but that the man had been shot?" Roger parried. "He was a blackguard. Enough came out at the inquest to prove that; plenty of evidence was found among his papers. The—the person who shot him probably had only too much reason."

Courtenay did not make any immediate rejoinder. He wriggled his chair backwards and forwards on the gravel, his eyes absently roaming over the park.

A terrible longing, an unutterable sadness, shook him. With a great effort he thrust the memory of the past behind him and leaned forward.

"You went down to Sutton Boldon the other day, Roger; did you hear anything of this there?"

Lavington was apparently immersed in a brown study. He roused himself with a start.

"Hear of what? Oh, the Bungalow murder. Yes, in a small place like Sutton Boldon, of course there is little else to talk about."

Courtenay wheeled himself a little backward into the shade of the great cedar that stood on the lawn beyond.

"What is the clue they speak of in the papers?"

"I don't know." Lavington's eyes wandered to the big copper beeches that stood sentinel-wise by the entrance to Daphne's garden. Farther down in the hollow by the stream there was the little bridge, the woods that hid Luxmore Hall from sight. "It—I believe they have found out that the girl who died at Northchester is not the one who shot Maximilian von Rheinhart."

"Not!" The word seemed wrung from Courtenay.

Glancing at him, Roger saw that his face was ghastly white, that beads of perspiration were standing on his brow. He sprang up with an exclamation of concern. Courtenay forced a smile to his stiff lips.

"Only a touch of the old pain, old fellow; it is passing now. You told me I must not expect to get rid of it all at once, you know! So the police have been on the wrong track all this time?"

Roger shrugged his shoulders.

"So it seems."

Courtenay was apparently in a loquacious mood this afternoon; he took out a cigarette and lighted it.

"I read what most of the papers said about the Bungalow murder when I was supposed to be getting better, before I realized what an absolutely useless log I had become. It seemed to me that I had got out of touch with things in my illness, and one of the first things I did was to send for a pile of old papers, and see what had happened while I was incapacitated. This Bungalow murder loomed rather large in the public imagination just then; and of course it was fixed in my mind by the fact that the murderer—murderess, I should say—was supposed to be killed in the disaster in which I was injured. Now you say that she was not."

Roger frowned.

"I don't say so. It is the police who claim to have made the discovery."

"At any rate, killed or not, I should imagine she has got clean away," Courtenay went on. "Even the most sanguine detective could hardly hope to trace the crime to the right quarter after this lapse of time." Roger knocked his pipe out against the stone balustrade; a tiny puff of wind caught the ashes and blew them over a Niphetos bud, staining its delicate whiteness a drabby, unclean brown. Roger's eyes rested on it mechanically.

"I should have thought so. But it appears the police are not of our opinion. I hear they have every hope of effecting an arrest shortly."

Courtenay wheeled himself off towards the house.

"It is rather hot out here. I fancy my head will he better indoors. When the police make a definite statement of that kind it generally covers a multitude of incompetencies. Probably this case will prove no exception. No, don't come with me, old fellow; I shall try to get an hour or two's sleep."

Roger waited a while. The day had been very hot; it was pleasant there in the shade, with no sound to break the stillness save the humming of the insects, the twittering of the birds in the trees, or the striking of the old church clock as it slowly counted out the hours. But peaceful though the scene was, Roger felt himself strangely out of harmony with his surroundings. It seemed to him that even the very calm held foreboding of sinister possibilities.

Though a week had elapsed since his first meeting with Miss Luxmore, he had not spoken to her again. Once he had walked past the bridge and caught a glimpse of Daphne's figure leaning over the rails, her face turned longingly to the house that was to have been hers. But when he had gone nearer, she had shown plainly that she did not wish to speak to him. At the first sound of his footsteps she had turned quickly away, and hastened up the slope to Luxmore Woods.

To-day, however, Lavington was restless and ill at ease. He was haunted by a feeling that the evil that threatened the Luxmores was growing nearer any moment the storm might burst over their heads. Possessed by this fear, it was impossible to sit still; powerless as he was to avert the catastrophe, any sort of movement seemed better than inaction.

He got up and, after pacing the terrace awhile strolled off into the park. This time he did not turn his steps to the stream; instead, he kept on the other side of the rose-garden, intending, on turning out of the park, to take the footpath to Norton, an outlying farm let to a man named Corbett, with whom the men Roger had seen watching the cricket on the village green a week ago were staying. He had ascertained that the one with the black beard, the one who had so strangely reminded him of Detective Collins, was no longer there; but the other, who was ostensibly an artist, remained. Mrs. Corbett gave out that he was in bad health, and had been ordered into the country for quiet.

Lavington determined to pay Mrs. Corbett a visit and ascertain what he could of her lodger's habits. He was racking his brains for a pretext when he became aware that some one was coming across the park as though to intercept him. As he caught sight of the tall, slight figure, of the white gown, the floating motor-veil, his heart beat quicker. He hastened his steps.

"Miss Luxmore!"

"Yes, I wanted you!" she panted, her breath coming quickly, her eyes glancing round in terror. The colour in her cheeks was heightened; her golden hair was disordered. "I—I have been frightened. Reggie told us at lunch that some man, a stranger, had been trying to talk to him, asking him questions, and just now when I came down to the bridge there was some one there; he was sketching. He looked up; I think he was coming to speak to me, but I was terrified and ran away. Then, when I was wondering what I was to do, how I was to get back, I saw you. Can you send him away?"

Roger's face turned a shade paler, with a throb of horrible misgiving. He wondered whether it was possible that this man—this detective, as he felt sure he was—could identify Daphne as the girl who had acted at Freshfield.

"One can easily get rid of him for the time being," he said slowly. "He has no right in the park at all. But were you very near him? Did he see your face?"

The girl shivered.

"I don't think so, clearly. I—I got away as quickly as I could, and he was not very near the bridge. But do you mean that if he saw me he might—"

"I don't know," Roger said dully. "One must remember that there was a large audience at Freshfield, and though the Japanese dress was to a certain extent a disguise, still, there must be a great risk of identification, if you should be seen."

All the pretty colour had faded in the girl's cheeks now, the fear in her brown eyes deepened; her lips moved inaudibly. At last, with a supreme effort, she regained her self-control.

"And then you fear—"

"The worst." The time was past for concealment. Roger could only avert his eyes from the girl's face as he dealt the blow. "That is why I begged you to go for your sister's sake, to spare her the shame."

A low sob burst from the girl's white lips.

"Ah, Heaven! My sister—my father! What shall I do?" She looked at him imploringly. "Can't you help me? I don't seem to be even able to think."

"If you were to go away from home, tell Lord Luxmore and your sister you have gone to be with friends and persuade your friends to keep your whereabouts a secret from every one," Roger suggested. "Couldn't it be done?"

The girl twisted her hands together nervously.

"I don't know. I can't see any way out of it. You—you saved me before; can't you help me now?"

Roger took the trembling hands in his warm clasp.

"Everything that I can do shall be done; you may rely on me to do the uttermost," he promised her.

"I will think—we will both think. There must be some way, surely, out of even this horrible dilemma."

"Ah yes!" The girl steadied herself for a moment by his arm. "I didn't mean to do any harm, you know," she moaned. "He was a bad man—a wicked man; you cannot know how wicked! He made me go; I could not help myself. And then in a moment I saw it was over." She shuddered and drew away, covering her eyes with her hand." But, if it came out, if my father knew that I was there—" she broke off with a little moan—"he might think as the world thinks, as you think—"

For the first time as he watched her, as he heard her words, a ray of hope lightened Roger's heart. Was it possible that all this time he had been making some gigantic mistake—that some deeper mystery lay behind the tragedy of Rheinhart's health?

He gazed at her.

"You do not mean—you cannot mean—"

She drew herself up; her brown eyes met his unfalteringly.

"I mean that I am absolutely innocent of Rheinhart's death; as innocent as you are yourself! When I begged you to save me, I did not realize that you thought—that the world would think—that I had done this horrible thing. I only knew that if I were found there, in his rooms at night, it would mean social ruin, ostracism. That people should imagine that I—"

"But, merciful heavens! Did you not see, did you not recognize—"

She shook her head.

"I never thought of such a thing. How should I? Maximilian von Rheinhart had ordered me to come. I dared not disobey. When I found the door open, I went in; he was lying there—dead! I was dazed with fright. Then I heard footsteps coming and hid myself. You found me—you know the rest."

"I—I know." The words came mechanically. Lavington was too thoroughly bewildered to reply coherently. Not for one moment had he hitherto doubted that the girl he had found hidden in the studio had killed Rheinhart. That, knowing something of the man's character, he had made excuses for her in his heart had not in any way affected his opinion of her guilt; the very possibility of her innocence had never occurred to him. He had often mentally pictured the scene that must have taken place before he was summoned, but always it had been this girl who, insulted, humiliated, goaded past endurance, had turned upon her tormentor. If she were indeed innocent, if matters were as she said, who had killed Rheinhart? His lips framed the question. "But who?"

There was a moment's tense silence. A shadow flickered over the girl's fair face. She caught her breath. Her fingers were interlaced and strained.

"How can I tell? I stole round to the window. He said it would be open, but it was fastened, and I went back to the door; that was open. I thought I had made a mistake; it was there I should have come. Then, in the room, he was lying dead!" She shuddered violently, and put out her hand as if to ward off the memory.

But there were certain aspects of the case that were puzzling Roger.

"But it was your glove, the diamond ring, the letters you burnt?" he said slowly.

There was another pause; the long, dark lashes were veiling the brown eyes now.

"Yes, the letters. I had come for them. I could not leave them to be found by anyone"—with another prolonged shiver—"so I took them. I—I had to!" she wailed.

Roger did not speak. His mind was busy with the past. Was it possible that there had been some terrible mistake, that he, as well as the police, had been on the wrong track all this time? That the murderer of Rheinhart must be sought—where?

Beneath the drooping eyelashes the brown eyes were watching his face closely.

"You do understand—you do believe me, do you not?" the sweet, trembling voice went on.

Then, with a jerk, Roger's mind came back to the present. He looked at the pretty, pleading face; the curve of the mouth, the delicately-modelled chin, reminded him of Elizabeth. He took both the slight, quivering hands in his once more, and bent over them.

"You are her sister!" he said simply. "I—I understand. I believe you—for her sake!"

A slight, jarring laugh broke the silence that followed. Miss Luxmore jerked her hands away; there was a certain defiance in the eyes that met his now.

"I know what you mean—I understand. The world would not believe me—the world that does not know—Elizabeth," with a slight sarcastic inflection.

A flush rose to Roger's forehead as he straightened himself; he felt chilled, disheartened.

"It is possible that after this time it might be difficult to prove your innocence," he said lamely.

Miss Luxmore had apparently recovered from her fright.

"Also, it would be difficult for them to prove I was there at all, I should imagine, she said, in a brisk, matter-of-fact tone. "I must go, Dr. Lavington. I am glad that you believe me, even if only for my sister's sake. Oh, I forgot," her voice changing. "The man—the detective—I dare not pass him!"

"I will send him away; he has no business here. If you will wait one moment." He strode off towards the bridge.

The girl stood still as he had left her, her eyes following the direction he had taken, her lips curved in an enigmatical smile.

Presently Lavington returned.

"The man had gone," he announced. "Not a sign of him to be seen. Perhaps one of the keepers may have warned him off; perhaps, too, we were mistaken, and he is not a detective at all. He turned with her towards the stream. "I think, perhaps, it would be wiser if you did not come here—to the bridge—again," he said diffidently. "If there should be any watch kept, if there should be any suspicion. It is known that you are here sometimes."

It seemed to him that her colour paled, but her voice did not falter.

"Perhaps it would be better; I believe you are right!" She paused with one foot on the bridge.

"Good-bye, Dr. Lavington!"

"One moment," Roger detained her. "How can I let you know if I hear anything—if I should find out anything about the detective?"

She paused a moment in indecision.

"Write! No, no; you must not. Let me think," wrinkling up her brows. "If it is anything of real importance—of great importance, mind—if you go through the wood there, keeping straight on, you will come to a wall with a little green door let in. It is kept locked, but if you should push a piece of white paper beneath any evening between six and seven I shall know. I will come to you." She flitted lightly across the bridge; on the other side she turned. "Thank you, Dr. Lavington, thank you for all you have done for me—for us!"

Roger waited till she was out of sight, then walked slowly back to the Manor, his mind busy with the ever-recurring problem of Rheinhart's death. If Daphne Luxmore were indeed innocent of it, the criminal must be looked for elsewhere; and, difficult though it might be to bring the guilt home to the right quarter, Roger felt that, at all hazards, it ought to be attempted. Elizabeth's young life ought to be freed from all danger of the vile charge that might at any time be brought against her sister. That the police were working with the preconceived notion that the girl who was known to have been in the studio on the night of Rheinhart's death was guilty of the murder, he felt certain. Even he himself had never doubted it. Would he have doubted it now—the question would make itself heard—if Daphne Luxmore had not been Elizabeth's sister?

Meanwhile, from beneath the undergrowth on the Luxmore side of the brook, a man was creeping quietly; his clothes were stained by moss and earth as he raised himself; in one hand he held a sketching-block; a knapsack was strapped on his shoulders.

"Well, I'm bothered!" he said, as he dusted his trousers with his pocket-handkerchief. "What is the doctor's game? And as for the girl"—staring at the wood in the direction of Luxmore Hall—"where does she come from—and who is she, anyway?"

Chapter Sixteen

CRASH! Swish! Roger Lavington awoke with a start. The night was pitch dark; he could hear nothing now, yet he felt certain that some sound had roused him. He switched on the electric light over his bed and looked at his watch—a quarter-past three. With some idea that Courtenay might be wanting him, he sprang out of bed and began to dress himself.

Swish! Swish! It was the same sound again, and this time Lavington could not be mistaken. Some one was throwing pebbles at his window. He raised the sash softly. Was it possible that Daphne was in danger, he wondered—that she had sent for him?

He put his head out. A man was standing on the terrace below, looking up.

"Is it Dr. Lavington, sir?"

"Yes; what is it?"

"I made bold to come to you, sir. Mrs. Hollingsworth, at the Courtenay Arms, has sent me. There's a lady that come by train last night been taken ill, and Dr. Arnold, down at Swarkeston, he has been sent for to Bardon to a bad case, and they don't know when he will be back. So Mrs. Hollingsworth, she said, maybe you would step down and have a look at the poor lady. I took the liberty of bringing a horse and cart; it is round in the drive, though, knowing as it is not your province, sir, but as it is a matter of life and death, for Mrs. Hollingsworth don't think she can last more than an hour or two—"

Long before this speech was finished, Lavington was completing his toilet.

Already their colloquy had attracted attention. He heard other windows being opened, then he cautiously let himself out at one of the side doors. A footman and a couple of grooms in different stages of undress were conversing with the messenger. He had brought down his portable medicine-case, and as he jumped into the cart and took it between his knees, he asked his charioteer, whom he now recognized as the old man at the village inn, what was the matter with his unexpected patient. But, though the man was loquacious to a degree, his knowledge of the details was of the slightest, and seemed to be confined to the fact that the lady had telegraphed for rooms in the afternoon, and had then followed it up by coming down "unexpected like" by the last train. It appeared to be surmised that her sudden journey accounted in some way for her subsequent indisposition, but Roger's informant knew little more than that the lady had been crying out as if she was in mortal pain, and that Mrs. Hollingsworth was "rare and frightened."

There was no exaggeration in this latter statement, Roger saw, when he arrived at the Courtenay Arms, The landlady met him, tearful, apologetic, apparently on the verge of hysterics. She tried to control herself as he assumed his gravest, most professional manner and asked for particulars.

"It is her heart, sir," she explained volubly, as she led the way to the patient's bedroom. "One only has to look at her to see that; and me knowing what it is, having suffered a martyrdom myself. 'Poor soul,' I said, when I found that Dr. Arnold was out, 'at any rate I shall take the liberty of sending up to the Manor for Dr. Lavington. Her friends shall have the satisfaction of knowing that she saw a doctor, though it's little enough he or anyone else can do for her.' But I'm much obliged to you for coming, Dr. Lavington, and it was put into my head through thinking the poor dear lady knew you, she asked so much about you when she first came this evening."

"Indeed!" Roger raised his eyebrows as she laid her hand on the door. "What is her name, Mrs. Hollingsworth?"

"Vonnerhart, sir. Mrs. Vonnerhart she put down in the visitors' book."

"I never heard the name," Roger said as he entered.

One glance was enough to show him that the woman who lay in the middle of the great four-post mahogany bedstead, propped up by pillows, and fighting desperately for every breath, was indeed very ill, though her case was scarcely so desperate as Mrs. Hollingsworth supposed. Fortunately, however, his little medicine-chest contained most of the remedies likely to be needed, and his administration of oxygen brought a certain amount of immediate relief. But the paroxysms of pain, though yielding to his treatment in a measure, were recurrent and terribly severe. It was broad daylight long before Roger could leave her with any feeling of security. When at last he came down the stairs, looking worn and weary in the clear morning light, his dark hair crumpled, red lines round his eyes, he found Mrs. Hollingsworth waiting for him at the bottom.

"You'll take a cup of coffee before you go, doctor," she said coaxingly. "And there's a beautiful dish of ham and eggs, and Will Jones has brought in some fresh mushrooms."

The odour coming from the kitchen close at hand was irresistible to a hungry man; Roger allowed himself to be persuaded.

"But, indeed, you are too good to me, Mrs. Hollingsworth," he said as he seated himself at the round table standing in the big bay window looking into the old-fashioned inn garden.

"Nay, sir, never say that." Mrs. Hollingsworth was bustling round pouring out a steaming cup of coffee and supplying him with provisions. "What we should have done without you this past night is more than I can tell. You think she will do well now, sir?"

"For the present, yes," Roger replied guardedly. "Is she quite alone here, Mrs. Hollingsworth? If she has any friends, I think they ought to know her state, though the immediate danger is past."

The landlady flung up her hands.

"And me knowing no more about her than yourself, sir. She wrote to me from London last week, saying she wanted to stay a week or two in this part, and as she had heard my house well spoken of, she would be glad to know if I would let her have two rooms, a private sitting-room and a large bedroom, from to-day— that is now, you understand, sir. Well, of course I wrote back and said I should be pleased to have her, and I would do my best to make her comfortable. But I got no answer, and I thought either that my terms did not suit her, or that she had given up the idea of coming into the neighbourhood at all; and I must say I thought she might have had the manners to write and tell me so. I am sure I never was more astonished than when I got her telegram, 'Coming 6.15,' yesterday afternoon."

"And you had no idea who had mentioned your name to her?" Roger interposed, when the worthy woman paused to take breath.

Mrs. Hollingsworth fanned her hot face with her apron.

"No more than the dead, sir. The idea did cross my mind before I sent for you as it might have been yourself; she was asking so much about you and seemed that interested in you."

"I cannot understand that; certainly she is a perfect stranger to me."

Roger was making a hearty breakfast. Mrs. Hollingsworth's viands certainly deserved the encomiums lavished upon them by the travellers who frequented the Courtenay Arms.

"And she did not say anything, sir, to tell you who she was, or how she had heard of you?" Now that Mrs. Hollingsworth's alarm was abating, her curiosity was having full sway.

Roger shook his head.

"She is in no condition to tell me anything yet, poor soul. Well, I must leave it in your hands, Mrs. Hollingsworth. If you can see your way to letting her friends know in the course of the day, I should do so. I will write to Dr. Arnold about the case, and no doubt he will be up some time this morning. If he should wish it I shall be pleased to meet him."

"She asked me last night," Mrs. Hollingsworth said, "whether you often came down to the village, and rare and disappointed she seemed when I said you didn't, sir. And then she asked me a rare lot of questions about you, sir—what you was like, and how long you had been here, and whether you and Sir James were old friends."

"I cannot understand it," Roger said musingly. Truth to tell, in spite of his very real sympathy with her pain and suffering, his new patient had not impressed him favourably. There was something in the glance of her big black eyes, a masculine strength about the modelling of chin and jaw, which he found almost repellent. He could not imagine what could be the secret of her interest in him, and could only surmise either that his name in the medical journals had attracted her attention, or that she might be a patient of his uncle's, and had possibly brought an introduction from him.

"She was anxious about a letter that ought to have been here waiting for her last night," Mrs. Hollingsworth went on. "From what she said I gathered that it was from some one in the neighbourhood. It put her out terribly when it didn't come."

"Oh, well, I dare say we shall hear all about her before long; and we shall find that there is no mystery about it at all," Roger concluded as he held out his hand. "Good-bye, Mrs. Hollingsworth, and many thanks. It is a curious name, Vonnerhart. I don't know that I ever heard it before."

Mrs. Hollingsworth followed him to the door.

"I am sure I never did, sir. I said to the lady last night it sounded foreign; and she laughed and said she was as English as I was."

"Oh, well, I dare say she is!" Roger turned down the village street towards the Manor. The school bell was clanging noisily behind him; he met the children running along the road. The girls in their clean, white pinafores smiled shyly at him, the boys touched their caps.

As he passed the Sturts' cottage, Mrs. Sturt stood at the door; he halted.

"How is Mary Ann, Mrs. Sturt?"

"Getting on nicely, sir, thank you." The woman smiled and moved aside. "Here she is, sir."

Little Mary Ann was sitting in a basket-work easy-chair piled with cushions, a doll, a couple of picture- books, two or three boxes of toys on a table beside her.

"Well, little one?" Roger laughed as he stepped over the threshold. "You look as if you were having a good time. Pretty comfortable, aren't you? You wouldn't mind breaking your arm every day at this rate, would you?"

"I'm sure she ought not, sir," the mother interposed. "Never a day but things come down from the Hall for her, and anything she fancies she is to have. And I have had to give up all my work to look after her. Miss Elizabeth is seeing to that. She has been untold good to us!"

There could have been no more congenial subject to Lavington. With some laughing remark to the child he took up a toy puzzle.

"So Miss Elizabeth sent you this, did she? I was sure she would be kind."

"Ay, she is that, sir," Mrs. Sturt assented heartily. "I'm sure in the old days, before Sir James's accident, when the young ladies used to come visiting us poor folk together, I always used to think I liked Miss Luxmore best; she was more sympathetic, I fancied. Miss Elizabeth was more stand off, besides being younger and livelier. But I have come to see as nobody could be better than she is. Not a day has passed since the accident but she has been in to ask after Mary Ann and pass the time of day with her. And I believe, when the child's arm was painful at first, it hurt Miss Elizabeth more nor it did her. Mary Ann, she says it herself. 'Mother,' she says to me one night, 'I don't want to cry; it makes Miss Elizabeth so sad.' It is gospel truth I'm telling you, sir. A gentler, kinder, more motherly young lady than Miss Elizabeth Luxmore I never wish to see. But"— her whole face brightening as she looked beyond Roger—"they say 'talk of angels and you see them appear'; we were just speaking of you, miss."

A shadow fell athwart the threshold; Roger turned, to see Elizabeth Luxmore regarding him with serious, surprised eyes. A little fleeting smile flitted across her lips as she answered Mrs. Sturt and touched Mary Ann's curly head caressingly. Then she laid her cool, ungloved hand for an instant in Roger's.

"You are early, Dr. Lavington; I quite thought I should be Mary Ann's first visitor."

Roger turned to greet Miss Luxmore; at the same moment his eyes met those of a man who was standing at the door of the little barber's shop at the other side of the street. For a moment he wondered why something in the steady gaze seemed familiar; then in a flash he remembered: transformed though he was by a longer, more unkempt growth of hair, by a straggling, sandy moustache, and by the discarding of his uniform, there was no mistaking Constable Frost's expression of stolid superiority.

Roger gave a great start of dismay. Why was the Sutton Boldon policeman here, spying on him?

Lavington's start of dismay and change of colour at the sight of Constable Frost were sufficiently obvious to attract Elizabeth's attention. She looked at him curiously as she settled herself on the seat beside Mary Ann.

"Nothing wrong, is there, Dr. Lavington? Mary Ann—"

"Oh, no! She looks all right," Roger constrained himself to reply with a certain cheerfulness.

But Roger felt rather than saw that all the friendliness she had shown him in their last interview had vanished; in its place the vague, intangible barrier of which he had been conscious formerly had reared itself once more. As he stood aside while she talked to Mary Ann, he puzzled himself as to what could possibly be the reason of the change. He was not conscious of having offended in any way, and yet the slight, conventional smile with which she responded to a remark of his had precisely the chill air of aloofness which had galled him when he first met her.

He could not tear himself away while she was there, though; it was absolute joy to know that she was present, to feast his eyes on the wealth of dark, bronze hair—bronze that the sun, kissing, turned to burnished copper; on the delicate pink and white of the half- averted cheek, to hear her pretty, caressing tones as she talked to Mary Ann.

"Do you know why I have come, little girl?" she asked. Then, as the child shook her head: "Because I am going to drive to Afreton with Mr. Reggie, and we thought somebody might like to come with us—eh, Mary Ann?"

Mary Ann's eyes sparkled.

"Oh, Miss Elizabeth!"

"You would? Then that is all right. Mr. Reggie will be here directly, and I know some one who will most likely sit between us on the front seat."

The child clasped her hands.

"Oh, Miss Elizabeth! Mother, where is my hat? Oh! But—"

"Well, what is it?" Elizabeth asked, as Mary Ann's face grew grave.

The little thing hesitated a moment.

"It—it isn't one of they motors, is it, miss? Because I'm frightened—"

Elizabeth laughed aloud, a ringing delicious sound that made Roger smile too out of pure sympathy.

"You funny mite! As if I did not know that. No; it is a dog-cart, and I believe I hear the wheels now. And Tompkins is going to sit behind. I believe if we asked Dr. Lavington he would lift a certain little girl I know of into the front seat, and then we should be quite sure the poor arm would not be hurt."

Mary Ann's face was a picture of delight as the dog-cart drew up, and the great Dr. Lavington himself lifted her in his arms. Reggie stared and laughed as they emerged, while Elizabeth lingered behind for a last word with Mrs. Sturt.

"New work for you, isn't it, Lavington? Here, give me the kid! Well, how do you find yourself to-day, Pollie?"

"Pretty nearly well again, sir, thank you. Mrs. Sturt answered for her offspring, curtsying her gratification behind. "And very grateful for all your kindness."

"Oh that's all right," Reggie said carelessly. "It is our place to look after her, you know, as we did all the mischief. Hurry up, Elizabeth!" with a natural desire to cut the interview short.

Elizabeth opened her lips as if to speak again, but Reggie was in a hurry to be off; he touched the horse with his whip.

Roger was left with, amidst his consuming anxiety, an underlying ray of comfort. Clearly her tone, her words, had expressed a measure of concern for him. Her farewell smile was infinitely more friendly than the one she had accorded him on entering the cottage.

He walked across the street; the man whom he had taken for Frost was no longer in sight. Apparently he had taken advantage of the moment when Lavington's head was turned to answer Elizabeth, to make his escape. Wilkes, the barber, was in the shop. Roger looked inside.

"I fancied I recognized a man who was standing at your door just now, Mr. Wilkes. Is he still here? I should like to speak to him. Tallish sort of chap with a sandy moustache."

Wilkes rubbed his stubby beard.

"Why, of course, that would be Mr. Barrington that is staying at Mrs. Corbett's, sir. He mostly comes in for a shave and a chat of a morning. Leaves his bicycle in the little yard at the back generally. I expect he has gone there now; that would be how you missed him." He lifted up the dingy blind that hung over the little window behind the shop. "No. He must ha' gone off without so much as saying good morning! It isn't often he does that."

Chapter Seventeen

IT WAS a week later. Roger was enjoying his cigar on the divan near the smoking-room window when a footman entered.

"The lady at the Courtenay Arms has sent up, sir. She wants to know if you will kindly call in and see her some time before night."

Courtenay had been specially trying all the morning; Roger had at last managed to quiet him and was now preparing to enjoy a well-earned rest. He was by no means inclined to welcome an interruption. An exclamation of impatience rose to Lavington's lips.

"I told Mrs. Hollingsworth that I should leave the case in Dr. Arnold's hands entirely.

"Yes, sir." The footman hesitated. "Mrs. Hollingsworth has sent word, sir, that the sick lady is that obstinate, she declares she must see Dr. Lavington. Dr. Arnold has been twice to-day, but she cannot content herself with him, and she is getting into such a state about it that she has frightened them all. Mrs. Hollingsworth thought, sir, that you might be so good as to walk down and explain things."

"Bother the woman!" Roger exclaimed irritably as he sat up. "Well, if I must, I suppose I shall have no peace unless I go. Who came up, William?"

"Mrs. Hollingsworth's daughter, sir."

A gleam of mirth lighted up Roger's eyes.

"What, the one I saw you walking with on Sunday? Don't let me keep you from her, William. Tell her I will come round and talk to Mrs. Vonnerhart as soon as I can."

"I am sure, sir—" The footman retreated, scarlet and embarrassed.

Roger stood up and proceeded to change his shooting-jacket for a more professional-looking coat. He only waited to put some statistics in order that he was preparing for his evening's work, and then, reflecting that since another visit to Mrs. Vonnerhart appeared to be inevitable, he might as well get it over at once, started across the park.

The Courtenay Arms was a pretty, old-fashioned inn. Its thatched roof and quaint mullioned windows had been the subject of many a sketch. The front was left untouched, as it had stood for a couple of hundred years or more, but at the back, yielding to Mrs. Hollingsworth's entreaties, Sir James's predecessor had built a new kitchen suited to modern requirements, and thrown out a pretty bay-window from the long, low parlour.

At first nobody seemed to be about; even the bar was deserted. Roger walked in. The sound of his feet on the stone passage soon brought Mrs. Hollingsworth out, however.

"Ah, Dr. Lavington, I do call this good of you!" she cried as she bustled forward. "Ever since Dr. Arnold called, and I told her it was your wish that he should attend her, we have not had a moment's peace with Mrs. Vonnerhart. She will hardly be decently civil to him, say what I will. Dr. Lavington should attend her, she said—Dr. Lavington and no one else. At last to-day I was forced to send up to you just to pacify her like."

"Perhaps I had better go up at once, then," Lavington said, turning towards the staircase. "I shall tell her she must be content with Dr. Arnold though; this sort of thing will not do."

Mrs. Vonnerhart was sitting by the open window in a big easy chair, propped up by pillows. Her breathing, though considerably easier, was still laboured. Her dark, hollow eyes lighted up when she saw Roger.

"Ah! Dr. Lavington, this is good of you!" she said faintly. "I told Mrs. Hollingsworth I would have you sent for." Slowly she turned her black eyes upon Roger. "Do you know why I came to Oakthorpe?"

"No!" The prejudice which Roger had unconsciously conceived towards her on their first meeting strengthened rather than abated as he waited, watching her expression the meanwhile in the clearer light. "That hardly concerns me, does it?" he went on, as she made no response.

"I came to see you." Her eyes, with their unpleasantly-secretive expression, were fixed full upon his face as though to mark the effect of her words.

"To see me?" For one moment Roger doubted whether he had heard aright. "I don't understand you, Mrs. Vonnerhart. Surely I have never had the pleasure—"

"You have never seen me before," the sick woman interrupted. "But when you hear my name, none the less, you will know why I have come—why I must see you."

Lavington felt thoroughly mystified. For a moment he wondered whether her mind was wandering; but no, her tones, though hoarse and low, by reason of her difficult breathing, were steady and controlled; her eyes met his fully, sanely.

"Your name!" he echoed lamely. "I don't think that I ever heard it before."

"No." The woman gave a hard little laugh. "You called me Vonnerhart just now, following Mrs. Hollingsworth's example. I suppose that is as near as those country yokels can get. You will know it as soon as you hear it, Dr. Lavington. I have no reason for concealing it, for keeping my whereabouts a secret—it is Von Rheinhart!"

"Von Rheinhart!" Roger's lips mechanically formed the words; his hands gripped the back of the chair he was leaning upon. His brain was in a whirl. Who was this woman? What was her connection with the dead man who was murdered in The Bungalow? Bewildered though he was, he retained some recollection of having heard at the inquest that Rheinhart had no near relatives. Certainly none of them had come down to the funeral.

Apparently the invalid was enjoying the spectacle of his astonishment. She even laughed a little to herself.

"Ah, I thought I should surprise you. Yes, my name is Von Rheinhart and I am Maximilian von Rheinhart's widow."

"His widow!" Lavington's expression was still one of blank amazement.

"I didn't know—I had no idea that he had left a widow."

"No, I thought not." Mrs. von Rheinhart nodded her head. "It was Maximilian von Rheinhart's pose to pass as a single man. Nevertheless, we had been married for some years when he settled at Sutton Boldon. And now, Dr. Lavington—now I think you will be able to guess why I came to Oakthorpe."

Though the room was whirling round for Lavington, though he felt absolutely dazzled by this sudden change of all his ideas, he managed to control his features, his expression remained absolutely sphinx-like.

"I cannot say that I do."

The feverishly-bright eyes watched his closely.

"You cannot say you do," mockingly. "And yet, Dr. Lavington, I should think you might imagine that Maximilian von Rheinhart's widow would wish to see the doctor who was called in at her husband's death."

"There is so little I can add to what was printed in the reports of the inquest," Roger said slowly.

The black eyes did not relax their eager scrutiny.

"So little can you add, Dr. Lavington, you say? And yet I think—I am sure—that, if you like, you can help me to the attainment of the object that brought me down to Oakthorpe. Do you know that I have sworn to avenge my husband's murder?"

There was a moment's tense silence; not a movement, not a sound, was heard save the laboured breathing of the woman by the window. Lavington, taken all unawares as he was, girded himself up for the conflict. He felt that it was to be a war of wits between him and this woman who called herself Maximilian von Rheinhart's widow; it behoved him to play the game warily; to calculate carefully the effect of each move before the piece was touched.

He raised his eyebrows slightly.

"I understand the police are taking the matter up again, madam. May I remind you that in your condition quiet and rest are above all things needful. You must endeavour to keep your thoughts as much as possible from this subject at present, at any rate."

"The police?" the woman echoed scornfully, clutching at the lace round the neck of her dressing- gown, as if to tear it apart, and ignoring the latter part of his speech. "The police would do nothing—see nothing—but what lay just before their faces. They have taken it for granted all this time that the girl killed at Northchester had shot my husband, and, secure in their belief, they have let the real murderess go scot-free!"

In her excitement she had raised herself; two red spots burned, hotly on her thin cheeks. Roger quietly laid her back in her chair.

"The amount of harm you may do yourself if you will not keep quiet is incalculable," he said sternly. "I at any rate, must refuse to be a party to it. I shall decline to discuss this matter with you in any way."

Mrs. von Rheinhart's laugh was not pleasant to hear.

"I don't think you will, Dr. Lavington. My chain of evidence is almost complete, but your testimony can supply the missing link, though whether you speak or refuse"—her voice growing emphatic—"the arrest of the real criminal is only a matter of days. Ah, you had no idea of that," as Roger involuntarily winced. "You don't know the strength of our case. No no! Wait, Dr. Lavington. You shall not go!" clutching at his coat with one thin, yellow hand. "You shall hear what I have to say. He; was a bad man, the world says. Well, I know what Maximilian von Rheinhart was, none better, though I was only a slip of a girl when he took me from home. I trusted him and loved him as few men are trusted and loved and when he told me, at the end of a month, that our marriage had been performed in a sham registry office and that he was tired of me, I thought my heart was broken. When he left me for some newer, fairer face, there was nothing for me to do, it seemed to me, but to die. Only fear—absolute physical fear of the unknown hereafter—kept me from putting an end to my life. But kind friends were raised up for me, and miserable, heartbroken, though I was, I lived on.

"Not until afterwards did I learn that the man who professed to be Maximilian's friend had duped him, not me. The marriage was legal enough, and I was Maximilian von Rheinhart's wife. When I heard of his murder I was living at Palermo with an old lady as companion. She was dangerously ill, and as she had been very kind to me, I could not leave her. I wrote to the police when the news reached me, but I had no money—I could do nothing." She paused and gasped for breath.

Roger watched her with a certain compassion. Presently he went over to the dressing-table, and poured out a dose of the medicine Dr. Arnold had prescribed.

"Drink this!" he ordered, holding it to her lips, "and remember that I have warned you that absolute quiet—"

She caught eagerly at the glass and drank off the contents.

"Ah, that is better! That gives me new life! Absolute quiet, you say, Dr. Lavington? Well, I shall have that very soon now, when the woman who shot Maximilian von Rheinhart is brought to justice. Then—then I shall have nothing to do but rest. Don't you understand that till then I can't lie still? The very thought that she is at liberty is torture to me. All the time we were separated, after I learned the truth, I always looked forward to going back to Maximilian. Perhaps he would be poor—lonely even. I should have said to him, 'I am your wife, Maximilian, your true and faithful wife.' I knew the old lady who had practically adopted me meant to leave me her money. I should have been rich, and Maximilian should have had a welcome from me. But she—Mrs. Scanlan—lived to last year; and Maximilian was dead; my dream was over. Do you wonder I swore the woman should be punished, that I would not rest until she had paid the penalty of her crime?"

Roger bent forward, keeping his eyes fixed on hers. "What good would that do you? It would not bring Rheinhart back to you? And, from your own showing, he was not a good man. Think what some one—man or woman—may have suffered at his hands! Think what the provocation may have been!"

"Why do you say man or woman," Mrs. von Rheinhart demanded, "when you know, and I know, that it was a woman."

"I do not know," Lavington contradicted her steadily. How much she guessed of his share of the events of that long past night he could not tell; but he realized that she suspected him, at any rate, of a more intimate knowledge of the circumstances than he admitted. "I know that the police searched everywhere for a woman who was believed to have entered The Bungalow that night, but I have seen no evidence to prove that she was guilty of the murder."

"What if I showed you some?" The pallid, clawlike hands were gripping the sides of the chair now. Those strange black eyes seemed as if they could read through his very soul.

Roger knew not how to answer while that curious gaze was upon him.

"My husband's effects were stored in London after the inquest," she went on. "When I came back to England my first thought was to visit the place, to see what I could learn from them. First, I found documentary evidence that he had sought for me, that he had not altogether forgotten me; next, hidden away in a secret drawer that the police had apparently overlooked, I came upon a letter—a love-letter—signed by a name I knew; inside the lining of the coat he wore the night he died there was a piece of paper; it had slipped down and been unnoticed until I found it by accident; it was only a scrap—'Yes, I accept your terms; I will be with you to-morrow at seven o'clock!'—but it was the same writing as the former note, there were the corresponding initials, and it was dated April 14th. Ah!" as Roger failed altogether to conceal the dismay with which he heard the announcement. "I thought you would see that I had more proofs than you guessed. Now, Dr. Lavington, we want your help; we want you to tell us how the murderess escaped."

Roger rose; he saw that it was impossible to over-estimate either the importance of the discovery that had been made or the danger in which Daphne Luxmore stood, should it be her name that was attached to the incriminating paper. Away from the influence of the girl's sweet, pathetic voice, too, the glamour of her appealing eyes, it was not so easy to persuade himself that she was innocent of the crime, that the murderer of Maximilian von Rheinhart must be looked for elsewhere.

"I regret I cannot help you," he said coldly. "I was merely concerned in ascertaining the cause of death. The hunting out and the tracking down of criminals is no part of my work, I am glad to say."

The dark eyes still kept up their hard, unwinking stare, the thin, bloodless lips moved in a ghastly attempt to smile.

"Perhaps the helping them to escape may be, Dr. Lavington— well, I think I shall be able to do without you. I have not let the grass grow under my feet, and they tell me—the detectives I have engaged— that the arrest is only a matter of a few days."

"Is that so? Your object will soon be accomplished, then." This time Lavington had himself well in hand. Even the keen eyes watching him could see no faintest change in his expression. He moved nearer the door. "In the meantime, let me warn you that nothing can be worse for you than this state of nervous excitement. You should endeavour to put the whole thing out of your mind if possible. Rest both mind and body if you are to recover your health."

"Ah, rest!" Mrs. von Rheinhart broke in in her harsh, uncertain tones. "That is so easy to recommend, so difficult to obtain. But when I see justice done to my husband's murderess, then—then I will try to follow your advice."

Lavington took up his hat and moved nearer the door.

"Take care that it is not too late," he said sternly. "Remember that I have warned you."

Mrs. von Rheinhart gave vent to a hollow, ghastly chuckle.

"Do you speak in my interests, Dr. Lavington, or in those of Daphne Luxmore?"

Chapter Eighteen

FARMER Corbett's land looked as if there was a scarcity of money. The crops were poor, the pastures were dry and arid. Half the cowhouses were empty; the door of one of the stables had lost a hinge; there had been a makeshift attempt at repairing it with some twine. Thomas Corbett, as he crossed the yard, a tall, gaunt old man, in a shabby suit of rough, brown cloth, with mud-bespattered gaiters, looked enfeebled and dispirited. Times were bad for farming, any of the men round Oakthorpe would have told you, but to Thomas Corbett it sometimes seemed that a double portion of ill-luck had fallen to his share.

That the Corbetts, in spite of the hard times, should continue to farm their own land in the midst of the Courtenay estate had been more or less of a grievance to successive holders of the Courtenay title for many years. Many of them had been offered much more than the land was worth for the farm, but hitherto the Corbetts had resolutely refused to part with their heritage.

Now, however, Thomas Corbett was beginning to fear that everything would have to go, that he would be unable to wage this unequal war with fate much longer. They had done their best—he and his wife, both; they had put their shoulders to the wheel with right good-will, but so far their efforts had accomplished little.

Mrs. Corbett had even for the past month let her two front rooms to an artist from London who was looking out for country apartments. It had been greatly against her husband's will. He liked to have his house to himself, he grumbled, though he had not denied that the lodger paid well, and that the money was useful. To-day, however, he had heard a report about this new member of his household that had displeased him exceedingly. He was pondering over it now as he looked down the orchard and marked the promise of fruit, deciding the while that he would tell the wife that, money or no money, the artist must go as soon as he could be got rid of.

His mind made up on this point, he turned back towards the house; at the same moment two men came in at the opposite gate and advanced to meet him. He recognized one of them—a short, stout man with a black beard—as a friend of his lodger's who had been to see him once or twice before; the other was a stranger.

"Ah, Mr. Corbett! A pleasant evening, isn't it?" the black-bearded one began politely. "I wonder whether we shall find Mr. Barrington at home?"

"I don't think so, Mr. Ward," returned the old man as they crossed the yard. "There was a note come for him an hour ago from the Hall and he started off in a fine hurry as soon as he read it. I have seen nothing of him since."

"Um! That is awkward." The spokesman stroked his beard thoughtfully. "I think we shall have to ask Mrs. Corbett to allow us to wait in his room. He is expecting us to-night, so that he is sure to be in before long. Perhaps there is a note for us."

"I dare say—I dare say!" Mr. Corbett did not seem very interested in his visitors. "You are welcome to wait for him if you like," he said, as he opened the door. "The room is his as long as he pays for it. But we are beginning to think, the wife and me, that we shall be wanting it before long. It is awkward doing without your parlour, we find, particularly when we are not used to it."

The two men looked after his worn face and bent form with something like consternation. The elder one whistled softly.

"So that is the way the wind blows, is it? Um! May be awkward. Well, Spencer, what luck have you had? It seems to me your coming here was a little imprudent."

Thus seen, close at hand, it was not difficult to identify Detective Collins. In spite of the disguising wig and beard, Lavington's eyes had been sufficiently keen that morning by the cricket field.

"I don't think so," the inspector differed. "It was important that I should see you, and no one knows me here but Lavington, and the chances were a hundred to one against meeting him at this time of night."

"I don't know about that. It seems to me the fellow is ubiquitous," the detective grumbled. "Well, I get your letter, Spencer. The manufacturers had been able to give you the name of the firm to whom this particular cigarette-case was supplied? I suppose you have interviewed them? Were they able to carry the matter any further?"

Inspector Spencer walked over to the window and closed it carefully.

"It is a hot night," he remarked apologetically, "but it won't do to run any risk of eavesdropping. Yes, Burnham & Matthews, of Bond Street, was the retail firm. I had a little trouble with them at first. The manager said it was against the rule to give the name of any customer. But I happened to have done some business for Mr. Matthews once, and when I saw him it was all right. They went to the books, and proved the sale of this particular case without any difficulty."

Collins drew a long breath.

"They did? Then our task ought to be considerably simplified. Go on, Spencer. Who was it?"

The inspector preferred to tell the story in his own way.

"They identified it because of the chasing. It seems their customer was not satisfied with what they had in stock, and wanted a particular design, of which they were given a sketch, which has made it easy to trace.

Detective Collins looked impatient.

"The name, inspector, the name! Was it—"

"It was sent down to Oakthorpe Hall on December 24th, 19—" the inspector proceeded calmly, looking at his notes for the date, and disregarding the other's start of surprise, "by Miss Luxmore's orders. The young lady stated in her letter that it must reach her by that date, as she wanted it for a Christmas present for her fiancé, Sir James Courtenay."

"Phew! This complicates matters considerably." Collins wrinkled up his brow and looked at the inspector. "We have never thought of this, Spencer. What is to be done?"

"Here is a communication received from Burnham & Matthews this morning," Inspector Spencer went on, producing an envelope from an inner pocket, and handing it to Detective Collins. "So, as I knew you were to be here to-night, I thought the best thing I could do was to bring it over and see what you would say to it."

Detective Collins did not unfold the note. He sat silent for a minute or two, his lips drawn together in a tight line amidst his bushy beard, one hand absently rapping the envelope on the table.

"So he was there," he said slowly at last. "This explains some things that have puzzled me but the old question is no nearer solution."

"Begging your pardon, I don't see much question about it," the inspector contradicted. "It was her ring and her glove, that's clear enough. Shows she was last there. And what was she doing if it was all over—if he was dead when she got there?"

Collins's expression showed that his thoughts were far away. He frowned heavily.

"On the other hand, what was he doing there, if it was he. The cigarette-case may have been stolen. I must put a man on for his doings that night—that is the next thing. Here is Frost. Now we shall hear what he has to tell us," as there was a step in the passage.

"I'm very sorry to be late, sir," Mr. Frost began as he entered, "but—well, the chance I had been waiting for so long came to-night, and I knew I ought not to miss it, so was sure you would understand, and did my best to get back as soon as I could."

"That's right." Detective Collins nodded. "Come in, and shut the door, man. You were wise, Frost. We can't afford to miss a chance in this business."

"That is what I thought, sir; so when I got a note from Clara, the head housemaid at the Hall—the one I scraped acquaintance with, according to your instructions, sir—that if I come up to-night she might be able to do as she promised. I knew you would have me take advantage of it."

Detective Collins pointed to a chair.

"Sit down, man, and tell us all about it. What was it she had promised?"

"Why, I had told her I was most particularly set on seeing Miss Daphne Luxmore; said as how I had heard how beautiful she was from a friend of mine as had painted her before her wedding was broken off. Clara, she takes me for an artist, you know, sir, like all the folks do about here"—with an apologetic smile—"and I wanted to see how she looked now. Well it wasn't easy to manage, Miss Luxmore shrinking so from strangers. But at last Clara thought she saw a way. That was what the note was about this evening."

"Well," the detective leaned forward, the interest in his face deepening, "what then? Do you mean that you saw her—"

"I saw her, sir, plain enough. Mr. Reggie was having some gentlemen to dinner, and to cricket on the lawn afterwards. Clara knew that he had made Miss Luxmore promise to sit in the arbour at the bottom of the ground with his lordship, to watch them. The servants were looking on, and Clara thought among them I should pass unnoticed until I got to the arbour and then I could apologise to my lord for my intrusion and say that I wanted to ask his permission to paint the Hall or something of that."

"Well, well, get on!" The detective could not conceal his eagerness. "You saw her, you say?"

"Yes sir. It all fell out as Clara planned." Mr. Frost was not to be hurried. "I got up to the arbour easy enough, and though my lord did not like it and told me I was trespassing, and that he never allowed anyone to sketch the Hall, for private reasons of his own, still, I saw the young lady, as I said before, and I heard her speak."

"Yes. You can identify her?" the detective said briskly. "Then that will—"

"Begging your pardon, sir, I did not say that," the other man interrupted stolidly. "I have never seen the young lady, Miss Daphne Luxmore, before."

"What!" the exclamation burst from the other two simultaneously. They stared at the speaker in incredulous astonishment.

Detective Collins was the first to recover his breath.

"You had never seen her before! Do you mean that she was not—"

"She was not the young lady who was at the doctor's having supper the night of the Bungalow murder. I saw her quite plainly then, and I could not be mistaken," Frost affirmed stolidly. "And it was not her that took part in the play at Freshfield, at Mr. Thornton's."

"Well, this beats all!" As if overcome by his amazement, the inspector dropped heavily into a chair and gazed stupidly at his quondam subordinate.

"Why, what did you tell me the other day? That you were all but sure that it was her, and that she was meeting this Dr. Lavington on the park."

Mr. Frost looked rather crestfallen.

"I did think so, sir; I thought it looked like her, as well as I could see for the trees. But, if it was, it wasn't Miss Daphne Luxmore, for I can swear I never saw her till to-night. There might be a little resemblance between the two—I think perhaps there was, and the hair was the same colour—but, if there is one thing more certain than another, it wasn't Miss Daphne Luxmore at the doctor's."

"Then what becomes of the letter the wife found—the note making the appointment for that night? The writing and the initials were hers." Detective Collins was puzzled and thoughtful.

Mr. Frost looked wise.

"I have been thinking things over as I came home, sir, and trying to piece it out. What if somebody as knew all about them, a maid or something of that, pretended to be Miss Luxmore, and maybe took Mr. von Rheinhart himself in. It doesn't seem likely as a young lady in Miss Luxmore's position would have been meeting him and writing to him on the sly."

"I don't know." Detective Collins deliberated. "No, no; it must have been Miss Luxmore herself. Her handwriting has been identified."

"On the other hand, Frost says positively that Miss Luxmore is not the girl he saw," Inspector Spencer observed, thoughtfully stroking his chin. "Of course we may have been wrong all this time. Miss Luxmore may have escaped in some other way, in the motor Wilson tells us was waiting in the lane behind the fields, for instance. And when we thought Dr. Lavington had helped her we may have stumbled upon a mare's nest."

He looked at Detective Collins.

That gentleman was still drumming abstractedly on the table with his envelope.

"Um, um! The girl wasn't his cousin, you know, inspector. If there is one thing more positive than another in the complicated business it is that."

A certain dry amusement twinkled in the inspector's deep-set eyes.

"No; but he may have had his own reasons for pretending she was. You and me are enough men of the world to understand that, Detective Collins."

"Just so!" But the detective's face did not relax; his eyes were turned to the window.

"Still, it is a pretty kettle of fish," Inspector Spencer went on, after vainly waiting for a word of encouragement from the detective. "Whether Miss Luxmore was there or not, what brought Courtenay into the business? I suppose he was there if we go by this cigarette-case. What do you say, Mr. Collins?"

"Say?" the detective echoed. "If you ask me, inspector, I must say that I think we have been wandering round in a circle all the time and are just as near finding Maximilian von Rheinhart's murderer as we were when we started."

"Oh, come! I don't know about that," the inspector dissented. "At least we know that it was Miss Luxmore who was at The Bungalow that night."

"We know she had promised to go," the detective corrected. "That is as far as we have got at present. Oh, I am not disputing your judgment, Spencer; I am only pointing out that our proof is of the slightest. We have no evidence that we could put before a jury; it is one thing to bring a charge of murder against a person in Miss Luxmore's position and another to prove it."

"Ay, that is right enough," the inspector assented. "Before we bring a charge, first we must bring evidence to show that Miss Luxmore was on the scene; secondly we must connect her definitely with the crime itself. If we could find the pistol now—"

"Ah, that would be something to go upon," Detective Collins agreed. The dreaming in his eyes had vanished; his face had resumed its usual keen, alert expression. "I wonder what became of it. Whoever shot Maximilian von Rheinhart carried it away with him or her. It was not left in the neighbourhood, either, I'm pretty sure, for we searched it rather closely—eh inspector?"

"And kept a close watch for it since. Still, it is not a big thing; it might have been disposed of in a hundred ways."

"Yes, yes." Collins got up and, pushing his chair back, took a few steps up and down the room. "The next thing to be done is to interview Miss Luxmore's maid, and to find out from her what her mistress's movements were on that April 14th."

"The young ladies, Miss Luxmore and Miss Elizabeth, they have the same maid," Frost observed. "I have thought of that myself, but the one they have with them has only been with them a little over a year; their last married and went to live at Birmingham. I have got the address, sir, if you would like to have it." He felt in his coat pocket.

"Yes, you might as well give it." Detective Collins held out his hand for the little slip of paper. "Mrs. Gere, 25 Bubbington Road.

Well, I think I had better look Mrs. Gere up myself. And if I don't get anything out of her I think I shall—"

The other two looked at him doubtfully as he paused.

"Well?" the inspector said questioningly.

"I shall look up Sir James Courtenay's valet and see if I can get any information about a certain pistol," Collins concluded significantly.

Chapter Nineteen

"I SEE there is a leader on police procrastination in one of the papers. It instances the Bungalow murder as a case in point," Lavington remarked.

He was walking beside the pony-chair in which he insisted on Courtenay taking a daily drive.

The latter was distinctly improving under Roger's care; the open-air treatment which Lavington had instituted was having its effect in better nights and lessened irritability; in a minor degree, too, in the brighter eyes and healthier hue of the skin.

He looked up now with a certain amount of interest.

"It is distinctly a contradiction of the proverb that murder will out."

"So far," Roger acquiesced.

He often wondered how much Courtenay knew or guessed of Daphne's connection with the Bungalow tragedy. That, in some way, the girl's association with Rheinhart had led to the estrangement of the lovers, he never doubted.

"Do you mean that you think they will yet trace the girl who disappeared so mysteriously?"

Lavington drove the ferrule of his walking-stick vigorously into the ground as he walked. Should he tell Courtenay of Mrs. von Rheinhart's presence in the village, of her discovery of the incriminating letters, he deliberated. In face of Daphne's danger, would her lover's heart turn to her again? Would he help Roger to prove her innocence, or would he accept her guilt as a foregone conclusion and harden his heart still further against her?

Roger felt that he could give no satisfactory reply; he temporized.

"I doubt whether they have not already done that, but it is not a foregone conclusion that she murdered Rheinhart."

Courtenay turned in his carriage to stare at him. Some of the healthy glow the summer sun had brought to his face had faded now.

"Do you mean—have you heard anything definite?" he asked incoherently.

Lavington took rapid counsel with himself. After all, nothing could be worse for Courtenay than his long fits of depression, his causeless outburst of anger. If he could be roused from the morbid contemplation of his own trouble, even though it were to a knowledge of Daphne's danger, it must make things better, it seemed to Roger.

"I have heard that a letter has been discovered making an appointment for that night—the night of the murder," he said slowly at last.

Courtenay leaned a little forward; he was breathing heavily. His face, so far as Roger could see it from his post at the side, was of a curious purple hue.

"An—an anonymous letter of course. The—the person who wrote it would not sign her name."

Roger considerately averted his eyes.

"There—I understood that there were initials; that they were those of a lady from whom the police had previously discovered a letter."

Courtenay stopped the chaise abruptly and turned. The purple flush had faded, his face was white, his eyes sought Roger's.

"Lavington, do they know—have you heard the name?"

"Yes." It seemed to Roger more merciful to strike the blow at once. "Yes! I have heard it."

"Ah!" Courtenay caught his breath. His face turned white as death, and he fell back in a dead faint.

It was some minutes before Courtenay regained consciousness. When at last he opened his eyes, he met Lavington's meaningly.

"It—of course, there is no truth in it, Lavington; you know that."

"I believe the lady whose name was signed to that note is innocent," Roger said steadily. "But, unfortunately, I do not count. It is other people— the police—we have to convince, and the time may be very short."

"Short!" Courtenay raised himself on one elbow.

"I don't understand, Lavington. You cannot fear—"

"An arrest!" Roger finished. "It seems to me that there may be grave danger."

"I cannot believe it!" throwing himself back with a gesture of angry impotence. "It is impossible. They would not dare to accuse her!"

Roger did not speak for a minute. It was evident that his surmise was only too well founded. Courtenay needed no words to tell him whose name the police had discovered.

"You cannot rely upon that," he said at last, choosing his words carefully. "Position and—er— that sort of thing might make the police take care to be quite sure of their ground before they preferred a charge; but once having ascertained that, it would be impossible to prevent their bringing it. No. The only way to be of real help is to find some reason to turn the suspicion into the right quarter."

"And that is, you imagine?" Courtenay questioned eagerly.

Lavington shrugged his shoulders hopelessly.

"How can I tell? It seems a horrible muddle. I can see no way out of it. The only thing I know is that Rheinhart was undoubtedly shot; that the lady to whom the suspicions of the police are directed is as certainly innocent; and that given these circumstances there must be some way of proving her so."

Courtenay groaned aloud.

"Ah, I see what you mean! But Heaven help us, Lavington."

There was another silence. Courtenay's face was rigid; his eyes, as he gazed out straight in front of him, were strained and tense. He jerked the carriage round.

"I must go back, Roger. I must look at the case in all its bearings. It—I think it is possible there might be a way of helping her, but I must go in; I must be alone. It is impossible to think clearly out here." He urged the pony on.

Roger dropped behind. When he reached the Manor, Courtenay had already disappeared, the pony-chaise was being led round to the stables. As he entered the hall, Mrs. Miller crossed from her master's room. She looked alarmed, disturbed. Roger was struck afresh by that curious sense of familiarity. Seeing him, she turned quickly towards him.

"Oh, Dr. Lavington, I am afraid Sir James is worse! He looked dreadful when he came in; and when Jenkins and William were lifting him into his chair I thought he was dying, his face was that white and drawn. I brought brandy and sal volatile, but he wouldn't touch them—just wheeled himself off to his study, and shut the door to, without as much as a word to me, though I was just behind. I can't understand it; something must be wrong. But perhaps he will tell you."

Roger was watching her closely; in his eyes incredulity was struggling with a dawning recognition.

"Perhaps—presently," he said slowly. "I think for a time Sir James will be better alone. He is not ill."

"I beg your pardon, sir, I am sure, for contradicting you." For once, in her anxiety for her master, the housekeeper seemed to have thrown off her timidity, her nervous, shrinking manner. "If you leave him—" She broke off with a cry.

A low exclamation broke from Lavington's lips; he stepped forward impetuously.

"Ah! Now I remember!"

Mrs. Miller looked at him in astonishment.

"I don't understand, sir— Oh!" Meeting his glance fully, she drew away from him, back against the dark wainscoting, her face growing white, her eyes fixed on his as if fascinated.

Lavington followed her up.

"Of course I know now. What a fool I have been not to see it before. You were Maximilian von Rheinhart's housekeeper at The Bungalow! It was you who summoned me, and I saw you again at the inquest!"

The woman did not answer, half leaning, half crouching against the dark background. Her pale face, her silvery hair, looked whiter, more ghost-like than ever; she stared up at him with wide-open eyes and parted lips.

"You must have known me," Roger went on. "When I told you that I thought I had seen you before, why didn't you speak? Why didn't you tell me that you had been Rheinhart's housekeeper?"

"I couldn't!" The woman drew herself upright against the wall; she put up her hands to smooth her tightly-braided hair, to straighten her little lace cap. "I wanted to forget all that time," she went on directly, recovering her self-possession as if by magic. "It—I wasn't proud of having had my name in the papers, of being pointed at as The Bungalow housekeeper; and when you did not recognize me I was glad. What good would it have done to tell you where you had met me before?"

"I don't know," Roger said mechanically. His mind was busy with The Bungalow question. Was it the hand of fate, he wondered, that was bringing so many of the actors in that mysterious tragedy together again? "But you did not call yourself Miller there—at The Bungalow?" he went on after a minute, certain facts striking him. "I am sure I remember—"

The housekeeper took out her handkerchief and wiped her dry lips furtively.

"No, sir, I didn't, worse luck for me; for John Miller was my first husband, and a better man never lived. I mourned for him truly. But then, after my poor girl went away and I was left alone, I was over-persuaded by a designing scoundrel for the sake of my bit of savings. I made a fool of myself, sir, in the second marriage; and when I came back to Sir James I was glad to forget about it, and go back to the name he had known me by when he was a child. But Sir James and Mrs. Melville, they both knew all about it, sir."

"Ah, yes. I am sure that is all right. But I should like to have a few words with you, if you please, Mrs. Miller!"

Lavington opened the smoking-room door and held it for her. She looked round unwillingly and hesitated.

"Another time, sir, I'm sure I should be honoured; but to-day there is a good deal for me to see to. And Sir James not being well it does seem to me that one of us—"

"You can leave Sir James to me. I will answer for him." Lavington motioned imperatively for her to enter. "I shall not keep you long," he added. "Just a question or two."

Shrinking as far as possible from him, the woman obeyed. He closed the door.

"You have heard, no doubt, that the police are taking up this matter of the murder of Rheinhart once more? Sit down, Mrs. Miller, please."

"Thank you, sir." She took one of the morocco- covered chairs standing near the door. "Yes, I did see something about The Bungalow murder in the *Telephone*, but didn't take any notice of it."

"Now I want you to cast your mind back to the night of the murder. I am particularly anxious to ascertain as far as possible the real facts of the case, and it seems to me that you are the only person who can help me. You know, of course, of the search that has been made for the woman who left her glove and ring beside Rheinhart's body, the woman who asked Heron the way to The Bungalow?"

Was it his fancy or did an expression of relief cross the face of the woman before him?

"Oh, yes, sir," she said quickly. "Of course I knew of that. They found out that she was killed in the railway accident at Northchester."

"No; that was a mistake," Roger contradicted her. "They are searching for her now, more closely than ever. But of late I have had some reason to doubt that that girl did really shoot Rheinhart. I am anxious should she be indeed innocent to prove her so. Can you help me?"

The woman hesitated; she looked away. For the first time a doubt of her good faith crossed his mind. Was it possible that she had some idea who was guilty—that she was screening some one? He watched her closely.

"I can't tell you anything, sir," she said after a pause. "Very often Mr. von Rheinhart had visitors I never saw. He would admit them himself by the window. I don't know who they were or whether he had anybody with him that night."

"Yet one visitor there must have been." Lavington's eyes did not move from her face. "At any rate some one must have taken the pistol away, and there is proof that the woman who left her glove was there. Do you know who she was?"

The suddenness of the question seemed to startle the woman's wits away.

"I don't know, sir," she said at last. "How should I? I didn't see her. I never knew she was there. As I found him lying there, my thought was that he had killed himself. I neither heard her go in nor come out. Even now I can't bring myself to believe there ever was anybody there at all."

Roger paused; he had no reason to doubt the woman's word. Yet, as she looked away again, he caught a twitching of the lower lip, and had an uneasy feeling that in some way he was being duped; that Mrs. Miller could have helped him if she would.

He waited a moment to frame his next question. Mrs. Miller slipped from her chair.

"I—it always upsets me to hear of that time, sir. It got on my nerves; many's the night I have not been able to sleep for thinking of it."

"Yes, I dare say." Roger moved forward to the door, and waited with his hand on the knob. "I am sure it must have been most trying. But, Mrs. Miller, you were in The Bungalow; if anybody is in a position to help me, you are. Can you not give me any hint? However trifling, however unimportant it may seem to you, it might yet prove of infinite service as a clue in tracking down the real criminal. Come, Mrs. Miller, think!"

The housekeeper moved a step or two forward; she threw out her hands as though to thrust Roger aside.

"No, I cannot," she said, her face working. "And let me tell you, Dr. Lavington, if I could, I would not. I would not move one step to punish Maximilian von Rheinhart's murderer. He was a bad man, a scoundrel. It was doing good work to rid the world of such a one as he. That is my last word. Will you let me pass, please, sir?"

"I beg your pardon." Roger stepped aside, his eyes still riveted on the white, defiant face. "But if the innocent should suffer—if the guilty should go free and the innocent should suffer?"

Mrs Miller hurried past him. She bent her head.

"The innocent!" she echoed in a whisper. "Ah, Heaven will defend the innocent, Dr. Lavington."

Chapter Twenty

"If you please, sir, a lady wishes to see you in the drawing-room."

"A lady!" Lavington echoed in displeased accents. He was hard at work perfecting an experiment upon which he had been engaged for months; after many failures, he seemed now to be on the high road to success, and he was in no mood to welcome an interruption.

"Did you tell her that I was busy and could not be disturbed?" he went on, as the footman hesitated.

"Yes, I did mention it, sir; but she was that set on seeing you, I thought maybe I had better come. She said it was most important, sir."

Roger uttered an impatient exclamation.

"Did she give her name?"

"No, sir." The man hesitated. "But I think—"

"Yes, yes!" Roger said testily. "What did you think? Out with it, man!"

"She asked for Sir James first, and, when I told her that was impossible, she would have me come to you, sir. I—I fancied she come from the Hall, sir; that was why I ventured to disturb you."

"From the Hall!" Roger's face paled. Was it possible that the blow he had been dreading so long had fallen at last? He turned from the man and busied himself among the crucibles and retorts. "Tell her I will be with her in a minute.

As the man withdrew, he threw off his mackintosh overall with feverish rapidity, and taking his coat from the peg near the door pulled it on as he hurried down the passage. In the drawing-room, though the windows were open, the green venetian blinds were drawn half-way down, excluding the, sunlight; to Roger, coming from the brightness of his laboratory, it looked dark and gloomy. He paused in the door-way, feeling dazed and bewildered; at the first sight of the tall figure standing in the shadow near the conservatory door his heart beat faster. He went quickly forward.

"Miss Luxmore, you sent for me—what can I do for you?"

The girl laid her hand in his a moment; she was paler than usual to-day; she looked as though she had been crying; her lips were trembling suspiciously. But the traces of trouble were only in Roger's eyes an added beauty. He waited for her to speak.

"Is there anything I can do?" he said simply.

Elizabeth raised her eyes to his.

"Dr Lavington, I must see James. Will you manage it for me?"

Roger hesitated.

"I would do anything in my power, Miss Luxmore, but I am afraid this is impossible—"

"Ah, no, no!" she interrupted him. "It—you don't understand. It is imperative—I must see him. Tell him that it is absolutely necessary. Tell him that I have come from Daphne—that as he refuses to see her he must listen to me!"

Lavington tugged restlessly at his dark moustache; the girl's agitation was infectious; a great pity grew and deepened in his grey eyes.

"I will do the best I can," he promised. "But so far I have not dared—no one has dared—to mention your sister's name to him."

"Ah, but now—now you must!" Elizabeth urged, her breath coming in short, quick gasps, two red spots blazing hotly on her cheeks. "Tell him that he knows—he must know—I would not trouble him lightly, and that by the memory of the old happy days I beg him to see me for five minutes with as little delay as possible. Please—please go to him, Dr. Lavington!"

Forgetting everything but the urgency of her errand, she caught Roger's arm and drew him to the door. With a strange feeling of unrest, an intolerable throb of mad longing, Lavington looked down at the white, ungloved hands tugging at his coat-sleeve. If he could press his lips to the cool fingers! For one moment he almost yielded to the overpowering impulse that possessed him; he bent his head. Then as he saw the girl's unconscious face, met the pleading in her brown eyes, his better self conquered; he drew himself upright, his forehead flushing darkly.

"I will try my best to induce Courtenay to listen to reason, Miss Luxmore. You may trust me."

"Thank you, I know I can," said Elizabeth quietly. Her hands dropped to her side; she looked up at Roger questioningly. Surely she was mistaken; he could not have made a movement to throw them off, to withdraw his arm.

He met her gaze unfalteringly, his eyes full of grave kindliness.

"Courtenay is in the study. If you will wait a minute I will go to him and see what I can do."

"Thank you," Elizabeth said mechanically. Surely she had made a mistake. He would not have dared. When the door had closed behind him she stood for a moment looking out of the window, then she turned and gazed round the room. It had been in process of being redecorated for Courtenay's bride when the news of the accident was brought to the Manor; she could remember going with Daphne to choose the design for the ceiling; the true lovers' knots that crept round and about so cunningly in the cornice; the rose-garlanded Cupids that peeped out coyly from the shadows.

Tears filled Elizabeth's eyes as she glanced round and saw a hundred mementoes of the past; the tragedy that had wrecked her sister's life seemed so causeless, so inexplicably cruel. Presently she heard Roger's footsteps returning.

"Sir James will see you, Miss Luxmore," he said, as he opened the door, "but he asks that you will be as brief as possible; and, as his medical adviser, I must warn you that all excitement is bad for him."

Elizabeth paused as he held the door for her. Her eyes were filled with tears.

"I am afraid what I have to say will excite him rather," she said with a new air of timidity which Lavington found adorable, "but it would be worse after if he did not see me, if he had to hear it from anyone else. I will try not to hurt him, Dr. Lavington."

"I am sure you will," he said as he preceded her across the hall to Courtenay's study.

Sir James sat in his wheeled chair in the middle of the room. By his orders the blinds had been pulled up to their fullest extent; the sunbeams, slanting across his head and chest, showed every line and wrinkle in the worn face, the droop of the round shoulders, the curving in of the hollow chest, with pitiless accuracy.

Elizabeth halted, her form swayed; for one moment Roger thought she was about to faint. Then she recovered herself and went forward.

"James—oh, James!"

A slow satirical smile overspread the cripple's face. Her pause had not passed unnoticed by him.

"What? You have made up your mind not to be frightened! Upon my word, your business must be urgent!"

Roger moved away, but as he closed the door he could not help hearing the pitiful quiver in the girl's voice, could not help catching her words.

"I had to come, James—I had to come, for Daphne's sake!"

He waited in the smoking-room with the door open, so that he could not miss her coming out. To him had ever seemed so long; more than once he glanced at the great clock in the hall—surely it must have stopped. But, no. Slowly, ponderously it was still ticking the moments away. Ten minutes, a quarter of an hour, twenty minutes. Roger tortured himself by picturing the scene going on in the next room. Had Elizabeth learned at last of her sister's danger? Had she come to beg Courtenay to put forth the power he had vaguely hinted he possessed to save Daphne—to save the girl he had once passionately loved from the terrible fate that threatened her? Roger asked himself in vain what could be Courtenay's answer.

At last he heard the door open, and Elizabeth's voice, clear, but with a sort of unutterable weariness:

"Then, that is all—I can do no more?"

"No, I am sorry to be disobliging, but you ask impossibilities."

Conscious they had no idea of his proximity, Roger hurried into the hall. Elizabeth glanced at him; even in the dimness of the shadow cast by the great staircase, he could see the pallor of her face, the big, blue marks beneath her eyes. She turned back for one moment.

"I did not think it was an impossibility I asked. But—well, if you refuse we must leave it there."

"What else would you have me do?" Courtenay's voice had the cold, sarcastic inflection that Roger knew and hated. "You must remember that I am heavily handicapped. The loss of both legs—"

"Ah!" Elizabeth's breath was strangled in a sob.

Roger drew her hand through his arm with scant ceremony, and guided her to the drawing-room. There, after he had seen her comfortably settled in a capacious arm-chair, he brought her a glass of wine, which he insisted upon her drinking, despite her mute protest.

"Rest there," he said authoritatively, when he saw the colour begin to creep slowly into her cheeks.

"Lie back against the cushion—so. Now I am going to leave you alone for a few minutes, and then I shall come back and see how my prescription works."

"Thank you; you are very kind," Elizabeth said faintly. Her upward glance thrilled his pulses.

He found Courtenay, to all outward appearance, unmoved; only a streak of crimson on his sallow brow, a faint quickening of his breath, spoke of his inward excitement. He was sitting before his desk, apparently engaged in writing some document which presented some amount of difficulty. The waste-paper basket was full, and the floor was littered with torn-up papers. There was a scowl on his face as he looked round.

"You may remember, Lavington, that I told you an hour ago that I had an important letter to write, and that I wished to be alone."

Roger stepped back,

"I beg your pardon. I was anxious to see—"

"Whether the interview upon which you insisted had proved as harmful as you expected!" Courtenay finished the sentence with a sardonic twist of the lips that was meant for a smile. "You are a nice sort of doctor, aren't you, Lavington? But, for your comfort, let me tell you that Elizabeth Luxmore is not so disturbing an element to me as to you. What"—as Roger, feeling as though he had unexpectedly received a douche of cold water, began a speech of incoherent indignation—"you did not know that I had guessed that? My dear fellow, must I remind you once more that the loss of my legs has not affected my power of penetration. You keep your secret somewhat after the fashion of a peewit's nest."

"I don't think you are entitled—" Roger said hotly.

"I'm sure I'm not," Courtenay agreed with ominous blandness. "I will take my misdeeds for granted, Lavington, for I'm particularly anxious to finish this letter, so—"

Roger would not trust himself to reply; he closed the door behind him with somewhat unnecessary violence. In the hall he paused a moment to collect his thoughts. Courtenay was evidently in one of his most captious moods; Roger had always found them trying. His introduction of Elizabeth's name, his jeers at the love which Roger had fondly believed to be unguessed by all the world save Daphne Luxmore, rendered him particularly exasperating to-day.

Presently, when he had cooled down a little, he opened the drawing-room door.

"I hope you are feeling better?"

There was no answer. He walked up to the armchair by the window—it was empty; the room was tenantless! As he gazed round in bewilderment, he realized that Elizabeth had not waited for him, that she had taken the first opportunity of slipping away. The open window, a stand of flowers that had been pushed aside, gave him the clue to the direction she had taken. Scarcely allowing himself time to think, to frame some excuse for attempting to overtake her, he hurried after her.

He followed the stream down to the bridge, realizing with a throb of disappointment, as he reached it, that Elizabeth must either have had too long a start or else had chosen to go back by the entrance gates; in either case it was hopeless to think of overtaking her now. He leaned against one of the supports of the bridge, and gave himself up to speculation. If, indeed, Elizabeth's errand had been to ask Courtenay's aid, he saw no ground—taking the latter's state of mind into consideration—for supposing she had been successful.

Roger was still meditating when he heard the swish of a woman's dress behind him. The thought struck him that perhaps after all he had been wrong—that Elizabeth had merely stepped out on to the terrace, crossed his mind as he turned. A woman of middle height, with an elaborate short gown of light silk and a much-befeathered hat, was regarding him intently.

"Good afternoon, Dr. Lavington," she said shortly.

He started violently as he raised his hat.

"Good afternoon, Mrs. von Rheinhart. I didn't expect to see you here."

"So I perceive." She smiled disagreeably. "This is the spot to which Miss Daphne Luxmore comes every evening, isn't it? I have heard of it."

Roger did not respond. If Mrs. von Rheinhart had made an unfavourable impression upon him when she was ill, it was considerably strengthened now. There was something sly, something underhand about the glance of her big black eyes, about the curve of her lips, he fancied; and the contrast between the peculiar pallor of her face—its pinched nostrils telling their own story of disease—and the gay hues of her attire struck him as particularly unpleasing.

"I suppose you are not aware that the park is private property, Mrs. von Rheinhart?" he said at last. "Sir James is always extremely annoyed at trespassing."

She did not look discomposed.

"I understood Monday was a free day."

"For the gardens and for certain parts of the park, in so far as they are shown to the public by the gardeners," Roger corrected her. "People are not allowed to wander about by themselves."

"Are they not?" The sly-looking eyes were watching him steadily now, a gleam of irony shining in their black depths. "I must apologize for my intrusion, then. Perhaps you would kindly show me the way to the part that is open. I have been anxious to have a little further conversation with you, and if you will allow me I will avail myself of this opportunity.

Roger paused a moment before he replied. But, profoundly as he distrusted and disliked Mrs. von Rheinhart, refusal was scarcely possible. He turned with her reluctantly.

"It will be best to make our way to the head gardener's house if you wish to go round; but I think it my duty to tell you that you are walking far too much, Mrs. von Rheinhart. You ought to rest much more than you do."

"Better to wear out than to rust out," she returned indifferently. "I wonder whether you will be interested to hear that we are getting on with our investigations, Dr. Lavington? The arrest of my husband's murderer is only a question of a few days now."

"Is that so?" Lavington's tone was studiously disinterested.

Mrs. von Rheinhart's eyes had a crafty glint as she glanced at him obliquely from beneath her dark eyelashes.

"We have found out what preceded and led up to the murder—the motive, I mean. As the French say, we have reconstructed the whole, and the rest is easy. The woman who murdered my husband is the one who, six years ago, stole his love from me. You may guess that now, more than ever, I shall not spare her."

Roger made no reply; his expression of stern gravity did not relax. Inwardly he was wondering what truth there might be in the story. In spite of his certainty that Mrs. von Rheinhart would stop at nothing to gain her own ends, to trip an admission from him, he had an uneasy feeling that there was something in what she said: there was an air of elation, of ill-concealed triumph, about her whole bearing.

The head gardener's house was nearer than the Manor; it stood in its own trim little garden, with a gravelled walk leading across the neatly-kept lawn to the front-door. A group of people waiting to be taken round the Manor grounds stood near the porch.

Roger opened the gate.

"If you will send in your card, some one will come to you." He was about to turn away, when Mrs. von Rheinhart put out her hand and clutched his arm.

"Who—what is that?"

Roger looked at her in amazement. Evidently she was labouring under intense excitement: her eyes were wide open and dilated, she caught her breath as if in physical pain.

"Ah, I warned you—"

"It is not that," she interrupted. "I thought I saw some one I used to know—some one who is dead." She was staring at the people who were moving backwards and forwards before the house. "It—you must come with me; I am frightened!" Her lean, muscular fingers were endowed with new strength as she tugged at his sleeve. "Come! You must come!"

Her voice, her clasp, were so urgent that Roger found himself yielding against his better judgment. She half dragged, half led him across the lawn. To all outward appearance the people who were now looking curiously at them were very ordinary folks indeed—a farmer's wife or two, stout and comely, with pretty, shy-looking daughters, a few prosperous-looking tradesmen who had driven over from the nearest small town with their families, attracted by the prospect of an afternoon's pleasuring in the Manor gardens. There was nothing that Roger could see to account for Mrs. von Rheinhart's excitement.

Suddenly, before they came up to the others, she stopped again and passed one hand over her eyes.

"Was I dreaming or mad?" she asked in a low, tense voice. "It—there is no one there!"

"You were mistaken," Roger said soothingly. "At a distance, one person looks very much like another. Was it a man or a woman you thought you recognized?"

"Mrs. von Rheinhart did not turn to him; her eyes, still looking scared and troubled, were fixed straight before her.

"It was a ghost!" she said slowly. "A ghost from the past—a shadow of ill-omen."

Chapter Twenty-One

DETECTIVE Collins sat in his private office; his brows were knit as he bent over a sheet of writing paper; his lips moved mechanically.

"Um, um! Blessed if I know what to make of it." There was a knock at the door; he hastily thrust the paper into a drawer in the desk.

"What is it?"

A clerk looked in.

"Inspector and another gentleman, sir—sailor."

Mr. Collins made a sound expressive of satisfaction.

"Matthew Wilson of course; the very man I was thinking of. Show them in!"

The offices of Messrs. Collins & Mason's Detective Agency were situated in a gloomy little street off the Strand. As yet the firm was only in a small way; Mr. Collins had not felt justified in making any considerable outlay.

The three dark little rooms which the agency occupied were furnished in the most meagre fashion, and were in curious contrast with the flower-surrounded police station at Sutton Boldon, and with Farmer Corbett's sunny little best parlour. But Mr. Collins was true to his instincts. On the table before him, looking strangely out of place in its dingy surroundings, there stood a tall specimen-glass holding one exquisite crimson rose. Detective Collins was smelling it as he greeted his visitors.

"Ah, I can't rival you, inspector, but I always must have a bit of something to look at. Well, Mr. Wilson, I was hoping that my note might catch you, but I wasn't sure, so I didn't reckon on it. But I'm glad to see you—very glad."

Matthew Wilson scratched his head doubtfully. Seen in the shabby office, he looked very big and burly. His weather-beaten face seemed to bring a breath of the sea into the smoke-laden atmosphere.

"I wasn't rightly sure that I could manage it, sir; but Inspector Spencer he came on purpose to see me, and he said it was necessary. I was just about signing for a voyage in the Mediterranean. It wouldn't be a matter of more than a month or so."

Detective Collins shook his head.

"I'm afraid it won't do." The detective opened a drawer and took out a number of photographs. "This is why I was anxious to see you this morning, Mr. Wilson. I wanted to know if you could identify any of these."

He spread out the cards on the table. They all represented men in different costumes. Matthew Wilson bent over them silently for a minute, scrutinizing them one by one, then he laid his finger down emphatically and straightened himself.

"That is him, sir—the man I saw get over The Bungalow wall. I didn't have much of a look at him, you may say, but I could swear to him anywhere."

Mr. Collins took up the photograph he indicated, and, after marking it, laid it aside on the mantelshelf, without making any comment. Then he shuffled the others again together and threw them aside.

"Once more, Mr. Wilson," taking another packet from the drawer and laying them out one by one.

The sailor looked at them carefully; his face brightened.

"There he is again, sir! I knew I hadn't made a mistake. You can see for yourself it is the same man."

Still with the same impassive air, the detective marked it and placed it beside the other.

"That is all, then, this morning, Mr. Wilson. I am much obliged to you. Now, if you will take a word of advice—I have an appointment with a lady in half an hour, and I must have a talk with the inspector here—if you could take a walk down to the wharf and tell them you have changed your mind about going to the Mediterranean, then come back here, and we will have a bit of dinner together at a quiet house I know of, and you could get the 3.20 train. What do you say?"

"Thank you, sir; much obliged to you, sir," Matthew Wilson said, as he made his adieux and got himself out of the room.

As the sound of his footsteps died away on the stairs, Inspector Spencer glanced at his colleague.

"Those portraits, Mr. Collins?"

The detective tossed them across to him.

"Nos. 8 and 27!" he announced. "You see the list here—No. 8, Sir James Courtenay, photographed in shooting costume; No. 27, Sir James Courtenay in ordinary morning dress."

The Inspector silently compared them.

"Umph! Seems rather to clinch matters, doesn't it?" he said as he returned them.

Mr. Collins drew in his lips.

"It is a corroboration anyway. I received a curious communication last night, inspector; I am anxious to hear your opinion of it."

He opened his desk, and, taking out the paper he had been scrutinizing when the others entered, handed it to him.

"Read it out," he commanded. "It is a queer start."

The inspector went over to the window.

"Having heard that you are engaged in inquiring into the murder of Maximilian von Rheinhart, the writer wishes to tell you that you are on the wrong track altogether. It has hitherto been assumed that there was only one visitor to The Bungalow, and that one was a woman. It has been brought to the writer's knowledge that there was at least one other—a man. Ask Sir James Courtenay's French chauffeur, Pierre Lamot, who is now in the service of the Duke of Alcester, where he drove Sir James on the night of April 14th, 19—. With this fact to work upon, a closer investigation of the circumstances will probably lead to a very different conclusion to that at which the police have at present arrived. No more at present.

"From,

"A LOVER OF JUSTICE."

The inspector droned it out in the deep tones in which he was accustomed to giving evidence at the police court. At its conclusion he laid it down and stared at the detective.

"Well, this is a new development! Who could have written it?"

"I might make a guess, and then again I might be wrong," the detective replied ambiguously. "I am expecting Mrs. von Rheinhart every minute"—glancing at the clock on the mantelpiece—"we shall see what she has to say to it."

The inspector did not seem much delighted at this piece of intelligence.

"It will be the first time she has been any good to us, if she has a sensible suggestion to make. She gets on my nerves, that woman. 'Arrest the murderer of my husband! I will have vengeance!' she says to me. And it is no good pointing out to her that we have got to find him first. Beats me why she is so keen on avenging her precious husband; he seems to have been a thorough bad lot, and from her own account he treated her like a brute."

"Women are queer creatures, the best of them." Mr. Collins was studying the anonymous letter closely.

At last the inspector looked up.

"Do you see one thing, Mr. Collins? This shows there is a third person we ought to find."

"A third person?" The detective's tone was distinctly puzzled.

The inspector's clean-shaven face looked triumphant; for once he had raised a point the astute Mr. Collins had failed to grasp.

"Yes. Don't you see, if anyone knows enough to send us this letter, the writer must know enough to be a valuable witness, if we could find him."

Mr. Collins was not wearing his black beard now; his thin lips twisted into an oracular smile.

"Ah, yes! I didn't see your point for a moment, inspector. But, yes, of course, the writer could tell us a good deal of the events of that night of April 14th; could clear up much of the mystery that overhangs it. But I don't fancy we shall get much more out of him."

"But this proves that some one else must have been hanging round The Bungalow that night," the inspector persisted, "somebody who knew Sir James Courtenay by sight too, probably. What is the postmark? West Strand, W.C. Um! That does not tell us much. Anybody might get it posted there. But the writer must be found."

"I don't think that will be necessary," Detective Collins said quietly. "I fancy I could make a pretty good guess here in London at the name you want."

"What! I don't understand!" the inspector questioned blankly.

"Don't you?" the other questioned blandly.

"Look at it again, inspector."

"I don't see the least clue to the writer," he said at last.

"I didn't say there was; still I would bet something I tell you the right name." The detective's smile deepened.

"Well, I give it up." Inspector Spencer's tone was distinctly haughty. At times, of late, he had been inclined to think that Mr. Collins was getting too big for his boots; it seemed to him to-day that his manner was almost offensively superior. "Who do you think it was?"

Mr. Collins was chuckling quietly to himself.

"It was meant for—I don't mind saying that—Hush! Here comes Mrs. von Rheinhart."

His ears were sharp. The other had heard nothing, but in a moment the clerk appeared to say that Mrs. von Rheinhart was in the other room. That lady was not given to ceremony. She followed closely on the messenger's heels. One glance at her face proclaimed the fact that her temper was not of the most amiable. Her look at the two men, the toss of the head with which she accepted the chair the detective placed for her, betokened that her mood was aggressive.

"Well, what have you done?" she demanded, without any preliminary. "Have you applied for a warrant for Daphne Luxmore's arrest?"

"No!" The detective's tone was curt.

Mrs. von Rheinhart looked at him contemptuously.

"Why not? I may as well tell you that, if you have not taken some decisive step before to-morrow night, it is my intention to take the matter out of your hands and apply to the Public Prosecutor myself."

A little smile crept round Inspector Spencer's lips.

"I doubt whether you would find that help your case much, madam! Still, of course, it is at your option to try it. The reason why we have not arrested Miss Luxmore is because we have not found sufficient evidence against her."

Mrs. von Rheinhart interrupted him with an angry laugh.

"There is evidence enough to hang her, I should say. There are the letters; the ring found beside the body has proved to have belonged to the late Lady Luxmore and descended to her daughter. Then you have the motive and the proof that Daphne Luxmore was on the spot. What more do you want?"

"On the other hand, there is Constable Frost's failure to identify her, and her maid's positive testimony that she was in bed at the time the murder was committed," the detective replied. "Testimony which, as we have ascertained, will be supported by that of Lady Folgate and the doctor who attended her. We can't fight against fact, Mrs. von Rheinhart."

Mrs. von Rheinhart put up her veil and it became apparent that her agitation was growing excessive.

"Do you mean to say you believe Daphne Luxmore to be innocent?" she demanded.

The detective coughed.

"It is not my business to promulgate theories, madam; I have to look at facts, and I say it is a fact that in face of Miss Luxmore's alibi we can do nothing. Our only course now, unless the alibi can be shaken, is to look for the criminal elsewhere. I should like you to read this." He handed her the anonymous letter, watching her closely as she looked at it.

Mrs. von Rheinhart's countenance exhibited several changes of expression as she studied it; astonishment, baffled malice, finally the gleam of gratified revenge.

"You have verified these facts?" she inquired, tapping the paper as she laid it down.

Detective Collins leaned forward, both elbows on the table, his chin resting on his clasped hands, his deep-set eyes fixed on his client's face.

"The main part of the story was known to us before," he said slowly. "That added to our difficulty in the matter of Miss Luxmore. The name of the chauffeur is a distinct gain—otherwise—"

"Otherwise you would do nothing, I know," Mrs. von Rheinhart broke in wrathfully. "Now, however, you will arrest Sir James Courtenay at once."

"We shall make a point of seeing the chauffeur, and I think the arrest will be the next step," Mr. Collins acquiesced. "We shall have to proceed cautiously, though. There is sure to be any amount of sympathy for a man who has been so terribly afflicted; though there is ample evidence now to warrant an arrest, I am doubtful— distinctly doubtful of conviction."

Mrs. von Rheinhart was not disposed to listen to any words calculated to damp her delight at the prospect of achieving the aim in pursuit of which she had been working so long.

"Other proof is sure to be found when the arrest is made. The pistol—"

"Ah! When we have found that, I grant you, we shall have something definite to go upon."

"We have something definite to go on now," Mrs. von Rheinhart declared emphatically. "You must arrest one of them, Inspector Spencer, either Daphne Luxmore or Sir James Courtenay, in either case I shall be avenged. Both"—with a discordant laugh— "have

wronged me, both have robbed me of the love which was my right."
Mrs. von Rheinhart rose; her suppressed exultation had dyed her
cheeks scarlet; her nostrils dilated, her eyes gleamed. "There is
nothing more for me to stay for, then. You will make the arrest at
the earliest possible moment, please." Detective Collins opened the
door for her.

"You may rely upon our doing our best, madam. Probably it will
be effected in the course of the next day or two." He preceded her
through the outer office and saw her into her cab.

Returning, he found the inspector still studying the anonymous letter.

"I can't make out who you think wrote this, Mr. Collins!"

"Can't you?" the detective rejoined carelessly. "Nice vindictive
woman that, inspector," nodding his head towards Mrs. von
Rheinhart's chair. "Upon my word, one can't blame the husband
for trying to get rid of her."

"I dare say not. But about this letter?" The inspector was not to
be led off into any side issues until the main question was settled.
"What do you intend to do?"

The detective spread out his hands.

"What can I do, my dear fellow? Our next step must be, I am
afraid, the arrest. There are one or two matters, though, that ought
to be cleared up first, in spite of Mrs. von Rheinhart, but I fancy a
few days will see the end of The Bungalow mystery."

"You mean the question of motive?" Inspector Spencer's mind
was moving slowly to-day.

Mr. Collins nodded.

"That—and you must remember that Rheinhart unmistakeably
had a lady visitor that night. If it was not Miss Luxmore—and her
alibi seems to prove conclusively that it was not—it must have been
some one else; we should at least get some light on the mystery."

"Mystery you may call it!" The inspector groaned. "Every clue
seems to lead to a blank wall."

"Each of them fits into its own little bit in the puzzle though. Now this letter—"

"Ah, now we are coming to it! Who wrote it, Mr. Collins?"

The detective glanced at the envelope.

"You will be surprised when you hear, I fancy, inspector."

"I dare say I shall," the inspector assented. "But I should like to know what you are hinting at, Mr. Collins."

The detective coughed. He looked round the room and lowered his voice as though to make sure that not a single word should reach the ears of a possible eavesdropper.

"What do you say to Sir James Courtenay himself?"

Chapter Twenty-Two

"Good afternoon, Frost!"

The ex-constable, stepping out of the post office, at Bredon, the nearest small town to Oakthorpe, found himself unexpectedly confronted by Inspector Spencer. His hand went up to his hat mechanically.

"Good afternoon, sir!"

"This is luck," the inspector proceeded genially. "I was just wishing that I could see you."

Mr. Frost's stolid face brightened.

"I've just been in to send a telegram to you, sir, as you charged me when anything of importance transpired."

Mr. Frost was rather fond of long words. In his own circle he was considered to have a pretty trick of speech.

"Ay! And you have made some discovery?" The inspector looked interested. "Come along, man, we will turn into the Dolphin and have a glass in the private parlour, and I will hear all about it."

He bustled into the old-fashioned inn standing opposite, Frost meekly following him.

There was little doing there. A stranger was a rare sight at Bredon, and his request for a room in which he could transact a little business with his friend was speedily acceded to.

He contained himself with difficulty until the land-lord had unwillingly withdrawn, after bringing the whisky and a siphon of soda, and set them on the tray beside the glasses. Then he glanced across.

"Well?"

Mr. Frost fidgeted. He had taken a chair at the other's invitation and now looked extremely uncomfortable.

"It—I do not know that it helps us much, sir. I've no doubt you will think I was to blame."

"I dare say I shall, but it is no use worrying about that," the inspector remarked philosophically. "Go on, Frost. I have no time to waste."

"Well, it is in this way, sir." A sudden thought struck Frost. He got up and shut the window, looking carefully down the cobble-paved path outside. "I—you know I told you that Miss Daphne Luxmore was not the lady I saw at the doctor's—the one acting over at Parson Thornton's."

"Yes." The inspector paused in the act of pouring out some whisky. "You don't mean to say—"

The ex-constable was not to be hurried. Never had his slowness of speech seemed more exasperating to Inspector Spencer.

"Well, that was true enough. I managed to get right up to the Hall windows the other day in the gloaming, and when the candles were lighted I saw my lord and the young ladies quite plain. Miss Luxmore sat with her face turned towards me. She might be a bit in the same style as the one I saw at Freshfield. I don't say she wasn't, and her hair was bright yellow, same as the other's. But I could take my oath it wasn't her. I wrote that to Mr. Collins, and that I didn't think I should do much by staying any longer here. He wrote back—I got his letter yesterday—and said I had better stop where I was a while. There might be some work for me to do in a few days, and in the meantime I was to keep my eyes open. So, yesterday, having nothing particular on hand, I thought I would spend the afternoon in the park. If there was anything to be picked up, I thought it was as likely to be there as anywhere."

"Quite right."

The inspector nodded as he paused. It was evident that Frost was not to be hurried. Left to himself, he would reach the point of his narrative in his own good time.

"Help yourself, Frost."

"Thank you, sir!" The man slowly filled up his glass from the siphon. "Your health, sir," he said to the inspector, as he raised it to his lips.

"Thank you," the other nodded. "Well, what did you see in the park? I thought Sir James Courtenay kept it strictly private, except on Monday."

"He does his best." Mr. Frost shook his head mournfully as he remembered sundry rebuffs at the lodge gates. "But there is a footpath to Norton that he can't stop—cuts across the northern corner, and once you are in, if there's nobody about, it is easy to slip among the trees. That is what I did yesterday. Then I made my way down to the bridge, keeping a cautious look-out for the doctor. He seems to be always hanging about. Presently I see him in the distance, so I slipped among the undergrowth like I did the time before that I told you about, and watched him. He walked about aimlessly for a while, as if he was waiting for some one, and I crouched down among the bushes wishing he was far enough. Presently he turned away. I gave him time to get out of sight and was just thinking it was safe to get up when I heard a woman's skirt catch in the briars along the path that ran just in front of me, and I waited. It was Miss Luxmore. I knew her in a moment. She wore a grey dress, and a floating veil like a nun, and as she passed me she was wringing her hands. 'Ah, James, James, you are very cruel!' she says to herself, with a sob like. Well, she went down to the bridge and stopped there the longest time, crying and moaning to herself. I daren't stir hardly for fear she should hear me, and I got that cramped and stiff before she had done that at last, when she had gone back, it was all I could do to raise myself. I came out, however, and stood on the path trying to brush off some of the green that had got on to my clothes, when I heard a little sound close to me, and there, just before me, on the same path, staring at me as if she had seen a ghost, was the very girl that was acting at Freshfield, and that I saw at the doctor's the night before. I could take my oath to her anywhere!"

He paused and looked at the inspector.

That functionary was leaning forward, his keen, eager expression showing the interest he took in the recital.

"You are sure it was not Miss Luxmore—that she had not turned back?"

Mr. Frost shook his head positively.

"I am positive of that, sir. I saw Miss Luxmore plain enough. She is older and thinner and sadder looking. Their hair is just about the same colour, that is all. Miss Luxmore, she was all in grey. This one was in white, with a motor-veil tied round her head. I knew her the moment I saw her, and she knew me, for as I stood still, what with the surprise and my pains, she turned and run back. Like a flash of lightning she was, and that quick on her legs that when I recovered myself, and made after her, she was out of sight round the bend of the path. I felt sure that I could catch her up in a moment, but when I came up to the turn not a glimpse of her was to be seen, and not a sign more of her could I And, though I hung about the wood for hours, laying the foundation of an attack of rheumatism for myself. But that is how the matter stands, sir. The girl that passed as the doctor's cousin at Freshfield is in this neighbourhood—or was last night—though where she is staying, or what she is doing, I can't make out. There's no doubt I saw her in the park with the doctor a while ago, and thought it was Miss Luxmore."

The inspector took a sip meditatively.

"I should say this case has had as many rum starts from first to last as anything I ever heard of," he said slowly at last. "And

I'm inclined to think you have hit upon one of the queerest, Frost. Have you no idea who this woman is?" The question was short and brisk; the tone strangely in contrast with the drawl of the preceding sentences.

The ex-constable looked at him in surprise.

"Why no, sir, I haven't. Do you—does that mean that you have?"

The inspector coughed and his eyelids dropped.

"It may be that an idea did cross my mind as you spoke. But I don't suppose there is anything in it. Still, I think you and I will take a look at the park to-night, and you shall show me just where this mysterious young woman eluded you."

"Very well, sir." Mr. Frost stood up and drained his glass. "Your health, sir. Why, there is Dr. Lavington! I declare, wherever I go, he always seems to be somewhere about—he might be shadowing me, he might. I suppose that will be Sir James Courtenay with him."

The inspector peered forth eagerly. The post office was on the opposite side of the street. A motor stood before the door; a man was just coming out with a sheaf of letters. The inspector's glance wandered past Roger's stalwart form to the stooping figure and hollow cheeks of the man who sat beside him.

"Poor fellow!" he said, as he turned away. "It —well, it seems a pity, but I suppose it can't be helped."

Meanwhile, all unconscious of this scrutiny, Sir James Courtenay was looking over the letters.

"One, two, for you, Lavington," he said lightly, as he tossed them over. "Five for me; all bills, I can see. Another begging epistle—faugh! And one for Miller; that makes up the lot."

"Miller!" Roger repeated. "I had no idea until the other day that she was the woman I had known as Mrs. McNaughton."

"Did you know her as Mrs. McNaughton?" Courtenay questioned.

The chauffeur was in his place now; with many creaks and groans, and not a few spasmodic starts, the motor was preparing to start. At the moment Roger glanced at the window of the inn. At the sight which met his eyes, he gave a great start.

When they were fairly off, Roger looked at his companion.

"Didn't you know that Mrs. Miller's real name was McNaughton?"

Courtenay's answer was sharp.

"How should I know? I have no list of your acquaintances—or Miller's either, for the matter of that."

"I did not suppose you had," Roger said huffily. There were times when Courtenay sorely taxed his patience. "But I should have imagined that you would know I should be sure to meet her in connection with The Bungalow case."

"The Bungalow case!" Courtenay glanced at the chauffeur, but the glass was sufficient barrier; it was not possible for him to overhear them. "I don't understand you. What connection had Miller with The Bungalow case?"

It was Roger's turn to look surprised.

"Why, surely you know that she was Maximilian von Rheinhart's housekeeper—that she was there at the time of the murder? It was she who summoned me!"

Courtenay stared at him.

"Miller was? My dear Roger, where in the world did you pick up such an extraordinary notion?"

His tone, his expression, nettled Lavington still further.

"It is not a notion at all; it is solid fact," he contradicted stiffly. "What is the use of playing up to me like this, Courtenay? You must have known that I should be sure to recognize her sooner or later." But Courtenay had turned more fully towards him now: his expression of absolute blank amazement was too genuine to be counterfeited.

"Are you mad, or am I, Lavington? It cannot be true; Miller never—"

"Miller kept house for Rheinhart under the name of McNaughton," Roger said with less warmth. "Is it possible that you didn't know?"

The chauffeur was driving quickly now. It was one of Courtenay's chief pleasures to feel rapid progression; it was to be feared that the time-limit was often disregarded; to-day, they seemed positively to fly over the broad, smooth road that had led ever since the days of the Roman supremacy from London in the south to the sea in the west. As they flashed by, Courtenay's eyes grew sombre, watching the flying hedges, the outlines of the grand old trees, quaint thatched farmhouses, tiny hamlets nestling in the shadow of the hills. The lines that suffering had graven round his mouth grew tenser, deeper.

"No, I didn't know," he said slowly. "She never told me—I have never asked her what she was doing just before she came back. We needed no reference with Miller; she was my nurse in my childish days; her love and devotion could not be doubted. I never wondered, either, that she preferred to call herself by the name by which we had always known her. She had seen so much trouble since she left us. Her only daughter, Alice, ran away with some scoundrel. Her second marriage was an unhappy one; it had lasted only for a short time, and she wished as far as possible to forget it."

"I wonder whether the police have any idea where she is?" Roger speculated.

Courtenay shook his head.

"I don't know—I never thought. I can hardly bring myself even now to believe that you are right—that she really is—"

"Maximilian von Rheinhart's housekeeper!" Roger finished for him. "Oh, there is no mistake possible there, my dear fellow. I taxed her with it, and she did not attempt to deny it. I thought it was possible that she might be able to help me; that circumstances might have given her some idea of the murderer's identity, but it was no use."

Courtenay touched the communication cord.

"Home!" he said briefly. "By Topham's Corner!"

Topham's Corner had a great reputation among the country folk. It was a curious-looking edifice, built partly of stone, partly of brick, with a superstructure of clay. There was a local idea that though the common belonged to the lord of the manor, if any man could build a cottage upon it in twenty- four hours it became his own property. Whether there was any foundation for this theory, in fact or not, in the early eighties a man of the name of Topham had taken advantage of it, and the before-mentioned curious structure was the result. He sat at the door this afternoon, a picturesque old figure, with a flowing silver beard and piercing dark eyes, wearing some strange patchwork-looking garment, which kindly time was rapidly mellowing into a deep russet brown. All along the country-side Topham was held to be a wizard. It was reported that no event of importance in the neighbourhood had happened for years without being foretold by Topham, and yet, when the lads and lassies went to him to have their fortunes told, he would drive them from him with contumely.

To-day, however, before they had any idea of his intention, he had hurried with an agility remarkable in one of his years, into the road, where he stood waving his arms and crying "Stop!"

With some difficulty, the chauffeur pulled up in time. Lavington looked at the strange figure in amazement. Courtenay stooped towards him.

"What is it, Topham?"

The old man was obviously labouring under great excitement; his face was working, his uplifted hands shaking.

"I have a message for you, Sir James Courtenay—a message for you. Listen, there is trouble coming to you—bitter, black trouble. But—and if you will walk warily—light will arise out of darkness; sweet will spring from bitter." He moved to the side of the road into his little garden. "That is all I have for you; but remember, Sir James Courtenay, that the message never comes to Topham for naught." And he disappeared into the cottage with dramatic suddenness.

The astonished chauffeur glanced at his master, and, receiving his nod, started once more. Courtenay turned to Roger.

"Nice cheerful sort of chap, isn't he? I scarcely know why I don't evict him from his tumble-down abode, only I suppose that long residence there has given him a sort of prescriptive right. However, if he takes to attacking people in this fashion, something will have to be done."

Lavington was aware that argument would only make him more determined; he contented himself by saying:

"His remarks seemed to be rather of an encouraging nature on the whole, I should say. I gather you are promised prosperity in the future."

"Rubbish! Hang the fellow!"

Courtenay relapsed into his wonted gloomy silence. Lavington, for his part, had plenty of food for thought. It seemed to him that the fact of The Bungalow housekeeper being in the neighbourhood constituted an additional menace to Daphne Luxmore's security; for, in spite of Mrs. Miller's protestations, he found it almost impossible to believe that she knew nothing of the former's visit to The Bungalow. Rather, he was inclined to believe that it was more likely to be Mrs. Miller who had put the police on Daphne's track at Oakthorpe. Though he had never hitherto availed himself of the means of communication she had provided, it seemed to him now that the time had come when he ought, if possible, to see Daphne, to explain to her as much as possible of the danger in which she stood, to persuade her of the urgency of making her escape.

He was obliged to wait until after dinner, however. It was never a cheerful meal at the Manor even when Courtenay was well enough to join him; to-day it seemed particularly gloomy. Courtenay was in an exasperating frame of mind; every fresh subject brought forward by Lavington appeared to provide him with new material for gibes and sneers. It was with a sigh of relief that Roger rose from the table and announced his intention of smoking his cigar in the park.

"Away from my lively society, eh?" Courtenay suggested, with a cynical smile. "Well, I have a good deal to do to-night, and I do not know how much time I shall have to do it in, so perhaps it is as well."

Once out of sight of the house, Roger quickened his steps considerably. So far he had not penetrated into the wood on the Luxmore side; but, though innumerable paths seemed to stretch on all sides, following Miss Luxmore's directions he had little difficulty in making his way to the green door.

There was a little stir behind him, too faint to reach his ears. When he had passed the first turning, two men, wearing soft shoes, stepped noiselessly on to the path.

"So far so good," Inspector Spencer remarked. "As I thought, this hiding-place has proved useful to the young lady sometimes. Well, she will find it occupied to-night."

He stepped lightly round an old giant oak, to all outward appearance passing it. It was firm and solid. Towards the wood, as the inspector had discovered, it was cleft nearly in two by a great hollow, one in which a man might well stand. A few threads of white were easily discernible. The inspector glanced at them as he waited.

In the wood Constable Frost was keeping carefully in the shadow of the trees as he endeavoured to keep Roger in sight. Lavington tapped lightly at the door in the wall that surrounded the Luxmore grounds, and pushed a paper beneath. Then he waited; it seemed to him a long time. He was telling himself that it was unlikely Miss Luxmore would be looking for him to-night, when the door was thrown open, and a white-robed figure looked out.

"You—you are here! What is it? What have you come to tell me?"

Something in the terror, the appeal of the tone, brought very forcibly to Roger's mind that never-to-be-forgotten scene in the studio. Just so had her brown eyes been raised to his, the same inflection had rung through her clear voice when she had pleaded to him for mercy. He caught the trembling hands in his now.

"Don't be afraid. I don't know that there is fresh danger. But I have come once more to beg, to implore you to get away while there is yet time. Think of your sister—of your father! If you should be accused—"

The soft hand rested in his a moment, then the girl seemed to regain her self-control as if by magic.

"They would not dare—Ah no! There is danger to others, and they will not see it. I thought—I feared that you had come to tell me—"

She broke off, shivering.

"Never mind others, think of yourself," Roger urged. He was unable to guess to whom she could be referring, neither did it seem to matter. The one thing important in his eyes was that by some means the girl before him should be got away—Elizabeth Luxmore's name should remain unscathed. "Your visit to The Bungalow is known to the police," he went on. "Your name is an open secret. Any moment they may take action. Now—now, if you would let me, if you would trust me, I could get Courtenay's motor and take you to a place I know of in London. You would then be safe there until we could think of some way of getting you out of the country."

"I can't! I can't!" the girl began.

Behind them in the flower-scented garden, on the other side of the summer-house which blocked Roger's sight, there was a cry:

"Daphne! Daphne!"

The girl slipped back into the garden, still holding the door in her hand.

"Go! Go! It is my father! He must not find you here!"

"But—" Roger began, bewildered.

"Hush!" The girl put her hand to her lips imperatively.

"Daphne! Daphne!"

Lord Luxmore's voice was growing nearer.

"Go! Quick! Hurry! For my sake—for Elizabeth's sake!"

The great door shut sharply, and Roger found himself alone in the wood. For one moment he remained staring at it blankly, then, remembering in whose name he had been begged to leave, he turned reluctantly back to the Manor.

On the other side of the closed door the girl in white leaned back her face pale to the lips, one hand pressed to her heart as if to still its beating. Lord Luxmore's steps were plainly audible, evidently he was coming down the very path which led to the gate.

"Daphne! Daphne!"

"Here I am, father." The answer came from the lawn beyond. "Come back to the veranda. We are going to have some music. Elizabeth will sing to us the new thing you like so much."

"Oh, well, my dear—"

Lord Luxmore's rejoinder was lost as the pair turned back to the house.

The girl by the door waited until the last sound of their footsteps had died away; then she ran fleetly along the path that twisted in and out of the shrubbery that surrounded the back of the Hall. Suddenly a dark form stepped out from the bushes, a firm hand was laid on her arm.

"One word, if you please, ma'am." The mellifluous accents were those of Detective Collins.

The girl repressed a scream with difficulty; in vain she tried to free herself, twisting and turning from side to side; the detective's iron clasp held her as firmly as a grip of iron.

"What do you want?" she panted. "What do you want?"

The detective's eyes were fixed upon her face, flushing and paling by turns, as, giving up the unequal struggle, she stood motionless before him. A smile of triumph lighted up his round, jocund countenance.

"Just a little explanation, madam," he said soothingly. "Just a little explanation!"

Chapter Twenty-Three

"Sir James desired me to say, sir, that he has still a little business to do, and when that is finished he is going straight to bed. He begs you will excuse him to-night."

"Certainly! I shall be off directly; it suits me better to work in the early morning than at night, I find."

Lavington pushed his manuscript together and leaned back in his chair.

The old butler waited.

"Shall you want anything more, sir?"

"No, nothing, thank you. Goodnight, Jenkins."

"Goodnight, sir." The man withdrew noiselessly and Roger was left alone.

He sighed as he fastened his loose sheets of paper together and laid them in his desk. He had made scant progress of late. It was impossible to discourse learnedly on the origin of certain obscure diseases when the fair face of Elizabeth Luxmore would keep obtruding itself between his eyes and the printed pages. He had even found himself idly sketching her face on the margin of the paper when he should have been reading an article in the *Lancet* on the most recent medical discovery.

He lighted his pipe and strolling over to the mantel-piece, took up a position with his back to the fire. It was early yet, only half-past ten, but with Courtenay's illness the household had fallen into invalid habits and early going to bed prevailed before Lavington's coming to the Manor.

Making up his mind, that, since he could not work, there was nothing to sit up for, he was about to turn out in search of his candle, when the sound of wheels in the avenue caught his ear. He paused; it was an unusual hour for a visitor to arrive. It struck him that it might be Ethel Melville, she had spoken in her last letter of hoping to come down to see her brother shortly.

There was a loud rat-rat at the front door, a peal at the bell, Roger crossed the room, and drawing back the curtains from the unshuttered window, looked out, He could make out a carriage standing outside the porch, two men sat on the box, another stood by the door. Then he caught the sound of voices in the hall;

evidently the visitors, whoever they were, were holding a lengthy colloquy with Jenkins. Then Jenkins put his head in.

"If you please, sir, I—they say—"

A glance was enough to convince Roger of the truth of his surmise that the visitors had brought bad news; the old butler's face was white, his eyes were staring, his head was shaking as if with palsy.

"What is it, Jenkins?" he said, moving towards him quickly. "Not Mrs. Melville?"

"No, sir, it—" the old man stammered; he seemed to have almost lost for the time being the power of coherent speech. "No, sir, it is Sir James, sir. It—oh Heaven save us, I can't say it! I think we must all be going mad!"

"Collect yourself, Jenkins." Roger spoke sternly. He saw this was no time for kindness, the man was on the verge of a womanish outbreak of hysterics. "What is wrong with Sir James?"

"One moment, my good man." A strong hand put Jenkins on one side. "I will explain matters to Dr. Lavington myself. Excuse me, sir." Detective Collins advanced into the room, closing the door carefully behind him. "It is as well to have as few mixed up in this business as possible," he remarked with a deprecating smile. "Dr. Lavington, I hold a warrant for the arrest of Sir James Courtenay. The police are in the hall with Inspector Spencer; we look to you to get the warrant executed as expeditiously as possible."

"A warrant for the arrest of Sir James Courtenay!" Lavington distrusted the evidence of his own ears. "You must have made some unaccountable mistake. What is the charge?"

Before the detective could reply Jenkins put in his head.

"Sir James, he heard the knock and he sent for me. He says will you please step this way; he will see you at once. You, too, sir, Sir James said," turning to Roger.

The library door stood wide open; Courtenay, sitting in his wheeled chair before his secretaire, commanded a view of the hall.

"Come in. I was expecting you," he said quietly. "You see I have been preparing for you," with a gesture towards the overflowing waste-paper-basket, the neatly-docketed packets on the shelves of the secretaire. "Roger, old fellow, close the door for a minute," for already the news that something extraordinary was taking place had spread to the servants' hall; frightened faces were peeping out from the passage. Before Roger could obey, however, Inspector Spencer and his colleague had followed him in. The inspector stepped forward. Courtenay met his glance fully.

"Do your duty, inspector. No preparation is needed, thank you!"

"Sir James Francis Lechmere Courtenay, I arrest you for the wilful murder of Maximilian Gerhard von Rheinhart, at The Bungalow, Sutton Boldon, on the night of April 14th, 19—" the inspector read in his clear, strident tones from the warrant in his hand. "It is my duty also to warn you that anything you say now will be taken down and may be used against you in evidence."

Courtenay bowed slightly.

"Thank you, inspector. I am much obliged to you. Where are you going to take me?"

"Only over to Bredon, sir, until the examination before the magistrates takes place. But Mrs. Cruikshanks, the wife of the inspector there, she will see that you are comfortable for the night."

"Comfortable!" Courtenay's smile was frankly amused. "I am sure she will be kindness itself," he hastened to add. "Roger, my dear boy, would you tell them to bring the brougham round. I suppose there will be no objection to that?" glancing at the police-officers.

"Certainly not, sir. We thought you would probably prefer it. One of us will go inside and the other on the box, if you will allow it."

Roger obeyed mechanically. The one thing that struck him amid the vast bewilderment that had overtaken him was that Courtenay's old genial manner had returned and that the cynical, sneering tone which he had adopted of late had vanished. He gave the order to Jenkins, never even observing in his utter preoccupation the old man's pitiful anxiety for further news. When he returned to the library Courtenay was already wheeling himself towards the door, the police closing in around his chair.

"There; I think there is nothing to wait for. One of the men can bring over what I shall want for the night." But the old friendship, the old love that had subsisted between the two lonely boys at school, and later on at college, swept over Roger in an overmastering flood now. Remembering Courtenay's high aims, the brilliant promise that his young life had held, the pathos of this pitiful tragedy seemed to be more overwhelming.

He turned from his friend with a groan to the men who stood beside him.

"I must see him alone. I will answer for him."

"You shall have your way, sir." Detective Collins took the answer upon himself. "But the door must be left open, and Inspector Spencer and me must stand in sight."

They moved into the hall. Courtenay wheeled himself back nearer the window. Roger's eyes were full of pleading, of tense, intolerable pain; the face that smiled back at him, the candid eyes, the mouth, strong yet sweet, were surely those of his childhood's friend and hero. The deep lines that the years of sorrow had graven were smoothed out. The long, weary time of ill-health, of sickness of body and mind was forgotten, as if it had never been.

"Courtenay! Jem!" The old name, never used since his coming to Oakthorpe, rose glibly to Roger's lips now. "This is a vile lie! I know you did not do it!"

A passionate appeal lay in the rough tones. Forgetful, Lavington's brown hand gripped his friend's thin shoulder like a vice.

Courtenay's upward look held something of wistful longing.

"I was at The Bungalow that night, Roger; that is true enough!"

"But you did not kill Maximilian von Rheinhart?" Lavington said hoarsely, his eyes fixed upon his friend as though they would force his secret from him, his muscles straining unconsciously. "It is no use you trying to blind me, Jem. I know you did not."

Courtenay winced involuntarily.

"That is for the jury to determine," he said slowly. "I knew—I have always known—that this charge might be brought at any time. Sometimes I have thought that the end might come first, and I have been glad. But, now, I fancy, after all, it is better as it is; for the rest, she will be safe, I think. That is what counts."

She! Lavington gazed before him, bewildered. He realized that for one moment he had forgotten Daphne Luxmore—had forgotten the girl he had found at The Bungalow. Before he had time to collect his thoughts, to realize with any coherency how entirely Courtenay's avowed presence in The Bungalow on the night of the murder must alter things as he knew them, his friend moved forward.

"Officer, I am ready. I hear the carriage outside. May I suggest I am a poor sleeper and I shall be glad to reach my shelter for the night as soon as possible."

"We are ready, sir." Detective Collins and Inspector Spencer kept close at hand on either side, while Courtenay wheeled himself across the hall and waited for the footman to bring him his coat and hat.

Old Jenkins stood near the door, tears standing in his eyes.

"If I had known what they had wanted I would have let them blow the house down afore I opened the door to them," he quavered. "You will forgive me, sir?"

Courtenay held out his hand.

"There is nothing to forgive, my old friend! You have nothing to reproach yourself with—I—" His words were drowned by a noisy outburst of sobbing from a group of frightened servants clustered round the doorway.

Detective Collins shrugged his shoulders.

"I did my best to get him away quietly; but once let these women know and there's no keeping them back. Who's this now?"

The sobbing maids were thrust on one side; a figure clad in rustling black silk, with a white, twitching face, staggered forward.

"What are you doing? Jenkins! Charles! Fools! Are you letting him be taken away without one struggle?"

Courtenay was signing to the men to lift him into the brougham. He turned his head.

"Miller, my poor friend, don't! Talk to her, Roger; show her it is all for the best."

But the waiting policemen interposed themselves deftly between the housekeeper and her master. He was placed in the carriage. Collins stood at the door waiting. Lavington moved forward. Courtenay held up his hand.

"Not now, Roger, dear old fellow; I would rather be alone. You can do as much for me here. Make my old friend there see that it cannot be helped; that indeed it is best so. And Ethel must be told." His voice quivered. "I was forgetting Ethel, Roger. There is a midnight express. Would you—could you—"

"I will go," Roger promised.

"Thank you. Tell her that I am sorry to have brought this upon her. If you come back, if you get the early train in the morning, I shall be glad to see you—if—if you care to come. Ready, inspector!"

Glad to end the scene, the two men got into the carriage and closed the door. Lavington stood in the porch until the last sound of the wheels had died away, then he turned heavily back to the hall.

The housekeeper was clinging to one of the doorposts behind him, her whole frame shaking as if with ague. He put out his hand.

"Come, Mrs. Miller, you must not give way; there is so much to be done! Let me help you back to your room."

But Mrs. Miller thrust his arm away.

"It cannot be true what they are whispering among themselves, Dr. Lavington"—with a withering glance at the weeping maidservants—"that they have arrested him for murder—arrested Sir James for murder!"

Roger paused a moment; then, conscious that it was useless to deny facts that by the morning would be ringing through the whole country-side, he bowed his head gravely.

"Ah!" Mrs. Miller fought down a strangling sob. "Whose murder? Whose murder, I ask, Dr. Lavington."

Roger drew her forcibly into the billiard-room at the end of the hall. If help was to be hoped for, surely it must come from this woman.

"For the murder of Maximilian von Rheinhart, at Sutton Boldon, Mrs. Miller!"

The woman interrupted him with a hoarse cry.

"Are they mad—mad? He murder Maximilian von Rheinhart! Sir James—he—I—" She broke off with a moan, struggled for breath, clutched wildly at the air.

Roger caught her before she fell. Laying her on the couch, he summoned the maids. Evidently nothing further could be hoped for from her now, and he had little time to spare if he was going to catch the midnight express.

A terrible thought was torturing him as he made his brief preparations. Now that Courtenay was accused of murdering Rheinhart, would it not be his duty to speak out—to relate the circumstances under which he found Daphne Luxmore on the night of April 14th? Would he be justified in disregarding his friend's wish and making public Miss Luxmore's share in the mysterious events of The Bungalow?

Another question insisted on making itself heard whether he would or not. It was evident from his own words that Courtenay, as well as Miss Luxmore, had been at The Bungalow on the night of the murder. As far as human probability could go, the death of Maximilian von Rheinhart must lie at the door of one of them. It was the old question he asked himself, the one that had been put by Detective Collins at Sutton Boldon, by Inspector Spencer at Corbett's farm—which?

Chapter Twenty-Four

THE LITTLE court-room at Bredon, in which the magistrates' meeting was held, was crammed to its utmost capacity. The news that Sir James Courtenay had been arrested for murder, and would be brought before the magistrates at Bredon that morning, had spread like wildfire over the neighbourhood. The interest that had been taken in The Bungalow murder was intensified from the accused man's wealth and position, and was raised in this case to fever heat by the romance that had gathered round Sir James Courtenay's name.

Roger elbowed his way through the curious sightseers on his way down from the station. He looked haggard and worn in the clear morning light; his mouth sternly compressed; his eyes sombre and set round with purple rims. He had not slept since Courtenay's arrest; he had scarcely sat down save in the railway carriage. The mental strain involved in breaking his terrible news to Mrs. Melville, in cheering her and encouraging her to believe that everything might yet turn out to be some terrible mistake, was considerable; and his determination at all hazards to be back by the hour fixed for the examination before the magistrates had necessitated two long journeys with barely an hour's interval between them. But, above all, his dark face betrayed the traces of inward conflict; the question he had put to himself last night remained unanswered; his line of conduct was still undecided.

As he neared the door of the court-house, guarded by two stalwart policemen, way was made through the crowd. The Luxmore carriage dashed by; he caught a glimpse of Elizabeth's face, looking pale and set; leaning back on the other side of the carriage was a deeply-veiled, shrinking figure. Lord Luxmore sat on the back seat, a benevolent-looking elderly man by his side.

Roger turned aside with a sick feeling of despair. Had it come to this, that he must either be false to his friend, or to the sister of the woman he had sworn to protect? Must he either betray the trust that had been placed in him, and bring shame and disgrace on the name he reverenced most on earth, or must he stand silent while Courtenay was accused of a crime of which his evidence would go far to clear him?

He looked round the room anxiously when he had been conducted to his seat beside Courtenay's solicitor; apparently neither Lord Luxmore nor his daughters were present, and he experienced a brief feeling of respite; even to himself he hardly acknowledged how tremendous would be the ordeal should he be compelled to betray Daphne before her sister's eyes. Nothing, he determined, but the last and worst eventuality should oblige him to disclose his knowledge of the crime; but should Courtenay's life or liberty be endangered, his conscience told him that not even his friend's positive commands ought to avail to keep him silent.

One or two minor cases were summarily disposed of by the magistrates, and then Courtenay was formally charged. His appearance, as his chair was brought into the court, created a buzz of excitement, under cover of which his solicitor leaned towards Roger.

"I hear that you will probably be called as a witness, Dr. Lavington; but we do not expect to require you to-day. This—this has been a terrible shock. That is Davenport Villiers, K.C. He is instructed by the Public Prosecutor."

The name was well known to Roger as one of the most eminent criminal lawyers of the day. He glanced across—the keen eyes, the prominent jaw and hard, firm mouth had become familiar through the illustrated papers; his heart sank.

As Courtenay passed him he leaned forward.

"Roger!"

"Jem!"

Their hands met in a long clasp.

A great silence fell upon the court as he was placed before the bench, and the charge was formally read out "that he, James Francis Lechmere Courtenay, did wilfully and of malice aforethought slay one Maximilian Gerhard von Rheinhart on April 14th, 19—"

There was a dramatic pause, and then Mr. Davenport Villiers rose, and in a few dry, concise sentences stated that the evidence proved beyond doubt that Sir James Courtenay was seen to enter The Bungalow a few minutes before the murder took place. The theory set up by the prosecution was that Sir James visited The Bungalow determined to put an end to the terrorism which Maximilian von Rheinhart was attempting to exercise over him and over others, and that Rheinhart's death was the result. Whether there might have been sufficient provocation to reduce the crime to manslaughter the learned counsel could not pretend to say; that would be for the jury at the assizes to determine; but he thought their worships would agree with him that there was ample *prima facie* evidence to justify them in sending the case for trial. Blackguard though he might have been, blackmailer though he undoubtedly was, yet Rheinhart had the right to claim the protection of the law for his life, and the law must step in to avenge his death.

Matthew Wilson was the first witness called. While he was making his way to the witness-box Roger caught sight of the elderly man he had noticed in the Luxmore carriage a few minutes ago; he was sitting on the bench a little to the right of the magistrates; a notebook was in his hand, and he was evidently prepared to follow the case with the greatest attention.

While Wilson was being sworn, Lavington leaned forward.

"Mr. Day, can you tell me who that man is—the man sitting next to Mr. Fernler?"

Courtenay's solicitor looked up fussily. Worthy family lawyer that he was, the present charge had taken him unawares, and he scarcely felt equal to coping with the situation.

"That—oh, that is Sir William Bunner; you must have heard of him; used to be called the 'Hanging Judge'; retired last year. I hear he is staying with Lord Luxmore."

"Sir William Bunner!" The name brought back a thousand memories to Lavington. So that explained Sir William's partial recognition of Daphne Luxmore at Freshfield; her agitation at the sight of him. Her escape had been even narrower than Roger had dreamt, he said to himself—if Sir William Bunner's memory had been one shade better.

Wilson gave his evidence clearly and well. It was perfectly obvious to Roger that the magistrates, who had been somewhat inclined to pooh-pooh the charge before, were considerably impressed. The jeweller's identification of the cigarette-case was next put in; the French chauffeur, Pierre Lamot, testified to having driven Sir James in the direction of Sutton Boldon on the night of the fourteenth, and to having waited for him in some such lane as that described by Wilson. Then there was a pause. Courtenay was reserving his right to cross-examine the witnesses until later. Mr. Day had telegraphed for a well-known barrister, versed in criminal law, to conduct the defence; he was expected down by the midday train. Until his arrival little could be done for the prisoner.

Mr. Davenport Villiers looked at his notes.

"Call Miss Elizabeth Luxmore!"

A thrill of surprise ran round the court. Miss Elizabeth Luxmore! What could she have to do with the case? Believing that the name of the wrong sister had been given through inadvertence, Roger stared at the tall girl who was following Lord Luxmore through the crowd up to the witness-stand. It was impossible—impossible, he told himself, that Elizabeth Luxmore's name should be mixed up in this horrible tragedy!

Then, as he saw that there was no mistake, that it was indeed Elizabeth who was standing there, taking the oath in her fresh young tones, the thought came to him that possibly she and Courtenay had been staying in the same house; that she would be called to testify as to the time he started on his drive to The Bungalow. It could not be anything else.

Courtenay was looking at her in evident surprise, leaning forward in his chair. Roger covered his eyes with his hand; it was nothing less than torture to him to see the girl he loved in this position.

Elizabeth was turning a little to the magistrates; her face was pale, but composed; the glance of her brown eyes was full and steady; with a little gesture she declined the chair the usher brought her.

"You remember the morning of April 14th, 19—?" Mr. Davenport Villiers began smoothly.

She inclined her head.

"Perfectly."

"Will you tell us where you were staying at that time?"

"At the Towers, Sir Gregory Folgate's place, about twenty miles from Sutton Boldon." The reply came without any hesitation. A close observer might have seen that the girl's ungloved hands were clutching tightly at the rail in front of her.

"Now tell us what particular reason you have for remembering that date?"

"My sister woke me early in the morning to tell me that she was ill; she had a terrible cold; and she was never strong." Elizabeth paused a moment, as if to arrange her thoughts in sequence, then she went on speaking slowly and deliberately. "She told me, too, that she was in great trouble. I knew already that three years before, when she was only a schoolgirl, she had drifted into a foolish, secret engagement with Maximilian von Rheinhart, who had taught painting at a school she attended for a short time. She had, however, found out his true character in time, and turned from him in horror; and she had held no communication with him for two years when her engagement to Sir James Courtenay was announced.

"Then, when he heard of it, Rheinhart sent to her; he demanded an interview. She had written to him foolish, romantic letters, addressed to the man she believed him to be; they proved, however, that she had at one time looked forward to marriage with Rheinhart; had even consented to a secret union. These letters Rheinhart had refused to return to her, and he was holding them over her, threatening to show them to Sir James Courtenay. He demanded a large sum of money for them—a sum she had at last scraped together.

"Not satisfied with that, however, when pretending to restore them to her, he had kept back several, among them the very one which Daphne most dreaded falling into Sir James Courtenay's hands. This, in a letter she received that morning of April 14th, he refused to give up unless she came to The Bungalow herself alone that very night. Before I saw her she had sent her answer. She had promised to go; she was frightened, terrified!"

Elizabeth stopped, and drew a quick breath. An usher brought a glass of water; she raised it to her lips, and drank feverishly.

Lavington straightened himself, and uncovered his eyes. It seemed to him that he was taking part in a play, a vision; he had no real consciousness of what he saw. Yet years afterwards his mind could reproduce faithfully every smallest detail of the scene: the tall, pale girl, in her sombre gown; the small head, with its wealth of dark hair closely folded; the stained and faded curtains behind her making a background for her clear, pure profile, her slight, rounded figure. Lord Luxmore, standing just beyond, waiting impassively; the magistrates leaning forward so that they might not lose a word; the absorbed faces of the spectators; Courtenay himself, listening, huddled up in his chair. All these were the merest accessories as far as Lavington was concerned; his attention, his interest, were for the girl in the witness-box alone.

The chairman was leaning towards her; he was saying something in a low tone.

Lavington fancied he was asking her to spare herself—to rest.

She shook her head as she set the water down, and turned again to Mr. Davenport Villiers. That gentleman had been looking over his notes. He raised his head.

"Your sister told you, then, that she had arranged to visit Rheinhart at The Bungalow that evening for the purpose of getting back her letters?" he began suavely. "Will you tell us what happened next?"

For one moment Elizabeth shaded her eyes with her hand, then she caught at the rail in front of her.

"I begged her not to go. I told her that it would only make matters worse, put her more completely in Rheinhart's power. But it was no use reasoning with her. Rheinhart had threatened that if she did not come he would send the letters at once to Sir James Courtenay, and she was frantic at the very idea. While I was talking to her about it she fainted. When she recovered, I told her that now her journey to The Bungalow was an impossibility; but she was obstinacy itself, and I could make no impression upon her. Then a sudden thought struck me."

"Yes," Mr. Davenport Villiers said encouragingly, twitching up his gown on his shoulders.

Elizabeth's glance wandered round the court, rested on Roger's sleek, dark head as he sat motionless, on Courtenay's face, upturned now, then came back to the bench. Sir William Bunner caught her eye, flashed a swift look of encouragement, then drew back with folded arms.

"We—we had been taking part in some theatricals a week or two before," the clear, sweet tones went on hurriedly, a little tremor here and there betraying inward agitation. "And we—my sister and I—had represented twins. I had worn a fair wig, and people had said that they never realized before how much alike we were, that they would have taken one of us for the other. I happened to have the necessary things with me. Lady Folgate had been anxious to see us. It seemed to me to give an opening of escape for Daphne. I begged her to let me go in her place; I was more confident of my own power of dealing with Rheinhart. He had already cheated Daphne once; I knew that he would not cheat me. My sister refused; she would not hear of my plan; but as the day wore on it became increasingly evident that to go herself would involve great risk to her health, and at last I prevailed. I could trust her with our maid Flood, who was devoted to us, and I told Lady Folgate that I was summoned to Oakthorpe afterwards. Fortune favoured me so far. I inquired my way to The Bungalow once when I left the Sutton Boldon station, and then found it without any difficulty.

"Rheinhart had directed in his letter that my sister should go round the house, and that the French window would be standing open; she was to go straight in. I crept round the house as quietly as I could, when I was startled by hearing the sound of voices raised loudly. I waited awhile, not knowing what to do; it must have been then that the man Wilson saw me as he described in his evidence. Then I made my way slowly round to the front of the house; it was not lighted up, and I did not know what to do. But time was passing; I had to get the train to Oakthorpe, and I took my courage in both hands and went up to the front door. It stood wide open; inside all looked dark and quiet. The thought came to me that either I or Rheinhart had made a mistake. I had thought he said window; probably he had meant door. I went in; the only light in the hall came from a room at the farther end, the door of which stood partly open. I pushed it wide and went in."

A thrill went through the court; on all sides men and women were craning their necks forward to get a glimpse of this long-sought-for witness; only Detective Collins and Inspector Spencer looked absolutely unmoved. Roger Lavington sat as if turned to stone. It was a dream, he assured himself—a bad dream from which he would presently awaken. The girl he had helped to escape from The Bungalow was Daphne Luxmore; why was Elizabeth, the woman he loved, taking the burden of her sister's sins upon her shoulders?

"You went inside?" Mr. Davenport Villiers prompted.

Elizabeth put up her hand and fumbled with the lace at her throat.

"Yes. He—he lay there on the floor—Rheinhart —dead! My first impulse was to give the alarm; I cried out, but no one came; the dead man was apparently alone in the house. Then I remembered my sister's letters; if they were found in his possession now, it would be worse than ever; they would be made public. I saw that a packet was sticking out of the dead man's pocket, and I went over and took it out. I must have dropped my glove, I suppose, as I felt in the pocket to make sure that I had left none behind." She swayed slightly, caught up the water, and drank eagerly.

Davenport Villiers waited a little to give her time to recover herself.

"There are two questions I must put to you, Miss Luxmore," he said at last. "How long an interval elapsed between your hearing the voices at the side of the house, and your entering the studio and finding Rheinhart dead?"

"I could not say exactly," Elizabeth hesitated. "I know I waited some time among the trees at the side of the house, trying to think what was the best to do. I should say, roughly speaking, from a quarter of an hour to twenty minutes."

"Um! Very well, thank you." Mr. Davenport Villiers made a special note in the margin of his brief. "My second question, Miss Luxmore, is this. Did you recognize the voices you heard when you were in the garden?"

"One was Mr. von Rheinhart's, I think," Elizabeth said with perceptible hesitation.

The barrister nodded as if well satisfied.

"Exactly! And the other? Had you heard that before?"

There was a distinct pause.

"I cannot be sure. I may have thought I did," Elizabeth faltered. "But I was frightened—terrified. I fancy now that I was mistaken."

"We should like to hear what you thought at the time," Mr. Davenport Villiers remarked quietly, his eyes fixed upon the girl's changing face.

"I thought—I thought—" The brown eyes wandered round with a passionate appeal. But there was no relenting in Davenport Villiers's keen face. He waited. "I thought it sounded like Sir James Courtenay!" It seemed as though the fatal words were wrung from Elizabeth Luxmore's pale lips.

Inspector Spencer stepped forward.

"That is as far as we propose to carry the case today, your worships. We are of opinion that the evidence amply justifies our asking for a remand."

Amply indeed! It was evident that their worships on the bench were emphatically of the inspector's opinion. They conferred with their clerk in low tones, then the chairman spoke.

"What day would you suggest for the adjournment, inspector?"

"We hope to be able to carry our case to a close before your worships next week."

"That will do, then. Sir James Courtenay, you are remanded until this day week."

A buzz of excitement ran through the court, the hum of many tongues released at last from the necessity for silence.

Never in the memory of living man had the gossips of the neighbourhood been regaled with so choice a dish of scandal. That not only should one of the magnates of the county be charged with wilful murder, but that the daughter of Lord Luxmore, the philanthropic peer, should turn out to be the mysterious woman who had been wanted for so long in connection with The Bungalow tragedy! The audience could hardly believe what they had heard her avow with their own ears! For a while it was doubtful which way the tide of public sympathy would flow, but the sight of Courtenay borne past by stalwart warders turned it in his favour: a murmur of commiseration arose. Roger caught one glimpse of his friend's face; to his amazement it was bright and hopeful; the look of pain, of melancholy, was gone; in its place was a quiet, serene light, a strong, cheerful endurance.

The crowd broke up, discussing the morning's extraordinary occurrences.

Some took one view, some another, but all were agreed that the real facts of the case were not yet come out; that Miss Luxmore could say much more if she would. One man, bolder than the rest, opined that if Sir James Courtenay did not shoot Maximilian von Rheinhart Miss Luxmore could tell who did. Another voiced the opinion of a large contingent that the matter lay between them. The old, oft-repeated question of Detective Collins and Inspector Spencer—which?

Walking down the corridor of the court still like a man in a trance, Roger found himself face to face with Detective Collins. The little man stopped him with scant ceremony.

"I was coming to see if I could find you, sir. That Mrs. Miller— we thought we might want her, and she is in the little room behind the magistrates, crying and going on till I don't know what to do with her. Perhaps if you—"

"I don't suppose I can do much good," Roger said, wearily. "Still, I—"

He paused. The door of the room they were passing stood open; inside he could see Elizabeth and her father talking to Sir William Bunner. A tall woman in black came swiftly down the passage; he stood aside for her to enter. The detective touched his arm.

"That is Miss Luxmore, the one that was to have married Sir James Courtenay."

Roger started and looked back. No, assuredly this was not the girl he had found in The Bungalow! The abundant hair was the same colour, the brown eyes were alike; but the face was longer, thinner. The full mouth too, the slightly projecting teeth altered the whole expression. Impossible, inconceivable as it seemed, Roger had to acknowledge that he had never seen Daphne Luxmore before; that the girl he had helped to escape from The Bungalow was Elizabeth, the woman whom he had mentally set on a pinnacle high above all others, whose cool, dainty air of aloofness had fired his blood. Another conclusion, too, was forced upon him. It was Elizabeth, not Daphne, who had been meeting him in the park; Elizabeth to whom he had spoken of his love; Elizabeth who had personated her sister, who had scoffed at and yet encouraged him; Elizabeth who had been amusing herself at his expense.

His face flushed darkly red beneath its tan; all the manhood in him rose in hot revolt against the trick that had been played upon him.

"This way, sir." Detective Collins was turning down a side passage. "She is more like a mad woman than anything else, saying she has come to get Sir James out, and goodness know what—"

"Good afternoon, Dr. Lavington!" The interruption came from behind. Roger turned. Mrs. von Rheinhart stood close to him, two hot red spots burning on her pale cheeks, her mouth curling in a sneer. "So, you see, we have succeeded, Dr. Lavington!" she said mockingly. "I prophesied we should, you may remember, and you contradicted me. Now, which of us is right?"

Roger turned away from her with barely concealed disgust.

"Everything is not settled yet, Mrs. von Rheinhart. You must excuse me. I have a patient here." Already his trained ear had caught the sound of sobs and moans from a room close at hand.

"Oh, yes! You are always in a hurry, are you not?" Evidently, in spite of the success she had achieved, Mrs. von Rheinhart was in no agreeable frame of mind. "Well, I will not keep you from your patient. You see for yourself—"

The door at which Roger was looking was thrown violently open.

"Let me go—let me go, I say! I must tell them that he did not do it! That they must let him go!"

"Now, now, my good woman," Detective Collins began to expostulate.

Mrs. Miller, looking strangely unlike her usually meek, frightened self, thrust him aside.

"Get out of my way, man! I tell you I—" She stopped short and thrust out her hand. "Who is that? Merciful Heaven, who is that?"

"My dear Mrs. Miller—"

Roger's tone was very pitiful as he advanced. He knew enough of the woman's devotion to her master to realize something of the blow his arrest must have been to her.

But she did not even glance at him; her eyes looked past him, beyond him.

"That—that woman! Who is she? It is not Alice, my own daughter! Ah, Heaven!"

"No, no!" Lavington spoke sternly now. Already the noise had attracted several loiterers. Sir William Bunner, coming down the passage, paused in surprise. "You are letting your imagination run away with you. That is Mrs. von Rheinhart."

At the first sound of the housekeeper's voice, Mrs. von Rheinhart had staggered back against the wall; as Lavington spoke, however, she pulled herself together and stumbled forward.

"I am Alice von Rheinhart, mother! I thought —they told me, when I went down to our old home, that you were dead."

"I wish I had been—I wish I had been!" the housekeeper wailed, shrinking away from her daughter's outstretched hand. "Alice von Rheinhart—Mrs. von Rheinhart! I did not know—I never dreamt— ah, Heaven, that I should live to hear it!"

Chapter Twenty-Five

"You sent for me, Sir William."

"Ah, yes, I want your help, Collins! Sit down, man. You and I have had a little piece of work together before now, have we not?" And Sir William Bunner leaned back and surveyed the detective with a twinkle in his eye.

"You are very kind to say so, Sir William."

Mr. Collins was evidently ill at ease as he took the chair to which Sir William pointed.

"Yes, yes! You have done some good work in your time, Collins," Sir William went on. "I sent for you this afternoon because I want your help in unravelling the mystery of The Bungalow murder."

"My help in unravelling the mystery of The Bungalow tragedy!" Collins forgot himself sufficiently to smile. "I think we have pretty well solved that now, sir!"

Sir William Bunner did not answer for a moment; a smile played round his clear-cut mouth as he drew a packet of papers towards him.

Detective Collins fidgeted a little in his chair. Years ago he had learnt that Sir William Bunner's smile generally meant that some point regarded by police and counsel alike as utterly insignificant had been seized upon by his keen eye as containing the whole crux of the matter; and Collins had never known Sir William Bunner to draw a false conclusion yet.

The "Hanging Judge" had not been wont to make mistakes. Collins had been secretly uneasy ever since he received the summons to the Hall. Sir William Bunner had left Oakthorpe the day of Courtenay's appearance before the magistrates, he knew; the news of his return had come as a surprise to the detective.

"You hold a warrant for the search of Oakthorpe Manor, I believe?" His tone was curt.

Collins looked surprised.

"Yes, Sir William. The police have been in possession of Sir James's private room since the time of the arrest."

"Good! And the rest of the house?"

Collins scratched his head.

"That hasn't been gone through very thoroughly, I believe, Sir William. You see, the circumstances of the case, Sir James not having been able to get about without help, it didn't seem necessary."

Sir William smiled again.

"Did it not, Collins? I think—I rather think I shall have to trouble you just to go back and do that part of your work a little more thoroughly."

The detective looked at him.

"I don't understand you, Sir William."

"Don't you, Mr. Collins?" Sir William's smile grew a little more pronounced. "Ah, I think you and the police have found a nice mare's-nest this time."

Mr. Collins's face deepened in hue.

"I hardly know how that can be. The case, it seems to me, lies between Sir James Courtenay and Miss Elizabeth Luxmore. I own for a long time we were puzzled; when we thought it was Miss Daphne Luxmore who went to The Bungalow it did seem likely enough that, provoked by Mr. von Rheinhart's sneers, possibly by his refusal to give up her letters and threats of showing them to Sir James Courtenay, she had caught up the pistol, which was probably lying near, and put an end to it all. But, as it was Miss Elizabeth, the motive was not sufficient, and we had to turn to Sir James Courtenay."

"Had you?" Sir William Bunner's tone made the detective wince. "How if I tell you it was neither of them, Collins?"

"I should say that it would be a difficult matter to prove, Sir William." The detective's tone was perfectly respectful, but there was a lurking amusement in his accent. This time, he told himself, Sir William Bunner would find that it was he, and not the police, who had discovered a mare's-nest.

Sir William Bunner was looking graver now.

"Ah, that is why I want your help, Collins. Together I think we ought to manage it. To begin with, you started with the hypothesis that, Elizabeth being innocent, Courtenay must be guilty. Well, the process of elimination often turns out satisfactorily. I began on much the same basis myself—only I broadened mine. Yours only admitted the guilt of two persons; mine embraced four. You said you were sure that Elizabeth Luxmore was innocent; I knew she and Courtenay both were. Still working on your line, I found that, having eliminated them, I had two possibly guilty persons left."

"Two others!" the detective echoed amazedly. "I think you are making a mistake. Sir William. I do really. I cannot imagine who you mean; but—"

The great judge surveyed his astonished face with amusement.

"And that is because you started with a preconceived theory, Collins. It seems to be assumed by everybody, police and public alike, that somebody from the outside came in and shot Rheinhart. You went looking for a murderer in unlikely and out-of-the-way places, while all the time the real criminal was close at hand. I do not say that I might not have done the same in your case, mind; coming fresh from the case myself I had the advantage of knowing Miss Luxmore and Sir James Courtenay, and of feeling certain that both were absolutely innocent. And I have been more mixed up in the case than you know—mind that, Collins. I wonder that I have never been arrested as an accessory after the crime myself"—with a jolly laugh. "It was I who brought Miss Luxmore away from Freshfield."

"You, Sir William!" The detective could scarcely find breath for more.

"Yes, I," Sir William repeated, enjoying the spectacle of his confusion mightily. "You never thought of that, did you, Collins? If you had arrested Miss Elizabeth Luxmore, I should distinctly have had to put in an appearance in the witness-box. Yes, I was among the audience at Freshfield, and though I wasn't sure of her in the Japanese dress, slanting eyebrows, and that sort of thing, of course she recognized me; she is my god-daughter, you know, Collins, and when she came to me and told me she was anxious to leave quickly and quietly, why, of course the thing was done. She came back with our party and left that meddling doctor in the lurch. If it had not been for him now, The Bungalow mystery would have been plain sailing from the first. I told my god-daughter yesterday that as far as I could see he had been doing his best to get her hanged," rubbing his grey hair irascibly.

"Dr. Lavington had!" Collins, unable to follow the judge's line of thought, was growing more and more bewildered.

"Why, of course!" Sir William was idly drawing a plan of The Bungalow on a stray piece of drawing-paper.

"If he had had a grain of common-sense when he found her hiding behind the window-curtains—as it appears she did when she heard he was coming—he would have said to her, 'My good girl, did you kill this man or did you not?' And when he had heard how she found Rheinhart he would have told her that she must stand her ground and tell the police. Instead of which, he hurries her off, takes her into his house, passes her off as his cousin, persuades her to act in those abominable theatricals so that the whole countryside may have an opportunity of identifying her; and goodness knows what he would have done next, if I had not fortunately appeared on the scene and carried her off. Upon my word, when I first heard the story I thought it looked as though he wanted to fix suspicion upon her, and for that reason, among others, I put him down among my four hypothetically guilty persons."

Collins was drumming his fingers absently on the tablecloth, his mind busy with the judge's theory. He looked up now.

"Dr. Lavington! Oh, I think he is out of the question, Sir William."

"Not at all," snapped the judge. "According to his own theory he was sitting alone in his consulting-room when he was summoned by the housekeeper; if he had had a quarrel with Rheinhart nothing would have been easier for him than to have gone to The Bungalow, walked in at the open door or window, and shot Rheinhart. I don't say he did, mind you—I don't think he did—but he went down as one of the four. Then came a name that never seems to have occurred to the police, and yet one would have thought that it was perfectly obvious. I allude to Mrs. McNaughton—or Miller, as she calls herself—the housekeeper. Now you have my four, Collins— what do you say to them?"

"I hardly know." The detective hesitated. "Until last Tuesday I should have thought that there were only two to be considered. Now I do not feel quite so certain."

"You are an honest man, Collins!" The judge glanced at him approvingly. "And you don't mind owning that you make a mistake occasionally like the rest of us. Well, to proceed: having put aside two out of the four, that left the other two to be dealt with. Well, I don't mind telling you that at first I thought the odds lay rather against the doctor; his conduct seemed so extraordinary for a sensible man. But there was the question of a motive; as far as that went I was at a standstill with both of them—until Tuesday, that is to say; then I found my motive." Comprehension was slowly dawning in Collins's eyes.

"You mean that Mrs. von Rheinhart—"

"I mean that Mrs. von Rheinhart's recognition by her mother supplied my clue," finished the judge. "We have been told how Mrs. Miller mourned for her lost daughter, how she had vowed vengeance on the man who had taken her away. I had an interview with Courtenay on Tuesday evening and told him what a fool he had been making of himself. It seems he had taken it for granted that Daphne was the murderess. She, knowing that Elizabeth had heard his voice, thought it was he. A pretty kettle of fish they made of it between them. Elizabeth went up to the Manor to warn him he was in danger and to beg of him to go away, while he, in order to save Daphne as he thought, sent an anonymous letter to the police as good as accusing himself. You know that, I suppose?"

"Yes, we knew that," the detective assented.

"I thought so. Well, I questioned Sir James as to his interview with Rheinhart. He told me that Rheinhart had written to him boasting that he had been Daphne Luxmore's lover, that he had told him if he came to The Bungalow that night he would find her in his rooms. There can be no doubt this is the revenge which Rheinhart had planned. It miscarried in a measure, because Courtenay arrived on the scene too early. Rheinhart's assertions as to his relations with Daphne he absolutely refused to believe, and threatened to administer summary chastisement. Rheinhart, however, insisted on him seeing the letters and, though he refused to read them, he recognized Daphne's handwriting. He recognized, also, that Rheinhart was the man whom he had seen with Alice Miller in Florence, and taxed him with it. That, if the housekeeper could have overheard it, would supply our motive."

"Yes, if—" Collins's tone was still doubtful. "Does Sir James say Rheinhart was all right when he left him, Sir William?"

"Perfectly. After hearing his story I thought it over, and went down on Wednesday to interview the Wilsons. I thought I should like to hear Mrs. Wilson's version of her husband's story. I wonder whether you have heard of her brother, the lad who has fits?"

"I think I have heard Wilson mention him," the detective said doubtfully.

"I saw him too!" Sir William went on. "I found that he had his first attack on the night of The Bungalow murder, just after the crime was committed. He has been fit for little since; 'a poor thing,' his sister called him. I asked to see him—it struck me that he might be useful to me—and after exercising a little patience, I got his story from him. A very interesting story. I should like you to hear it, Mr. Collins." He touched the bell.

"Why, you don't mean that he—I declare I never thought of that!" the detective began excitedly.

Sir William motioned him to be silent; as the door opened a tall, comely-looking young woman, whose pleasant face was overclouded now by distress, entered. She was closely followed by a thick-set, loutish-looking youth, who glanced at the two men in evident trepidation.

Sir William pulled forward a chair.

"Sit down, Mrs. Wilson. Now, Edward, my boy, I want you to tell that gentleman what you saw on the night that Mr. von Rheinhart was shot."

Edward shuffled his feet about uneasily, and glanced appealingly at the judge. Mrs. Wilson laid her hand on his arm.

"Speak up, Ned. Nobody is cross with you. The gentleman only wants to know the truth. He's frightened, sir. I'm sure there isn't a more obedient boy in general."

"I'm sure he is a good boy," Sir William assented gently. "You were in the garden, Edward; now tell us what you saw."

"I had been walking about a bit, looking for our Polly, sir. I got up to the hedge between the doctor's and Mr. von Rheinhart's, hearing voices and not being very sure where they came from. At last I made out it was two men in The Bungalow, quarrelling. At last they got that loud and angry, and me being curious, I got over the hedge, which wasn't very high, and went near the windows. Before I got up, though, a tall man came out, in such a temper that he brushed up against me almost without seeing me. Mr. von Rheinhart, he came out and shouted something after him—I didn't make out what. Then he went back and closed the windows, but didn't draw the blinds down. As he was fastening the clasp a woman came into the room. I knew her; it was the housekeeper. She—she—"

The lad stopped; his fate twitched painfully; he jerked his elbows up and down.

"Now, now, Ned!" His sister put her arm through his. "You go on. It will soon be over, and then we will go right away home. You are a good boy for telling the truth. Come!"

Her touch and voice had a soothing effect: the boy grew calmer.

"She was in a rare way about something; I could make that out, sir. She was talking that fast and waving her arms about. Once she went up to Mr. von Rheinhart as if she would hit him, and he laughed at her. Then she caught something up from the table and pointed it at him. The next moment there was a loud bang and Mr. von Rheinhart fell back. She—she jumped about, sir. Her face looked awful. That—that is all I can remember, please, sir; something seemed to go wrong in my head then, but I s'pose I got back to the house somehow."

"Ah, poor lad, that you did." Mrs. Wilson interposed, getting up and drawing her cloak round her. "That was a bad night's work for us, sir. He was as bright a lad as you ever see till then, sir, though a bit mischievous. Now—"

"Ah, well, he will be better now that he has got that off his mind," Sir William interposed kindly. "You have been a good boy, Ned and I am much obliged to you. Good afternoon, Mrs. Wilson; good afternoon, my boy. Well, Collins—" as the door closed behind the two—"what do you say to this?"

"Say, sir? Why, that me and Spencer must have been a couple of blind asses never to have thought of this before!" The detective's tone was one of hearty self-contempt. "I can't imagine how it was it never came into my head!"

"Well, it wasn't easy to make it out until after Monday's recognition," Sir William conceded. "I don't think that you have been much to blame, Collins. The question is, what is to be done next? I say, search the Manor, and see whether we can find any incriminating proof among Mrs. Miller's possessions. Your warrant will cover that, I imagine?"

"I suppose so," the detective said thoughtfully. "It is a question that hasn't come my way before. But I think we might stretch a point."

"And at once," said Sir William Bunner emphatically. "Before any notion of this boy's story reaches the housekeeper. It is sure to get about, now the sister knows of it. Never was a woman born, I believe, capable of keeping such a secret to herself."

"Ay, and we ought to have other evidence," Collins agreed. "This lad is a doubtful sort of witness; sure to break down or have a fit at the sight of the judge or jury; we couldn't get a conviction without corroboration. With your leave, Sir William, I'll telephone to Spencer—he is at the village police-station here to-day—and will tell him to go up to the Hall with a couple of policemen and the warrant, and I'll walk over and join them."

"I'll come with you myself, Collins," Sir William declared, rising. "I want to see this business through."

It was October 1st; autumn was setting in early; already there was a touch of frost in the air; the evening was beginning to draw in as the two men entered the park. They crossed the grass, keeping in sight of the avenue, and looking behind now and then for sight of the police from the village. Sir William was pointing out the various points at which, in his judgment, the boy's story would need confirmation, when suddenly the keen-sighted detective touched him.

"Do you see that, sir? It looks to me like her— Mrs. Miller."

"What!" Sir William paused and adjusted his pince-nez. "It is Mrs. Miller," he declared. "What is she up to? No good from the look of her. We must keep her in sight, Collins."

Mrs. Miller was moving along in a curious, secretive manner, keeping in the shade of the trees and glancing about her from side to side. The two men turned and followed her down, treading softly and keeping at a safe distance.

She walked on, quickening her pace from time to time until she came in sight of an opening amidst the trees, from which a view of the village could be obtained. Then she stopped and fumbled in the bosom of her dress.

Suddenly Sir William uttered a sharp exclamation—the detective was before him. He sprang forward and caught the woman's arm. Something bright slipped from her hand and fell on the grass at her feet as she fought and wrestled with Collins.

The detective's strong arms held her firmly.

"Not so fast, not so fast, Mrs. Miller. Sir William, might I trouble you to glance at that pistol? Ah, I thought so!" as the judge picked it up and looked at it, raising his eyebrows as he saw the initials on the silver mount. "The very weapon we have been looking for so long—the one with which Rheinhart was shot. I think it will clinch matters for us, sir."

"I think so," the judge acquiesced gravely.

Mrs. Miller ceased to struggle; she stood motionless, quiescent, in her captor's grasp. Her white face was blotched with weeping, her reddened eyelids quivering automatically. Her upper lip twitched to one side, leaving the yellow, prominent teeth exposed. As Sir William spoke, she turned to him imploringly.

"Ah, let me do it, sir, let me do it. They will let him out then, and then perhaps Alice will forgive. He was her husband, you see, sir, and I never knew it. There isn't anything left for me to do but to die!"

Chapter Twenty-Six

"Among Mrs. Miller's effects at the Manor, labelled to be opened 'immediately,' we found the following." Inspector Spencer handed up a paper to the magistrates, amid the breathless silence of the crowded court.

It had been a day of surprises. No hint of the discoveries made by Sir William Bunner had been suffered to leak out previously, and their disclosure had been the more dramatic. Apparently, the one person who was most unmoved when Sir William Bunner and the detective were giving evidence was the prisoner himself. Only the very closest observer would have noticed the beads of perspiration on his brow, the nervous grip of his hands.

The crowd, the witnesses who had been called to give evidence as to Courtenay's movements, the magistrates themselves, had listened with supreme amazement to the gradual unfolding of the mystery of The Bungalow murder. Now that the key was in their hands, the solution seemed so simple, so obvious; so much that had looked dark and sinister was shown to be capable of an absolutely innocent interpretation. Their interest reached its culminating point when, after Edward Plummer had repeated his evidence— stumblingly indeed, but in a fashion that unmistakably bore the stamp of truth—after Sir William Bunner and Detective Collins testified to finding Mrs. Miller on the very brink of committing suicide with the pistol with which Maximilian von Rheinhart was shot, and to her words when they seized her, Inspector Spencer had entered the witness-box and detailed his search among the housekeeper's property, and the discovery of the papers which he now placed in the magistrate's hands.

The chairman opened the envelope, and glanced over the contents with his colleagues; then he looked at the barrister for the prosecution.

"I think perhaps it would be as well to read this aloud at once, Mr. Villiers. It so entirely exonerates Sir James Courtenay that, in my opinion, it should be made public in his interest with as little delay as possible."

Mr. Villiers bowed.

"I am quite of that opinion, your worship."

"To be opened immediately," the chairman began, after the usher had twice called "Silence" peremptorily and unnecessarily.

"Because my beloved master has been falsely accused of the crime I committed, and because, all unknowing, that I was thereby wrecking my daughter's happiness, I shot my daughter's husband, Maximilian von Rheinhart, on April

14th, 19—, I, Hannah Frances McNaughton, or Miller, write this last plain statement of fact—the truth as it is known to me and to the God before whom I shall shortly appear.

"When my daughter fled from home in secret with some unknown lover, I swore I would punish the man to the utmost of my power. But do as I would, I could find no trace of them. The only word I ever had was that Sir James Courtenay once thought he saw them—or, at least, Alice—in Paris. Little did I think, when all my efforts had proved unavailing, and, having come to the end of my savings, I settled down at Sutton Boldon as Maxmilian von Rheinhart's housekeeper, that I was so near the object of my search. I knew him to be a bad man, I despised him, but in some ways the situation suited me and I stayed on. On the fatal day, I had taken Mr. von Rheinhart's tea to the study as usual. Half an hour later I was crossing the hall, when I heard him speaking in a loud, hectoring tone. A voice I knew well answered him—that of my former nursling, Sir James Courtenay. I stood still and listened in amazement. 'You scoundrel!' I heard. 'Do you think I don't know what sort of a man you are? The very moment I saw you I recognized you as the man I saw in Paris with Alice Miller, my old nurse's daughter. You ruined that girl, and broke her mother's heart!'

"I do not remember what followed. When I realized that I had been living in the same house with the man who had taken my daughter from me, that I had been serving him, something seemed to snap in my brain, my blood took fire. I swore that if the law could not touch him I would take the matter into my own hands. I waited till I heard Sir James Courtenay leave; then I opened the study door and walked in. Mr. von Rheinhart turned upon me angrily. He was flushed and excited. 'What do you want, woman?' he cried roughly.

"I do not know what I told him, how I accused him of ruining my child; but the jeer with which he answered me, the words in which he told me that she was ready enough to leave me to go with him, will remain burnt in my memory for ever. I lowered myself to beg him to tell me where she was, and he laughed in my face, and said he did not know or care. Those were the last words he ever spoke. The pistol with which he had been practising earlier in the day lay close at hand. I caught it up, and as he crossed the room I fired at him. He fell at once; my aim had been true enough—he was dead! As I looked at him lying there, I felt no regret. He was a bad man, I told myself; he deserved his fate. I never regretted his death until Sir James was arrested. Then I knew that my time had come; I must speak. Yesterday I learnt that my child was living—that, all unintentionally as far as he was concerned, he was her husband. I must go without even bidding her farewell; I could not bear that. From the spot where I shall die I shall see the roof that shelters her. I should like her to know that her mother's last thought was of her.

"HANNAH MILLER."

There was a dead silence in the court for a minute. It was broken by a long-drawn breath from the spectators. So the mystery of The Bungalow murder was explained at last; all surmise and questioning were at an end. The world knew by whose hand Maximilian von Rheinhart had died.

The chairman spoke.

"This is the end of the case against Sir James Courtenay, of course. You will go no further at present, I presume, inspector? With regard to Mrs. Miller—"

"She will be brought before your worships tomorrow. This, of course, concludes the present charge, sir." Inspector Spencer stood down, with a bow to the bench.

The chairman cleared his throat.

"Sir James Courtenay, you are discharged. And it is my duty to tell you, voicing the sentiments of my colleagues as well as my own, how entirely rejoiced we are that the charge against you has been shown to be without an atom of foundation. You leave the court without a stain upon your character and, in the name of my colleagues and myself, I wish to congratulate you most heartily, and to join with your friends and neighbours in hoping that you may soon be restored to health sufficiently to take up your position once more amongst us."

Sir James sat with bent head during this speech; at its conclusion he looked up with misty eyes and lips that trembled in spite of his self-control.

"I thank you," he said simply. "Then I am at liberty?"

"Certainly."

Lavington moved forward on one side, the solicitor, Mr. Day, on the other. Courtenay's chair was wheeled quickly, not through the crowd at the back, but out by a side door into the corridor, and from there to the justices' private room beyond.

As Roger stepped aside to allow the chair to pass through the doorway, he found himself face to face with Elizabeth Luxmore; she held out her hand.

"Oh, Dr. Lavington—"

Roger made no answering movement; he bowed stiffly.

"Miss Luxmore—"

Elizabeth's face was very pale; her great brown eyes were raised to his appealingly.

"I wanted to see you—to explain."

In some inexplicable fashion Roger's expression hardened.

"That would be a mistake. Explanations are unnecessary, as it seems to me! I prefer"—bitterly —"to let facts speak for themselves!"

"But I want to tell you—you were always so kind to me, and I want to make you understand." The sweet voice quivered pathetically; she laid her ungloved hand softly on his arm.

Roger made a quick backward movement; the girl's hand dropped quickly.

"That is extremely kind of you," he said, with a hard sarcastic inflection in his tone. "But I do understand perfectly, thank you. It will always be a source of gratification to me to reflect that for quite a considerable time I must have afforded great amusement to Miss Elizabeth Luxmore. If that is all"—he turned away—"I believe Sir James Courtenay wants me. You will excuse me?"

"Amusement!" the girl echoed drearily. "Ah, if I could only make you see—if you knew—"

"Elizabeth!" It was Lord Luxmore's voice. "Daphne is asking—"

Roger went into the room to Courtenay. He found his friend leaning back in his chair, white, indeed, and exhausted, but with a light in his eyes, a patient smile on his lips. He held out his hand to Roger.

"So that is finished, Roger, old fellow. The nightmare is over, and we are all sane once more. Ah, Heaven! Daphne—"

He was facing the door; Lavington looked round. Daphne Luxmore stood on the threshold, her golden tresses gleaming against her black dress, against the shadows beyond. She held out her hands appealingly.

"James! Oh, James—forgive!"

Sir James raised himself.

"It is I who should say forgive, Daphne! Do you know that I have thought—"

"I don't care what you thought." Daphne crossed the room with tottering steps and sank down beside the chair. "It was my fault—all my fault, James. Tell me that you forgive me, that you love me just a little still."

"I have loved you always, Daphne. But I am only a miserable wreck of a man, child. You must forget me—be happy with some one else."

"As if that mattered." As Roger stole out of the room he caught the girl's whisper as her soft arms twined themselves round

Courtenay's neck, and her head sank on his bosom. "As if anything mattered to me, so long as we are together. You—you will let me help you to bear it, Jem?"

In England the lilacs were in bud, the birds were building their nests, the first fresh leaves of spring were unfurling themselves, rejoicing in the cool air, in the welcome sunshine; but at Sermoneta, in Italy, it was hot and airless. Up on the hill, where the great hotel was built resplendent in all the latest modern improvements, it was cooler. The company that had floated the Sermoneta Hotel had been wise; they had chosen their site near an old cypress grove, and now in the hottest weather the gardens were shaded and pleasant.

The travellers who were coming in by the old diligence that was toiling up the steep, dusty road looked at the green shadows of the garden longingly.

Giuseppe Varconi, the driver, cracked his whip as he pointed out the hotel with pride.

"Ah, there is not another like it in the whole countryside! Little wonder that it is always full, that some days I have to take away a whole diligence full of disappointed ones," he said.

But there was only one passenger for the hotel today; the rest were going to a little hamlet higher up. The solitary one who alighted, a gaunt, bronzed Englishman, seemed in no way impressed by Giuseppe's eulogies; he stood by, taciturn and gloomy, while they handed down his valise to the hotel waiter, and then, touching his hat slightly in farewell to his fellow-passengers, strode off in the man's wake. In the hall he was met by a gorgeous belaced official, who begged milord to write his name in the visitors' book.

Shrugging his shoulders resignedly, the Englishman obeyed. "Dr. Roger Lavington, 45 Weymouth Street, W."

Then he looked up.

"Sir James and Lady Courtenay are here?"

The man spread out his hands.

"But yes; they are expecting Monsieur with impatience. The *déjeuner* is ordered in their private apartment. If Monsieur will give himself the trouble to follow me I will conduct him to his room to make his preparations."

In spite of his gloom, a smile curled Roger's lips at the man's phraseology as he followed him up the polished uncarpeted stairs.

It was nearly two years since he had seen Courtenay. After the latter's reconciliation with Daphne, he had wrung from Sir James an unwilling consent to his departure. He had been a witness at Mrs. Miller's trial, which had resulted, of course, in a verdict of manslaughter and a small sentence of imprisonment.

And after that he had gone to Germany to assist in some researches which were just then engaging the attention of the civilized world. It was hard, unremitting toil, and when it was brought to a successful issue and the long strain was over, Roger had felt the usual reaction. He had long since promised himself a holiday in the South and this visit to Sermoneta was the result.

When he was at last shown down to their little salon, prepared though he was for the improvement in Sir James's health, he could scarcely forbear a start when he saw his friend standing up to welcome him, looking once more, though thinner and older, like the Courtenay of old.

The Italian doctors, the latest improvements in modern surgery, had done much for Courtenay; happiness and the relief from an ever-gnawing anxiety had done more; and though it was impossible for him to walk freely, it was wonderful to him to be able to move about again even with the aid of a stick.

Lady Courtenay was standing behind him. Roger was inclined to think her as much improved as her husband. Her hollow cheeks had filled out, happiness had brightened her eyes, brought back the colour to her cheeks.

"Roger, old man!" Courtenay said no more as he held out his hand, and Lavington took it in a firm grasp.

Lady Courtenay was waiting for him with her pretty smile when he turned.

"Welcome to Sermoneta, Dr. Lavington! I can hardly tell you how delighted we are really to have a visit from you at last!"

"You are very kind." Roger bowed low over her hand. Remembering the past, he could not but be conscious of a certain awkwardness.

How much Lady Courtenay had heard of his meetings with her sister, how much she knew of what had passed between them, he had no idea. Beyond an occasional reference in the columns of the fashionable intelligence to Lord Luxmore and his daughter, Lavington had heard nothing of Elizabeth Luxmore since Mrs. Miller's trial; he had never spoken to her since the interview in the tiny court-house at Bredon.

Only a month ago, however, a paragraph in one of the papers had caught his eye. "We understand that a marriage is likely to take place shortly between Mr. Guy Whitstone and the Hon. Elizabeth Luxmore." That was all, yet his hand shook as he laid the paper down, and when he stood up his face had a curious grey look.

He was thinking of that paragraph now as he replied to Lady Courtenay's kindly greeting. As his eyes wandered from her golden hair to her brown eyes, he felt a sudden pang—the resemblance between the two sisters was more marked now that Lady Courtenay was in better health than when Roger had seen them together—it was possible this morning to imagine that, apart from the different hair and complexion, it might be possible to mistake one for the other.

"There is another person I must ask after," he said, forcing a smile. "How is—"

Lady Courtenay coloured.

"Why, how did you know? I mean—" stammering as her husband flashed a playfully warning glance at her.

"Ah, the son and heir!" laughed Courtenay. "We are deferring your introduction to him until after *déjeuner*. He is a fine boy, Roger; you would never guess he was my son."

"Jem!" Lady Courtenay slipped one hand through her husband's arm. "How dare you, sir! When you know that every one says he is your very image!"

"Do they indeed?" Courtenay laughed. "You see what good order I am kept in, Roger. But come, you must be famished."

Déjeuner was served in the big *salle-à-manger* overlooking the garden. The Courtenays had a round table placed near the window. Roger glanced with some interest at the other family groups, but the Courtenays had apparently made few friends at the hotel, and they exchanged only the barest greetings.

Conversation during the meal was, of course, restricted to the baldest commonplaces. They talked of their travels, of the beauties of Sermoneta, of Roger's labours in Germany. At last, when all had finished, Courtenay pushed back his chair with an air of relief.

"Now, come, Roger, we will have our cigars on the veranda where it is cool and quiet; Daphne can bring little Jim to us there."

Lady Courtenay made some laughing remark as she glided away, and Roger followed his host through the window. Two hammock-chairs stood outside; Courtenay motioned Roger to one, and sank in the other himself.

"Well, Roger, old boy," he said when they had lighted their cigars, "don't you want to ask after your old friends at Oakthorpe?"

"Well, you see, you keep me pretty well posted up in the news." Roger watched his smoke curling up to the roof. "I saw a paragraph concerning Miss Luxmore's forthcoming marriage in one of the papers."

Courtenay looked at him curiously beneath his lowered eyelids.

"Ah, you saw that!" He lay back and idly blew his smoke into gay twists. "Roger, I know you'll think I am a lazy fellow; but even with the best of artificial limbs walking is not an unmixed joy, and my soul pines for a particular brand of tobacco. There is a jar of it in the *salon*, where we were before lunch. I wonder whether you would mind fetching it for me."

"Of course not!" Roger rose. "Don't you think of getting up while I am here."

He found his way across the hall to the *salon*. As he opened the door he heard a slight movement; a tall, white-clad figure rose from the low seat by the window.

For the moment Lavington's eyes, coming from the dimness of the hall, were dazzled by the sunshine.

"James sent me for his tobacco, Lady Courtenay," he began. Then he stopped short, his face changed.

"Miss Luxmore! I did not know—I had no idea—"

Elizabeth moved forward. Roger stood still. His heart was beating wildly; he did not know what to say; and it was Elizabeth who broke the embarrassing silence.

"I wanted to see you," she said tremulously, "and so I made James and Daphne promise—I told them not to tell you. I knew you would not come if you knew."

She was looking a little older, a little thinner, Roger saw now that he was becoming accustomed to the light. There were faint hollows in the perfect oval of her cheeks; there was a pathetic droop about the corners of the sweet, curved mouth; but in the eyes of the man watching her she had never looked lovelier, more adorable. With a supreme effort he pulled himself together.

"You were quite mistaken, Miss Luxmore," he said gravely. "I was extremely rude to you the last time we met. I have often hoped that some day I might have the opportunity of apologizing. I can only assure you now that the words were no sooner spoken than they were regretted."

"Oh. You were quite right to be angry!" Elizabeth said with a little sob. "That—that did not matter."

"I had no right," Lavington contradicted her stiffly. "But since you are good enough—" He broke off abruptly. "I must not forget to congratulate you, Miss Luxmore," he resumed in a lighter tone.

"Oh, that!"—Elizabeth interrupted him—"that was all a mistake. It was contradicted the next day. Didn't you see it?"

The joy light leaped into Roger's eyes. Could he hope after all? Was the prize still to be won?

"There has been no question of an engagment with Mr. Whitstone. The notice was a mistake on the part of the paper." Elizabeth Luxmore's beautiful eyes were fixed on Roger's changing countenance as she spoke.

"A mistake!" Roger caught his breath. "I beg your pardon. I didn't know."

The girl pouted as she glanced up at him for one moment from beneath her upcurled brown lashes.

"I—think you ought to have known better."

A flash of swift, incredible joy swept over Roger, then it passed, leaving him white and cold.

"I don't understand," he said, bewildered. "I quite thought—"

But Elizabeth had seen and understood the change in his face, a misty gladness was shining in her brown eyes, her lips were trembling.

"You—you won't understand," she whispered. "Oh, Roger, I have not forgotten"—she paused, the swiftly hot colour flashed over face and neck and temples—"what you told me when you thought I was Daphne."

The man's dark, rugged face lighted up; he made one swift forward movement as if to gather her in his arms. Then he remembered, and stopped short.

"But it was hopeless then!" he groaned. "It is hopeless now. I am only a poor man, a comparatively unknown scientist."

"Father said the services you had rendered humanity in the recent researches had placed your name on the foremost list of men of science," Elizabeth quoted demurely. "He said you were a match for anyone. But, of course, if you don't want—if you have changed your mind"—in a small voice.

"I? Changed my mind?" The man laughed aloud recklessly. "When for every moment of these two years I have been hungering for you, for the touch of your hand, for the glance of your eyes."

Elizabeth drew a little nearer.

"Then why don't you tell me again? O–h, Roger!"

For the man's arms had closed round her, had crushed her against his breast, his lips were pressed to the mass of wavy, brown hair that lay across his shoulder.

THE END

Lightning Source UK Ltd.
Milton Keynes UK
UKOW06f1629070416

271768UK00001B/22/P